I0831924

THE AMATEUR ASSASSIN

A TALE OF DECEPTION AND DELUSION

By Jack Warner

Published by
Quatrefoil, Inc.
312 Four Seasons Lane, Montvale, NJ 07645

ISBN: 978-0-9778056-9-3 (Hardcover Edition)
ISBN: 978-0-9778056-6-2 (eBook Edition)

WARNING—

The ideas, information and techniques detailed in this book are presented for entertainment value only, and are in no way intended to influence the behavior of the reader.

Any and all crimes committed by the reader are the reader's sole responsibility, and the author and publisher of this book disavow any and all claims to the contrary.

If this unrestricted disclaimer is unacceptable to the reader, this book SHOULD NOT BE READ. It should be returned to the library or bookseller un-scanned and unread in its original pristine condition. If downloaded as an eBook, it should be deleted.

THE AMATEUR ASSASSIN

A TALE OF DECEPTION AND DELUSION

By Jack Warner

"Fear of death drives all our other fears
and fuels all our emotions.

"Our doomed desire for self-preservation
compels us to seek immortality through
fame, power, fortune and in physical
relationships. All of which ultimately
abandon us in the end.

"Death is our only lasting legacy.
And in creative hands, it is our
only permanent art form."

Ian Kirk

"Death may be the greatest of all human blessings."

Socrates

Contents

1.

George Trecott

NEW JERSEY--

HE GROUND OUT his third cigarette of the morning and swigged down the dregs of his cold coffee. He hit "save" on his desktop and rolled back his chair. This was another "thrilling" start to another "thrilling" day...if by "thrilling" you meant boring grunt work with no end in sight.

George Trecott lived alone in a small 2-bedroom house in a run-down section of a dreary New Jersey town. He didn't know his neighbors and didn't really want to. Those few friends he once had, had long ago moved away. And a series of layoffs had ended all his ties with former co-workers. Now he worked alone, lived alone, and rarely ventured out--except to check the mail, buy groceries, or empty the trash.

Making another pot of coffee, George Trecott thought back with growing anger to that day almost thirty years ago when he had graduated with honors from Columbia with a BA in English Lit. He recalled painfully the dreams he once had. Dreams of becoming an accomplished author...or at least one with reviews good enough to support himself as a full-time writer. All those grand hopes had faded and been taken away, as rejection slip after rejection slip met his every effort.

Those few publishers who actually read his manuscripts called them "too esoteric" or "too derivative" or "not commercial enough". Nothing he wrote ever made it into print. Idiots! Didn't they recognize his budding genius? Obviously not! They deserved his scorn… and one day maybe something far more!

Try though he may, George couldn't help obsessing over that stupid old question— *"If a tree falls in the forest and there's no one there to hear it, does it make a sound?"* Which led him to the more painful question—*"If there's no one out there allowed to read my novels, do they even exist? Or are they all just blank pages?"*

During all those years of thankless writing, George had made his living as a substitute teacher at a middle school. And later as a freelance copywriter at a small NJ ad agency that handled a few retail accounts. It was at one of them where George met Janet. A year or so later they were married. And pooling their salaries they could just afford to buy the small house where he still lived.

Then, after eight years of a barely tolerable marriage, George received his ultimate rejection slip. Janet's note on the kitchen table—

I've Had It!

Nothing more. No good-byes. No explanation.

She had emptied out her closet, her dresser, and their joint bank account. She had taken their one good car, leaving him the old junker that he drove to the post office, the market, and for a while to his workplaces.

That was nearly two years ago. Not long after, his substitute-teaching job was abolished due to budget cuts...and the ad agency where he worked had folded.

Desperate for funds, George had searched the internet for a possible new employer. Ultimately he found a publishing company in Texas that was looking for a free-lance editor. They called themselves *Ripper Publishing*...and said they specialized in thrillers and mysteries *"by new and promising authors"*. George knew that probably meant...books written by anyone with enough cash to actually pay *Ripper Publishing* to print their stuff.

The deal was that *Ripper* would send George the manuscripts online. He'd fix them up and email them back. There was to be no contact or consultation with the authors. George would be paid a flat rate by the page. The more pages he edited, the more he could make.

George took the job...actually the only one he could find. But soon it started eating away at him. It was not so much the hours of correcting punctuation and spelling, reworking run-on sentences and fixing the most glaring confusions in the narrative. It was the sheer trash he was asked to edit.

With few exceptions, it seemed that most of *Ripper*'s clients were cretins or drunks...spewing out yarns of malice and mayhem. At times, he seriously questioned the mental state of those who penned the perverse sex scenes that popped-up every few chapters. And beyond that...most of the key figures in their plots were so stupid or clueless in their actions that the Feds, or CIA, or local cops, or rival bad guys would have nailed them almost before they got started.

For months, George had managed to hold in his frustration...burying it deep inside. But for some reason, today his anger started to build. Perhaps it was the weeks of terrible weather, or his acid stomach, or his running out of cigarettes...but today his anger began to rise, then churn, then explode into a fury he had never felt before. Until he could no longer contain it.

In a rage he couldn't control, he leapt to his feet...grabbed the full pot of coffee off the burner and smashed to the floor. Then, at the top of his lungs he screamed out—

"No! No! No! No more!
Enough!
I am the one who has finally had it!
This has to end...and it will !!!"

Pacing the room, he fumed aloud—

"Life has been dealing me a totally crap hand!

"I'm a brilliant writer. And it's about time that the entire world wised up to that fact!

"The publishers say today's market wants 'Thrillers'...OK then, I'll give them the ultimate 'Thriller'!

"I'll create one so-compelling, so-exciting, so-alarming that it will totally redefine the genre.

"A work of such brilliance that even the most elitist literary critics will acclaim it!"

Still trembling a bit...but then suddenly overcome by a feeling of surging euphoria...George forcefully swept away everything on his desk. Pulled the plug on his computer. And grabbing paper and pen, feverishly began sketching out the concept for his masterwork.

The hours flew by. And by morning, he had it! A staggeringly brilliant concept…with plot twists so bold that every publisher in the world would come begging to sign him.

Then he scrawled down his working title—

"The Assassin."

Over the next several days, working with little sleep or food, George had made great progress outlining the plot details of the novel. And it was now time for his vital next step.

With every fiber of his being, George believed that a great writer must actually live the experience. Just making things up was not an option. He had to get out into the field if his work was to be truly honest and not just a new version of things he had read about before. So without hesitation, he committed himself to several months of actually living the life of an assassin.

He had to learn the best ways to kill, obviously. But he also had to know how to secure the right clients…and how to collect payments from them. All with virtually no risk of being found out or captured.

George started the process by researching assassination kill methods on the internet. He drew up a list of the four major techniques… weapons, explosives, poisons, and apparent accidents. While he personally favored poisons, he knew that a truly professional assassin should be expert in a full repertoire of killing techniques. Each target deserved their own select treatment…something that matched their transgressions or lifestyles. Anyone could kill, but a master assassin should do so with artistry. The premium assignments always went to those considered the best in their field. And as in any other business, referrals would be important. So a reputation for brilliance in the elimination of the target was essential!

Still, of all the killing methods, George innately favored poisons… or more broadly, toxins. While not opposed to using weapons like guns, knives, garrotes, etc., George considered them a bit too risky. And with the exception of a sniper rifle, they required being up-close and personal. This increased the odds of being caught or blocked in some way. And it gave the target an opportunity…perhaps a small one…to fight off the attack and survive.

Certainly, explosives had the advantage of killing at a distance…not only in terms of miles, but also in terms of time delays. Yet, there was some risk in planting a device without detection. And the blast site would leave significant forensic clues that could be traceable.

Accidents would seem an ideal killing method. Because at face value, an accident is an accident and not a killing. But staging one properly is not so easy. And depending on the target's importance, investigators would search aggressively for foul play. Once found, tracing things back to method and opportunity could pose a problem.

Which led George back to poisons. Some of which are untraceable. Some of which kill hours or even days after being administered. Some of which are so potent that death is almost immediate and absolutely guaranteed.

Yes, one had to get close to the victim to add a drop or two to their beverage or food. Or close enough to give them a quick pinprick while passing in a crowd. But there were other ways, too. A dried coating in their coffee cup or wine glass, a switched tube of toothpaste, a replaced container of mouthwash or face cream or hair gel.

With proper planning, poisons gave one the greatest degree of anonymity. Certainly, that was their great appeal. But to George, a far more compelling reason was their role in literary history... ranging from Cleopatra to Catherine de Medici to the poison apple that the Wicked Queen gave to Snow White...and thousands of legends more. These gave poisons their unequalled charm. So without question, poisons would be the specialty of George's title character!

But even while he was exhaustively researching the full scope of killing methods on the internet, George was multitasking to determine how best to find his first real "client" and "victim". And the technique he was currently testing had already proved amazingly simple and successful.

And that meant that very soon he would be heading south to Florida, where he would begin his active fieldwork!

TARGET # 1—

The Young Wife

2.

The Letter

BOCA RATON--

HOWARD DIXON SORTED through his stack of afternoon mail, all of it business related except for one envelope. This was hand addressed in block letters, with the word "Personal" underlined twice.

When he slit it open, the single-page typed letter sent a chill through his body. It read---

---

Mr. Dixon,

Your wife is having an affair. But that's not the reason I'm writing to you. I'm writing because she and her lover have attempted to hire me to kill you, so that they can collect on your recently revised Will that names her as your sole heir.

Throughout my career I've done many questionable things. But I've always drawn the line at targeting people who have done no wrong. It's a personal code of honor that I've tried to live by! And as far as I can determine, you have done no wrong—except perhaps in choosing poorly in the choice of your new young wife.

Thusly, I'm writing to warn you to take precautionary steps for your safety. If you wish—be so forewarned and just leave it at that. But if you'd like to take preemptive action to permanently remove the threat, I'd be honored to take on that task on your behalf. To give me the go-ahead, simply place the following listing on eBay within the next two weeks. It should read—
"For Sale—A 6-inch 17c bronze statue of St. Michael The Avenger. Starting bid-- $10,000."

If I see your listing, I'll be in further contact to finalize the terms of a possible contractual arrangement.

Stay well,
Your Guardian Angel

With hands trembling, Howard Dixon read the letter twice. Was it a hoax? A sick practical joke? And if so, who could have done it?

He absolutely couldn't believe that his sweet young wife had a lover…and even more so that she could be part of anything like this. But then why this letter with its accusations?

Surely this was the work of some psycho. And a dangerous one. Should he just ignore it and try to forget it? No! For the rest of his days it would prey on his mind and poison his marriage.

Should he show it to his wife…laughing it off as some sort of practical joke…while carefully watching her reactions for any telltale signs? No! That would only compound the problem. To do so would be an acknowledgement that he half-believed the accusations. And it would so upset her that their relationship would be tainted forever.

He'd become like some modern day Othello, with suspicion and jealousy destroying them both.

Should he hire a private detective to track her? And hire someone for his personal protection? That would be going pretty far, if it was just a hoax designed to unsettle him.

Clearly, he needed some good and highly confidential advice. And that meant calling his lawyer, Doug Sullivan.

Yes, Howard Dixon had remarried 6-months before. At 74, many thought he was being foolish to wed the 32-year old Tilly Brown. But she'd been there for him during those difficult times after he lost his dear wife of nearly 50-years to cancer.

Tilly had been Howard's executive assistant and closest colleague in the firm that he had founded when he was still a young man. They had spent more time together over the past 3 years than anyone else in either his business or personal life. His respect and admiration for her had grown steadily over that time to become something far more. A true fondness. Increasingly, he found himself simply delighted to be in her company during their long business hours together.

And then, after losing his wife, the way she consoled him had awakened feelings that he thought long gone. She brought him youthful joy. And as he finally realized…love. Love in all its illogical and magical forms.

At first, Howard feared that expressing his love to Tilly would so upset her that she would want to end their relationship. But to his amazement, she wept and told him that she had been in love him for more than 2-years. She said people would no doubt talk and gossip over a

May-December romance, but that really wouldn't matter if they truly loved one another. They were true soul mates, and she hoped for nothing more than spending the rest of their lives together.

They were quietly married on a business trip the following month. People learned of their union only upon their return.

With a wink, the guys at the Club saluted him for his good fortune... no doubt privately making snide little jokes about the questionable prowess of a septuagenarian with a new young bride. And his only child...a long estranged son...called him a stupid old fool for marrying someone who was young enough to be his grand-daughter.

But Howard was still fit and in great health. He looked like a man in his early 60s. With luck, he had a good 10 or more years ahead of him. Years that he'd rather not spend alone!

Tilly was certainly attractive, although many would call her a bit plain and bookish. She dressed conservatively and wore her light-brown hair in a simple pixie-cut. Soft spoken, she was smart-as-a-whip in both financial and legal matters. It was she who had put together many of the firm's most successful business ventures.

'Dixon Holdings' was a Florida real-estate investment firm in Boca Raton that Howard had founded in 1986. Over the years he had grown it to a $138-million enterprise. A key to its success was Howard's reputation for being scrupulously honest and fair dealing...a relatively rare commodity in Florida's entrepreneurial real-estate world. He was active in local charities, on the board of several foundations, and extremely well liked as a pillar of the community.

Those in real estate and banking had increasingly viewed Tilly as Howard's right-hand and junior partner. She was very talented and a very professional businessperson. Though their marriage raised eyebrows because of the age difference, no one would have called her a "gold-digger". That would have been clearly laughable!

Howard arrived at Doug Sullivan's office a little after 6:00PM on the same day he received the letter. Tilly was in Atlanta visiting her mother, and Howard wanted to see Doug and get his advice before she returned home the next morning.

After reading the letter and silently mulling its contents, Doug began with three direct questions—

"Do you think she's having an affair?"

"Absolutely not! That's simply unimaginable!"

"Do you think she wants you dead?"

"No. That's ridiculous!"

"How sure are you of all that?"

"I'm very sure. But the claim in this letter is so unnerving that I needed to talk it through with you…in utter confidence, to decide what I should do. And beyond that, I want to know who sent me this vicious letter and why. Whether it's a nut job, or a competitor, or part of some shakedown scheme, I want to know. I can't just toss the letter away and forget it. It's an attack on me and my happiness and I can't just leave it at that!"

"OK"…Doug nodded. "Then here's what I think we should do--

"First of all, let's rule out the affair thing. I have a very discreet and capable investigator who can monitor Tilly's movements and also look into her background…from before you first met her…right up until today. Who knows? Rather than an affair, there could be someone from her past, or present, who is putting pressure on her… blackmail or whatever. Or conversely, perhaps this letter is intended to destroy <u>her</u>…and not you. Someone who is holding a grudge against Tilly. Someone wanting to ruin her life. My investigator will uncover all of that, to see if there's anything there.

"Next comes the question of a hired killer. Finding one and hiring one is far easier said than done. And a search for one leaves obvious tracks. My investigator can shake the trees and find out if anyone has been in the market recently for a hired killer. If the answer is 'No'…that knocks down a likely threat against you. But just to be safe, I'll have him assign a discreet security team to watch your back for the next few weeks. You'll never see that they're there. But believe me, you'll be kept safe!

"Now let's talk about the letter itself. Who wrote it and why?

"It appears to have been computer-printed on a common ink jet printer. No real clues there. We'll do a forensic analysis of the paper, looking for fingerprints. The writer no doubt wore gloves. But it's possible there may be residual prints on the paper that was loaded into the printer, possibly some weeks before. That's something often forgotten and therefore overlooked.

"Then there's the postmark. New York City. That doesn't tell us much. Even if this person is local, it may have been mailed from there to throw us off.

"The contents of the letter itself are more than a little strange. It's signed 'Your Guardian Angel'. It talks about a 'personal code of honor' and being 'honored to take on that task on your behalf'. And it asks you to give them the go-ahead by offering to sell a 17th century bronze statue on eBay. A statue of 'St. Michael The Avenger'. I'm no Biblical scholar, but I've never heard of any such Archangel. But we can look into that more. Does all of that give us a personality profile? Maybe. But it could all be just some mumbo-jumbo designed to throw us off.

"Howard, do you know anyone who thinks like that…or talks like this? Angels? Saints? Avengers? Does any of that ring a bell, no matter how vague? Possibly someone from your past, someone from the Club or your Church? Someone from business, possibly an old client or competitor? Or maybe someone with a connection to your first wife?

"No? OK then!

"If you draw a blank there, there's really only one way to learn more about the writer. Only one way to smoke him out…assuming it's a 'he' and not a 'she'. And that's to actually do that posting on eBay.

"It's my recommendation that we move ahead with that…exactly as he specifies. And then, when he responds, we'll have far more to go on.

"If there's no offer to buy the statue, then we can conclude it's all a hoax and we can rest easy. And if there is a reply, there'll no doubt be a request for payment. That's where these things almost always go south for the bad guys. When they try to collect, we can nab them. All that stuff in novels about untraceable wire transfers, and multiple drop-off points, and burner phones sounds good, but the authorities can usually break them wide open. And we will bring in the authorities…probably the FBI…once we get this guy's reply.

“Those are my recommendations. Are you comfortable with them?

“Howard…?”

“Yes, Yes, and Yes to them all, Doug! I’m really grateful for your advice on all this. Frankly, I didn’t know what to do, or where to start. Thank God I came to see you!”

“Howard, don’t worry. We’ll see this through. We’ve been friends since college, and I’ve been your lawyer since even before you started your business. As you know, I was really delighted when you married Tilly. And I absolutely hate that you’re being put through all this. We’ll nail this bastard! You can count on it!”

3.

The Client

NEW JERSEY--

"St. Michael The Avenger!"

George Trecott's smile broadened when he saw the listing on eBay. "So that guy in Boca Raton is the one who has taken the bait!"

George had mailed his letter to seven men in different parts of the country. All in their 70's or older. All fairly recently married to far younger women. All in affluent communities like Boca Raton. He had narrowed his search to these seven after researching a far larger group on the internet. It's amazing how much you can learn if you know how to access the staggering amount of personal data in the Cloud.

May-December weddings among so-called industry leaders were easy to find. Changes to Wills a little less so…but much could be inferred from changes in property-ownership documents and changes in the beneficiaries of financial accounts. Then a deep dive into the social and family and community life of the individuals and their spouses would yield a short list of likely candidates. George particularly liked to study their photos…not only the published ones, but also those stored in the Cloud. From childhood, through yearbooks, to those just recently taken. All could shed revealing light on the personality of the individuals.

Obviously, ex-military and ex-law enforcement types were culled out. Also those with a "tough guy" reputation or appearance. Not that they wouldn't want a cheating wife taken care of…it's just that their response might be less predictable.

No, George wanted guys like Howard Dixon…at least in this first test of "client development". Nice guys with reportedly kind natures and stellar reputations. Guys who might be so shaken by his letter that they would not know what to do. Guys who would just want the problem to go away. Guys who if properly handled could become "clients".

All seven of the letters that George mailed out were basically the same…differing only in the item to be sold on eBay. Now two weeks later, only the-- "17c bronze statue of St. Michael The Avenger"-- was listed. That acknowledgement made Howard Dixon officially "the client".

Now for the next step—

No, George Trecott would not reply to Howard Dixon. In fact, no contact of any kind would ever be made. This was still the basic research stage. Not yet the real thing. In this, the initial stage, George was only looking for a fairly safe and easy way to attract and communicate with potential clients. And eBay seemed to be the perfect way to receive their messages without revealing his location. The whole 'payment step' could be deferred until much much later. Thanks to the advent of Bitcoin and the other cryptocurrencies, that would be fairly safe and easy. But for now, George wanted no money…just knowledge. And he was increasingly anxious to get rolling on the most dangerous and unnerving part of the whole process…the actual kill.

And to begin that phase of his research, it was time for George to finally pack up his bags and drive to Florida.

4.

The Wife

BOCA RATON--

GEORGE PREPARED THE dose. Just enough to send Tilly to the Emergency Room and not the morgue. He didn't want to actually kill her. And in this case, he wanted the toxin to be highly traceable, so that the hospital lab would immediately suspect foul play. This was an important part of his research because he wanted to see the reaction of the authorities. He wanted to see how soon Tilly's husband would be implicated and how the broader investigation would proceed.

And to add a little spice, George had tossed in a nice diversionary twist. Right after receiving the EBay response, he sent Howard's estranged son a separate backdated letter. This one stressing that -- "your gold-digging stepmother is about to steal your rightful inheritance". In this letter, he didn't ask for an eBay response, just that he would be in further contact. Hopefully, this letter would give the cops a second family member to suspect. That would prove interesting!

George had driven to Florida and paid cash at all the gas stations, small motels, and fast food restaurants on the way. He avoided major highways that had EZPass toll cameras. He wanted no electronic records of his travels. He checked into a motor court about five miles from Boca and spent the next week doing surveillance.

Before departing from home, George had filled a suitcase with items of disguise. Used clothes and hats from a thrift shop…in both men's and women's styles. And importantly, he also bought a few pairs of distinctive shoes and sneakers.

From the websites of costume shops and theatrical supply houses, he bought wigs, fake mustaches and beards, along with a kit of stage makeup. And from drug stores, he bought both sunglasses and clear readers.

Ideally, he would also have liked to have fake IDs and other documents. But they would take time to secure. Getting them would have to be deferred until his next "project".

Once in Florida, he rented a different car each day…from different companies at different locations. And each day he assumed a different persona while he surveilled Howard and Tilly. This proved to be a wise move, because he spotted the same black SUV across from their condo when they were home… which was then re-parked near their offices during the day. Whenever Howard left the office, the SUV tailed him. It was clear that Howard had requested some type of protective surveillance. Not the police. This looked to be private.

Because George used a different car and changed his appearance each day, he wasn't spotted. However, he had to use his real drivers license and credit cards for his car rentals…creating a potential problem. But he had carefully picked the rental locations in a way to establish a plausible explanation, should the need arise. He would claim that he was a retiree from up North, thinking about a possible move to Florida. And that he was visiting different communities on the East and West Coast to compare them. Unfortunately, he had to rent cars on a few occasions, because his own car kept having erratic engine problems…and he didn't want to get stranded in an unfamiliar location.

Once sure of Howard and Tilly's daily routine, George then firmed up his plan and his timetable. They almost always left their condo shortly after 7:00AM…Monday through Saturday. They drove in separate cars, even though both started off their day at their company offices on South Federal Highway. Separate cars allowed Howard to visit his real-estate properties during the day, and Tilly to take out-of-the-office trips for meetings with their accountants, lawyers, city land departments, bankers, etc.

But on her way to the office, every morning without fail, Tilly stopped first at a place called the "Boca Bean Coffee Shop". She always ordered a latte and a croissant. Then she sat at an outside table, checking messages on her iPhone. Only if it rained did she take her order to-go.

Of all the other possible locations…at their Club, at a favorite restaurant, in their offices, in their home, or on the road…George concluded that the Boca Bean was the ideal and safest place to poison Tilly.

To prepare, George surveilled the place on three successive mornings… arriving before Tilly, listening to her order, and watching how the baristas served up each order.

The first barista would take the order and accept payment. That order would then be passed along to a second barista, who would prep the order and then set it out for pick up at the far side-end of the counter. With heavy morning business, it usually took 3 or more minutes until the coffee order was set out…with an indication of the specific brew written in marker on the white plastic lid. And in Tilly's case, that was always Chai Latte.

On the morning of the deed, George was particularly nervous. This was a real person, not just a character in his fiction.

Watching Tilly these past few days, he had actually grown a bit fond of her. She seemed a genuinely nice person. A person that he wished he had known. The type of person he would have liked to have as a wife. But he kept telling himself that she wouldn't be seriously harmed. Yes, the toxin would cause her to pass out, but it would cause no lingering damage. It might even make her husband love her more! Howard's fear over her health and his display of devotion would likely bring them closer together. So in doing this, George told himself, he was actually doing her good, not wrong.

Reining in his nervousness, George entered the "Boca Bean Coffee Shop" the moment he saw Tilly pull into the strip mall parking lot. He ordered a Chai Latte, paid cash, and moved down to the end of the counter to wait for his order. When it came, he popped open the lid…feigning a glimpse inside to see if his order was correct… squirted in the toxin and quickly recapped the cup. Stepping back from the counter and moving toward the milk and napkin station with the cup, he waited until the moment Tilly's order hit the counter. He then swiftly moved back and switched the cups. If his timing was off, he could always walk out with the doctored latte and try again the next day.

But this morning, his timing was perfect. Tilly had lingered a few extra moments to check her cellphone before going to the pick up. The switch was made with no one the wiser.

George left the coffee shop with his cup and went directly to his car. He watched as Tilly took an outside table, sipped her latte and started going through her email. Three minutes or so later, she seemed to swoon and her head hit the table. Her phone fell to the ground. Those seated around her rushed over to help. Then someone from the Coffee Shop staff ran out, surveyed the situation and started to dial 911.

In his car, George took a sip of his Chai Latte, made a face at a taste he certainly did not like, opened up the door and poured all the remaining liquid onto the ground. He placed the empty cup and lid in a plastic bag, started up his rental car and drove away.

He would retrieve his own car, change motels, and stay in the area to monitor the local news. All the while thinking to himself—"This will be really fascinating!"

5.

The Investigation

WEST PALM BEACH--

THE PALM BEACH Sheriff's Office has over 4,200 employees, serving over 1,400,000 Floridians through 20 district offices across Palm Beach County. The scene of the incident...Boca Raton...was in District 7, located at 18901 State Road right in Boca. But due to the nature of the case, and Tilly and Howard Dixon's prominence in Palm Beach County, it was quickly bumped up to Headquarters in West Palm Beach.

When the call first came in, 911 dispatched both EMS paramedics and the local police to the "Boca Bean Coffee Shop". They transported the still-unconscious Tilly Dixon to the ER at the nearby Boca Raton Regional Hospital, a highly ranked 400-bed facility. After the attending team quickly ruled out trauma, brain injury, stroke, heart attack, and anaphylactic shock, their suspicion immediately turned to poisoning. That's when the Sheriff's Office in Boca was first notified.

Fortuitously, the first-responding police officer to the scene of the incident had secured and bagged everything on and around Tilly Dixon's table...including both her cell phone and tote bag. But even so, the local Sheriff's Office dispatched a team to process the area and take statements from the Coffee Shop employees.

With a suspicion of possible poisoning, the hospital team worked swiftly to stabilize Tilly's airway, breathing, circulation, and neurological status. Blood and urine samples were rushed to pathology to assess her electrolytes, kidney function, liver function, and to provide a complete blood count. Meanwhile, her GI tract was decontaminated using activated charcoal, and a total bowel irrigation procedure was run to remove any possible toxins that were still unabsorbed by her system.

These procedures bore fruit. Tilly's vital signs stabilized and within little more than an hour she regained consciousness. Her first words—"What happened? Call Howard!"

Moments later, the Deputy Sheriff in Boca called his superiors at the West Palm Beach Headquarters. His first words— "We've got a probable VIP poisoning!" And because it was the wife of one of the county's most prominent business leaders, the word of the poisoning quickly spread all the way to the top.

Primarily known by its acronym—PBSO—the Palm Beach Sheriff's Office was a huge complex on Gun Hill Road in West Palm Beach. Located in the 12-story South Tower, it was flanked by twin 6-story East and West Towers. In addition to its 2,166 inmate Detention Center, the complex housed the Crime Lab with a staff of over 100 scientists and support personnel and state-of-the-art capabilities in both toxicology and latent print identification. It was here that all the samples and test results from the Boca Raton Regional Hospital were sent...along with all the forensic materials gathered and bagged at the scene by the local police.

The Crime Lab confirmed initial suspicions. Tilly Dixon had indeed been poisoned. A fairly exotic alkaloid had been introduced into her latte. It was a compound that could cause short-term paralysis, but would almost never prove fatal. Whether the intent was murder…or instead to simply incapacitate her…could not be initially determined.

At this point, the investigation was labeled "a potential homicide attempt"…and it was turned over to the PBSO's Violent Crimes Division… where it was assigned to one of the 4 squads in the Homicide Unit. In addition, the FBI was briefed.

Though the PBSO had clear jurisdiction in this case, the FBI had asked to be kept fully informed because there could possibly be one or more Federal crimes involved. While the FBI Regional Field Office is located in Miami, they had a Satellite Office right in West Palm Beach, not far from the PBSO. And unlike all the territorial disputes and infighting often portrayed in the movies, the PBSO and the West Palm Beach FBI Satellite Office had always worked cordially and extremely well together.

Because of the prominence of the Dixons, everyone recognized that the case would draw extensive media coverage…and that they had to get ahead of that coverage. So three days later, a joint meeting was held in the PBSO main conference room. Convened at the request of the Sheriff himself, it brought together the heads of the Special Investigation Division, the Violent Crimes Division, the Homicide Unit, and the Crime Lab. The Chief of the Homicide Unit brought along his chief Lieutenant and the two detectives he had assigned to the Tilly Dixon case. Also present was the PBSO's Communications Director and the FBI Director-in-Charge of the West Palm Beach Office. The purpose of the meeting was to give the Sheriff a full and comprehensive report on progress to date. And to make sure the entire team was "on the same page" and doing everything possible to bring this case to a successful conclusion.

The general public was not yet aware of the poisoning. The press had reported that Howard Dixon's wife Tilly had collapsed at a local coffee shop and been rushed to the Boca Raton Regional Hospital. It was further reported that while now out of the ICU and resting comfortably, she remained at the Hospital for observation and further testing. That was how the PBSO had managed the story so far.

But the press and the public could not be kept in the dark much longer. And the potential for a media frenzy was enormous—

"The mysterious poisoning of a prominent Florida businesswoman!"
"Is there poison in your latte?"
"Are our Coffee Shops no longer safe?"
"Is this the work of homegrown terrorists?"
"Is there a deranged murderer in our midst?"
"Police have no clue!"

If not properly handled, this could become the lead story on every news broadcast in the Nation...and become fodder for weeks of sensationalist follow-up stories and articles in the press and online. And just as with the Tylenol capsule poisoning crisis back in 1982, the hysteria that this might cause could last for months...doing damage not only to South Florida's reputation, but doing economic damage to the entire Fast Food industry.

With all that hanging in the balance, the Sheriff had scheduled a 10:00AM Press Conference for the next day. And prior to that, he had to brief the Governor, the two State Senators, and key county and local officials. To accomplish that, he had scheduled an afternoon conference call. To prepare for these events, he needed...and demanded...a detailed, candid, and up-to-the-minute report from his people!

Lieutenant R.C. Nichols of the Homicide Unit was put in charge of the briefing. And he organized it in a chronological sequence.... bringing in his Detectives and others as needed, should questions arise. He had provided all attendees with a full kit of reports and reference documents for their review prior to the session.

After introducing his people and providing an outline of his presentation, Lt. Nichols started at the beginning—

"911 got the call at 7:24AM last Tuesday morning. A woman, subsequently identified as Tilly Brown Dixon, had collapsed at an outdoor table of the Boca Bean Coffee Shop. She was unconscious and unresponsive. EMS personnel and the local police arrived at 7:29AM. After checking her vital signs, the still unconscious woman was transported by the EMS to the Boca Raton Regional Hospital. The first-responding police officer had secured the area. His report is in your packet.

"The Hospital suspected poisoning and took successful measures to revive her and clear her system of any toxins. There's a full report from the Hospital in your packet. They state that she appears to be fully recovered.

"She was discharged on Friday and is now resting at home with her husband Howard Dixon, the CEO of Dixon Holdings. The press calls Howard Dixon 'The Dean of South Florida Real Estate'. And our current and past Governors have honored him for his many humanitarian and civic good works. He's also been honored by various State and National organizations for his business and personal achievements.

"I understand, Sheriff, that you're acquainted with Mr. Dixon socially?"

"Yes, Lieutenant. But that's of little relevance here. In this job, you meet a lot of people socially. Mr. Dixon appears to be a model citizen. And though you can't always tell a book by its cover, we do know that there are some in the press who'd love nothing more than to tear down the reputation of a so-called 'model citizen'. And dare I say…the reputations of law enforcement and public officials! That said, please carry on with your presentation, Lieutenant."

"Yes Sir! To continue—

"The Crime Lab has done a complete work up on the 'poison' found in Mrs. Dixon's system. Their full report is in your packet. They've identified the substance as an alkaloid compound once fairly widely used by Veterinarians to anesthetize larger animals for surgery and in pain management for other procedures. While not preferred for those uses today, it's still available and can often be obtained without a prescription. And there are probably old bottles of it in many stables and barns across the State and Country. As such, there's almost no way to determine where this specific material was obtained.

"Mrs. Dixon ingested the 'poison' in her chai latte, purchased minutes before at the Boca Bean Coffee Shop. The concentration in her cup was strong enough to render her unconscious, but was below a potentially lethal dose, per the Crime Lab. In fact, even at a larger dose, its effects would likely have worn off in a few hours, with no lingering medical issues. That's a calculation based on her size and body weight and general health history. However, lethal intent cannot be ruled out. The perpetrator may have simply misjudged the compound's effect.

"I don't want to minimize what happened here. But some of the lab guys have quipped that, in effect, someone gave Mrs. Dixon a giant 'Mickey Finn'!"

At this, the Communications Director perked up and nodded with a smile to the Sheriff...while franticly making notes.

"The Crime Lab also did a full work up on the coffee cup, its lid and all the other materials on and around Mrs. Dixon's table at the Boca Bean Coffee Shop. The only prints found were from Mrs. Dixon and the coffee shop employees. However, smears over the employee's prints on the cup and lid suggest that someone with gloves or using a napkin may have handled the cup after it was placed out for pick-up. Nothing significant was found on any of the other items on or near the table where Mrs. Dixon sat and drank her chai latte. Only the coffee cup had the 'poison'

"The key question, of course, is who put the substance in Mrs. Dixon's cup? And to determine that, we started our investigation at the Boca Bean. Detectives Bert Carlson and Harry Rodrigues interviewed the shop's employees...retrieved and analyzed the shop's security camera footage...and made copies of all the credit card and cash register transactions that morning.

"Mrs. Dixon ordered her chai latte at 7:13AM. This was her usual order. Interestingly, another individual ordered a chai latte at 7:10AM...just 3-minutes before Mrs. Dixon entered the Coffee Shop. That was the only other chai latte ordered that morning. This individual paid in cash, so we have no credit card records to follow up on. But the security camera captured a quarter-angle rear view of that person. It was a middle-aged, fairly heavy-set woman, wearing a short blazer-type jacket, dark red pants and blue and white Nike sneakers. She wore a tan sunhat and wore dark sunglasses with large lenses. We estimated her height at about 5' 6" and her weight about

180-pounds, her age in the early 60s. Her hair was dark brown going to gray. Unfortunately, the security camera was in the far corner of the Coffee Shop, so we have no clear or full-face images to help identify her. The store employees said she was not a regular customer and they don't believe they have ever seen her before… or since.

"Our yet to be identified 'mystery woman' picked up her latte at the far end of the receiving counter and left the Coffee Shop just before Mrs. Dixon picked up her cup. It was at this receiving counter that we believe a possible cup switch was made!

"Security cameras in the parking lot let us identify the car that our female suspect was driving. After leaving the Shop, she got behind the wheel of a late model white Ford Fiesta sedan…where she sat sipping her latte until Mrs. Dixon actually collapsed at her outside table. That's when our suspect opened her driver's side door, poured out the rest of her latte, closed the door and drove away. Forensics were unable to find traces of the poured out latte.

"We thought we really had something when the parking lot security footage gave us her license plate numbers. But that proved a dead end. It seems those plates had come off a junker car parked out back of the Pompano Beach Car Body Shop. She had obviously switched the plates from that car to avoid detection. This pretty well confirms that this woman was our likely perpetrator.

"Who is she? As of yet, we do not know.
"What was her motive? That's still unclear.
"Was she working alone…or on behalf of someone else? That's still to be determined.
"Was she specifically targeting Mrs. Dixon…or just anyone at random?

"We're still early in our investigation...and while we don't as yet have very much to go on, we're confident that we'll eventually find this woman and answer all those questions.

"In addition to our efforts to identify our 'mystery woman', we've explored the possibility that the Coffee Shop employees or the owner himself might somehow be involved.

"Our investigation has uncovered that the two baristas working there that day were selling drugs out of the Coffee Shop. A buyer would order 'four special javas'...and when paying in cash, would slip an extra $100 bill into the first barista's hand.

"Receiving a high sign, the second barista would pour out 3 hot coffees and slip a drug packet into an empty 4th cup. All four cups would then be put in a cardboard carrying frame...and the happy customer would just walk away with his or her stash.

"We sweated these guys over a possible attempted murder rap... and they quickly told all. They gave up their scheme in an effort to show that they were just low-level street guys and nothing more. We've turned all this over to the Narcotics Division, who think they can keep these guys talking...possibly leading up the food chain to some major distributors. Do any of us think that the Tilly Dixon 'poisoning' is somehow related to the drug trade? No. But we don't want to rule out anything.

"The owner of the Boca Bean Coffee Shop is one Carlos Jarman. And we've determined that he is in serious debt to the Sanchez Syndicate. What started as a typical monthly protection squeeze grew into a debt of over $100,000. When no one else would lend him the money he needed to keep his Coffee Shop operating, he unwisely borrowed the money from them. And we understand that he's been unable to repay them. We can't yet tell if this in any way has a bearing on the

Tilly Dixon case. A warning to Jarman, perhaps? That is something we'll keep pursuing. But effectively destroying the business would seem counterproductive...a very unlikely way to collect on owed money. Then again, it may be part of a plan to take over the business.

"Now, getting into the most critical and revealing part of our investigation...our focus on the victim and her husband.

"We interviewed Mrs. Dixon at some length in the hospital. She said she couldn't think of a single person who might want to harm her. No one from her past life in Atlanta. No one from her single or married life in Florida. No one from business. No one from her social circle. Definitely not her husband.

"But bells went off when we asked her husband if he could think of anyone who might want to harm his wife. He was at her Hospital bedside day and night and appeared very distraught. But rather than taking a few minutes to directly answer our questions, he asked if he and his lawyer Doug Sullivan could meet with us the next morning at his lawyer's office.

"That's when they showed us the 'Guardian Angel' letter and their investigator's detailed report. Their investigator's name is Chuck Daily. He's a retired Miami PD Detective Sergeant with a solid reputation. You've already seen the 'Guardian Angel' letter and the investigator's report. And you'll find duplicate copies in your packets.

"We asked Dixon and his lawyer why they decided to reach out to this 'Guardian Angel' individual directly with a posting on eBay... rather than to call in the authorities. A transcript of their response is also included in your packets.

"Bottom line—they wanted to see if this was just a hoax. And if not, to flush the guy out and have something more solid to bring to the authorities. Dixon said his prime concern was to not upset his wife and their relationship needlessly. He said he wanted to protect her from all this, if it turned out there was no real threat.

"They claim they received no response whatsoever. No contact. No calls for payment. Nothing. So they chalked it up to being a sick practical joke.

"Frankly, we believe them and have tentatively cleared the wife's husband from any direct involvement in his wife's poisoning. He was certainly foolish to not bring us in at the outset. But other than that, the advice given by the lawyer, and the work done by the investigator Chuck Daily, was all pretty sound. What they did was pretty close to what we would have done if they had brought us in. Obviously, we're revisiting all their findings…in the Crime Lab and in the field. Also, we've asked our PBSO and FBI profilers to analyze the letter for any clues about the writer.

"We next interviewed a number of Tilly and Howard Dixon's business associates and friends. Nothing relevant uncovered there.

"But when we interviewed Howard Dixon's son…Willard Dixon… low and behold, he showed us a second, and different, letter that he had received from the 'Guardian Angel'. A copy of that letter is also in your packet. This second letter claimed that Tilly Dixon was conspiring to have his father's Will changed, to steal his rightful inheritance. There was no eBay mention. It just said that the sender would be in future contact. Per Willard Dixon, that never occurred. He said he therefore concluded that it was just a crank letter.

"He also claimed that because of his lifestyle, his father had rarely spoken to him in over 6 years…and that he had never met Tilly

Brown Dixon. He said he considered their marriage none of his business and none of his concern. And that he wanted none of their money. He runs a successful charter boat business, is single, and has a good reputation. To date, we have not cleared him. Our uncertainty revolves around that second letter. Why was it sent to him? A diversion from the sender? Or did he write both letters himself to throw off suspicion? We're digging into his background and finances in an attempt to know more.

"One more possibility— Is it possible that this poisoning of Tilly Dixon was in actuality a random act? That the perpetrator was not targeting Tilly Dixon specifically? But that she just happened to be in the wrong place at the wrong time? That instead, this was the work of some disgruntled person or persons wanting to make a protest statement? A statement against 'the one-percenters'...or against 'latte drinking liberals'…or against 'Boca Raton fat cats'… or who-knows-what?

"While unlikely, it's a remote possibility that we can't dismiss. But if this indeed was the case, it would be one pretty remarkable coincidence, considering the 'Guardian Angel' letters. And as they always drum into us at the Police Academy…'there really are no such things as coincidences!' But even so, we'll keep our minds open on this one.

"So in summary, where does our investigation now stand?

"Unofficially—We're a long way from solving this case. A long way from charging anyone. A long way from proving anyone's guilt. A long way from even knowing the motive!

"We're certain that our 'mystery woman' from the Coffee Shop is the person who actually added the substance to Tilly Dixon's latte. But we have no hard admissible evidentiary proof. From her evasive actions, we can clearly see that she's no amateur. That's incriminating, but only circumstantial. From day one, finding her has been a top priority. But she seems to have vanished into the wind. To date, our APB on her has produced absolutely nothing.

"She could have acted alone. But what if she's just a hired operative? We can't and shouldn't rule out the possibility that there's someone else…someone bigger…behind all this. And finding that person hinges on our finding out specifically why Tilly Dixon was targeted.

"That brings us to those two 'Guardian Angel' letters… finding out who wrote them and finding out what they were really up to. Without doubt, they offer to eliminate Tilly Dixon. But the obvious question is motive. With no request for payment, it clearly wasn't money. But what then was the motive? Do we have someone with a major grudge against the Dixons? Someone who possibly sees themselves as some kind of grand chess master…making clever moves to get others to fail? We're working on that assumption.

"Is our 'mystery woman' the 'Guardian Angel'? Or is she an accomplice, or just someone the 'Guardian Angel' had hired? Was the poison intended to kill? Or was it just a warning? Is there a 'second act' yet to come?

"To determine all that, we're conducting an intensive multi-pronged investigation that continues…but that to date has produced only questions and no definitive answers. This is a tough one and the prospects of closing it soon are uncertain…unless the perp makes further contact or does it again.

"That's my '<u>Unofficial Report</u>'. But recognizing why we're all here, let me now give you my '<u>Official Report</u>'.

"It's a short-form summary that hopefully will keep the Press and the Politicians satisfied enough...at least for now...so that we can keep doing our job. Doing our job without turning this whole thing into a circus! Here's a printed copy. But let me read it aloud—

"The PBSO has reported an incident at the 'Boca Bean Coffee Shop' in Boca Raton, where a local businesswoman, Mrs. Tilly Dixon, lost consciousness and was taken to the nearby Boca Raton Memorial Hospital. After being revived, she was kept overnight for observation and released in good health the next day. The specific cause of her short-term loss of consciousness is still under investigation, with the possibility of some form of food poisoning or food contamination. Further findings will be released when the investigation is complete. "

"That's all I have! Any questions?"

From the Communications Director—

"I like it. But, of course, the Press will swamp us with questions. So if I'm really, really pressed... off-the-record, I can feed them that quip from one of the local cops. I wrote it down. He said—

> *"Who knows, maybe some sad sack guy slipped her a Mickey so that he could play hero! But then he panicked and ran off!"*

At that, the Sheriff showed some annoyance and just shook his head. He then directed a question to Lieutenant Nichols—

"The Press will certainly be going after Howard and Tilly Dixon for their comments. Where do we stand with them?"

"They very definitely want to avoid publicity of any kind. In fact, they've said that they plan to refer all questions to the PBSO for comment...and that they also plan to refuse all interview requests. It's not that they're camera shy. They're as anxious as we are... actually even more so...to find out who is doing this to them. But they believe we're in the best position to find that out. So they're putting their full trust in us. And in exchange, we've promised to keep them fully informed...which should keep them from going off the reservation."

At that, the Sheriff stood up, thanked Lieutenant Nichols, and leaving the room, turned to make one final comment—

"Keep the pressure on. And keep me fully informed. I want this case solved ASAP!"

6.

Fly-on-the-Wall

NEW JERSEY--

BACK HOME IN New Jersey, George Trecott delighted in all he had learned in his little Florida experiment. Seeing his plan in action. Tingling with the excitement of possibly being discovered and arrested. Actually being immersed in all the detail and texture of real-life locations.

George savored and relived every step in the process. The mapping of his route to Florida and around Boca Raton…so that no record of his presence would exist. The tricky mechanics of pulling off daily car rentals, motel changes, and persuasive disguises. All without a hitch. These were real-life experiences that no author just sitting at home could realistically conceptualize or express.

And then there was the deed itself! Dressing as a middle-aged woman for the benefit of the cameras and coffee shop staff. More than the clothes and makeup, it was mastering the walk, talk and gestures. To perfect these, George had practiced for hours before a mirror, copying what he saw in his tapes of old movies.

Once home, George organized and consolidated all of the field notes he had made during his Florida trip. They filled several notebooks…

and this was only the first of the several in-the-field experiments he was planning to make.

He also made a list of the flaws in his planning and execution. Things he must correct going forward. Obviously, he needed a full set of fake ID documents…starting with a driver's license, social security card, and more. All could be obtained for cash in NYC if you knew where to look. A few sets of car license plates would also be helpful, eliminating the need to secure them in the field. That would be fairly easy, since most people never bothered to turn in their old plates when getting rid of an old car. He'd also like to add a few extras to his costume and makeup kit. A homeless person, a security cop, a chef, a waiter, maybe a nurses aide, maybe even a priest.

Then he sat back to reflect on all he had learned…not just the stagecraft…but also from the still ongoing actions of the Dixons and the Police. Having planned well, he had created a primary, real-time source. A week before traveling to Florida, George had successfully installed spyware in both Howard's and Tilly's laptops.

It's amazing how foolish even the most experienced computer users are. How easily they can be enticed to open an email attachment. In Howard's case, it was an attached article presumably from his Golf Club. In Tilly's, it was a piece about "Women in Business" from the AMA.

Once the spyware was installed, George could read all of Howard and Tilly's email. Email between themselves, to and from their lawyer…and of greatest interest…emails to and from Lieutenant Nichols in the Palm Beach Sheriff's Office.

Talk about being a fly-on-the-wall! This put George right in the center of the whole ongoing investigation. And he was totally amazed at just how extensive it was. At the onset, George hadn't really considered that his 'spiking' of Tilly's latte in a little coffee shop would be treated as a 'VIP Poisoning'...and that it would draw the attention of the entire PBSO and the Sheriff himself. He would never have imagined how many avenues the PBSO would explore... how many alternate theories they would consider. The number and range of resources they would employ. Just how high up the law enforcement and political food chain this simple case of a spiked cup of coffee would climb. All this made his little maiden experiment vastly more productive!

George was not particularly concerned that the police would ever discover his role in planning and carrying out this "poisoning"... though he did want to carefully monitor how they were proceeding in their investigation. But what he really wanted to see and experience was the emotional reactions of Howard and Tilly after having their lives turned upside down.

Did he feel a bit guilty? When it came to Tilly and Howard...admittedly "Yes". They both seemed pretty decent and undeserving of the pain and turmoil he might be causing them. But as they say..."You have to break a few eggs to make a good omelet." So it's only fair that a writer might have to disrupt a few comfortable lives to create a great novel!

Only next time...for learning experiment Number Two...he decided that he would choose an unrepentant bastard as his target. And even more important, that this target be surrounded by high-security personnel. It was one thing to walk into a public coffee shop uncontested. The vastly bigger challenge was to perfect a way to penetrate a high-security location, make the 'kill', and come away undetected.

And his search to find that person and situation had already begun!

TARGET # 2—

The Con Man

7.

'Tex' Bickford

INDIANAPOLIS--

SEYMOUR DOLLAN (AKA 'Tex' Jay Bickford) sat quietly in his cell in the Marion County Jail #1 on Alabama Street in Indianapolis. At 6-foot-three and beanpole slim...with a sweep of longish gray hair, a deep tan, and silver blue eyes...the 54-year old Dollan had looked every bit the part of the Texas millionaire he had claimed to be when they arrested him three weeks ago.

But today, in his ill-fitting prison-issued jumpsuit, he looked more shifty than genteel. Gone were the trappings of his image—the cream-colored Stetson hat, the thousand-dollar buckskin jacket, the custom-made python boots, the bolo tie, and the gold Rolex Oyster watch. All these were locked away in the prison's storage lockers, along with his iPhone, a bulging money clip of cash, and his wallet filled with credit and debit cards.

Also gone...at least for today...was his signature million-dollar smile and folksy baritone drawl...both of which he had perfected watching old John Huston films. But he was never without that razor-sharp mind and wide-eyed empathetic gaze that he had learned to combine in a way that had put so many under his spell.

Some lucky ones seem to have been blessed with natural-born talents. His was the ability to persuade and manipulate. As a child, he found he could con his parents and teachers almost at will. In high school, he could persuade his classmates to take tests and write papers for him…to "loan" him cash and their cars…all while working his special magic on some of the most unapproachable girls in school…getting them to go "gaga" and then to go "all the way".

With talents like these, Dollan knew that he was destined to far greater things than his small Upstate New York town could offer. Before becoming 'Tex' Bickford, Seymour assumed a number of personas and roles. Dropping out of high school at 17, he went to Utica…where claiming to be 21 he became Billy Sweeny working on commission doing estimates for a shady furnace repair company. With few exceptions, he turned a simple tune-up job into a full furnace and boiler replacement. Winning him the gratitude of the homeowner for saving them from a potentially disastrous house fire…but more importantly, earning him thousands in commissions.

From there he moved to Poughkeepsie, where as Will Collins he became a "water control engineer"…persuading dozens of homeowners that the water seepage in their basements, if not corrected, would result in dangerous mold, critical foundation settling, and a major loss in their home's resale value. He not only sold them expensive French drain installations…on a profitable no-money-down financing plan…but in several cases, also convinced them they needed complete asbestos abatement and radon gas protection systems. Typically, he could make the sale in one call, with commissions averaging nearly $5,000 per customer.

Then in Pittsburg he was Colin Wilson, selling penny stocks. In Atlanta he became Cole Thomas, with his own investment-counseling firm—'Wealth Builders International'. All this was before Seymour turned 27.

From there he moved to bigger and bigger things. Which eventually led him to Dallas, where he became 'Tex' Bickford...Founder and CEO of 'Galileo Global Partners'.

Sitting in his cell, Dollan ran through a series of possible strategies he could use to get out of this one. He had been charged many times before, but never indicted. Now he was jailed here in Indianapolis facing multiple charges of both fraud and embezzlement. This morning they told him his hearing would be delayed for at least another six weeks, because prosecutors in three other States were claiming jurisdiction. And the Federal Prosecutor here in Indianapolis was also looking into the matter.

A request by his local attorney to release him on bail was soundly denied. He was considered a Grade-A flight risk!

Dollan had no way of knowing how many of the other five members of his team had been arrested and charged. Clearly, here in Indianapolis both his CFO and his Administrative-VP were probably in custody. Hopefully, Ginger Morgan...his fiancé and Assistant Manager of 'El Paso Trust'...had not been discovered. And once word of his arrest reached them, his Regional Managers... Sid Lafontaine and Ed Montagne...were probably both "into-the-wind". But then again, they may have been swooped up and might be asking for a deal.

Dollan's 85-square-foot cell was a tad smaller than the 1,635-square-foot suite he had occupied at the 'JW Marriot' when his scam began in Indianapolis a little over a year ago. But his cell had all the basics…a cot, a stainless steel sink/toilet combo, and a wall hung desk topped by two shelves. They had granted his request for a few books, a dozen ruled pads, pencils, and his address book. These he put to good use in mapping out a defense strategy.

From his local attorney, he knew the structure of the Criminal Justice System in Indianapolis's Marion County. And also at the State and Federal levels. As of yet, he didn't know how things worked in the other States that wanted a piece of him—Louisiana, Oregon and Maryland--but he assumed they were all fairly similar. His early guess was that he might have the best chance of escaping real jail time if he could somehow maneuver things to help Louisiana win jurisdiction. He had friends there…with friends who knew friends!

It would be tough though, considering that three groups were targeting him in Indianapolis…where the local media were still having a field day over his arrest. And where some want-a-be "investigative reporters" were trying to further their careers at his expense.

The biggest problem was the local DA who saw this case as his passport to higher office. And he had almost unlimited resources at his disposal. Right next door to the jail was the Marion County Sheriff's Office…with over 800 employees, including a large force of seasoned detectives and a media-savvy communications unit.

Also headquartered nearby, right in Indianapolis, was the US Attorney for the Southern District of Indiana. And the FBI had their main field office here too. They had assigned two agents to the case. Yes, it would be a real challenge to get the jurisdiction switched to Louisiana!

Clearly, Seymour Dollan…aka Billy Sweeny…aka Will Collins… aka Colin Wilson…aka Cole Thomas…aka 'Tex' Jay Bickford…and many aka's in between…had his work cut out for him. But hey, he was a master world-class persuader…and today he felt fully up to the challenge!

8.

Harley Quirk

INDIANAPOLIS--

'Tex' Bickford had arrived in Indianapolis for the first time eleven months before his arrest. He had come there to meet with and swindle Harley Quirk, a man he had never before met. But his research on Quirk was solid and the proposition he was offering was extremely compelling.

Harley Quirk was the president, owner and creative director of 'The Thomas Quirk Advertising Agency'...a highly respected 32-year old firm founded by his father. With a staff of 82 and billings in excess of $130-million dollars, the agency represented some of the region's most important advertisers.

On the surface, it would appear that the Agency was extremely successful. For the sixth straight year it had swept up an impressive number of the industry's top creative awards. The Agency's hallways were lined with over 100 framed award certificates, and a large display case in the reception area displayed over a dozen award trophies...including 3 Clios.

The Agency's name was frequently in the press. And like his father, Harley kept the flag flying by its pro bono work for a number of the region's top charities.

In the terms of the trade, Quirk Advertising was a "hot agency" and a great place to work to further your career. Getting a job there was considered a plum! Whenever there was a job opening, the Agency was flooded with applicants. And hoping to get an inside track in advance of future openings, the heads of key departments were being constantly bombarded with requests asking for permission 'to drop off my portfolio' or asking for 'a get-acquainted sit down'.

But beneath the surface and unknown to the staff, problems were emerging. Recently, the Agency's financial position had grown a bit shaky. They were now fairly consistently spending more than they were taking in. And that had Harley increasingly worried.

Harley was a creative guy and administration and finance were not his strong points. Those areas he had always delegated to others. As president and owner, Harley was fully committed to a 'maximum growth' strategy. People were hired in anticipation of future income. Harley believed that it took top talent to attract top clients...and that talent had to be already in place when making a new business pitch. It would all work out when the income from that new account flowed in! The key was signing bigger and bigger clients with bigger and bigger ad budgets. That was Harley's strategy to make The Thomas Quirk Advertising Agency a truly national powerhouse!

And so far that strategy had worked...almost tripling the Agency's size since Harley took over the reins from his father. Up, Up, Up was his track record!

But the advertising business is notoriously a roller coaster business...with huge wins followed by abrupt downturns. The challenge was to always keep forward momentum by having a new client ready to sign up just before an old one departed. And Harley prided himself in having always made that happen. It's just that things were moving a bit slower right now than Harley would have liked. Time to step on the gas!

But then suddenly and without warning, things spun wildly out of control. Instead of growth, the Agency was facing a major reversal. In a single week, four of the Agency's largest accounts had called Harley with dramatic cuts in their budgets.

- The Agency's largest account, 'Indiana Cellular', told Harley they were being acquired by AT&T...and AT&T's agency would be taking over the account.
- 'Family Pride Markets' called, cancelling their $5-million dollar 'branding' campaign because their new CEO just ordered that all discretionary spending be slashed.
- Then, 'Olympic Runner Shoes' cancelled everything due to a catastrophic drop in their business when the press reported that their shoes were being made in Chinese slave labor shops.
- And the very next day, 'Pontiac Insurance' called to say they had decided to drop all print and broadcast advertising and redirect their entire ad budget into online marketing.

While no one other than Harley was yet aware of these major setbacks, he knew that the news would spread quickly within the Agency. So it was essential that he head off any rumors of doom-and-gloom by holding a full-staff meeting ASAP.

In making his notes for the meeting, Harley planned to make four points—

1. Client circumstances beyond our control have just given the Agency a little hiccup!
2. All four of the clients involved have extolled the Agency's work on their behalf and pledged that they would fully honor the 90-day termination clauses in their contracts. They also asked that I pass on to you their sincere appreciation and best wishes!
3. Thanks to our considerable war chest, I want to assure you that everyone's job here is secure.
4. The challenge now is to leap aggressively into high gear… accelerating our new business efforts to replace all the lost business with bigger and better accounts!

The staff meeting went a little better than expected, with the Creative Director and the VP of Account Service adding their own little 'go-get-em' pep talks. But Harley knew that most on the staff were uneasy. And probably some were dusting off their resumes!

They say that bad news comes in threes. But for Harley, bad news didn't stop at just the four pieces of bad news he got from his budget-cutting clients.

After the staff meeting, Harley asked his CFO to calculate the potential financial damage that the Agency was facing. He was shocked to learn that the Agency's forecasted income would be slashed by far more than one-third. And he was even more disturbed to learn that those four big accounts delivered a full 120-percent of the Agency's profitability. In other words, all of the Agency's smaller accounts actually operated at a loss. Nice to have on the client list, but not paying their way based on the amount of time and talent being devoted to them. Bottom line? Without some significant new business, the Agency was facing financial disaster!

But what about those millions that they had in the Agency's bank accounts? After all, Quirk Advertising was a $130-million dollar ad agency and its latest bank statements showed they had over $32-million in cash. Couldn't that give them the breathing room they needed until new accounts signed on?

Harley, of course, knew the answer. The $130-million was fiction... and virtually all of the $32-million in the bank was untouchable. It was almost entirely made up of cash pre-payments from clients... cash that was already owed to the media.

While the Agency claimed 'billings' of over $130-million dollars, that didn't mean their income was anywhere near that amount. In ad agency parlance, 'billings' were the combined ad budgets of an agency's clients...an often-inflated number designed to impress. And typically, only 15-percent of the advertiser's spending was agency income. In other words, for every $1,000 that the client actually spent through the agency, the agency's gross income was only $150.

In Quirk Advertising's case, their reported billings of $130-million dollars would yield, at best, an annual gross income of a little over $19-million dollars. And in less than a month that would drop to about $10-million dollars. Even now, in any given month, Quirk had only about $1-million dollars in their operating account. And that was before the impending cuts!

While Harley mulled the possibility of tapping into the millions of dollars in media pre-payments that the Agency managed for its clients, he knew that would be dangerous. Under strict financial guidelines, an ad agency has a legal fiduciary responsibility to keep its own income separate from the monies they receive from a client...monies to be subsequently paid out to the advertising media.

That's part of the very definition of their status as an 'agent' rather than a reseller. And it comes from a very long tradition.

Certainly, Harley was tempted to utilize some of the over $30-million of client pre-payments just sitting in the Agency's bank accounts, awaiting payment to the media. Tens of millions of dollars flowed through the Agency's hands every month. And yes…strictly speaking the agency was legally bound to not use it on its own behalf… but couldn't it be utilized as a kind of very short-term 'bridge loan' to help the Agency straddle the problem?

The CFO told Harley that the Agency was already taking full advantage of this 'float' in meeting their cash flow needs. Yes, if they delayed payment to the media to the maximum extent, they might double or even triple that 'float'. But if they did so, the media would soon be screaming about late payments, and blow the whistle with clients.

So the basic answer was that tapping into client media pre-payments to any greater extent was out of the question. Not only was it legally risky business…but even if employed, it would not solve the Agency's cash flow problems.

In fact, Harley was now embarrassed to have even brought up the question with his CFO. And in retrospect, he was somewhat ashamed to learn that they had already been using the Agency's 'client float' to fund his 'maximum growth' strategy. He vowed that whatever the future held, the Agency's reputation for integrity and ethical standards would never be compromised. He owed that to his father's memory and to the people they employed!

After a night of troubled sleep, Harley faced head-on the fact that all he had built was now crashing down around him. Even if he cut his staff to the bone, the Agency would probably still default on some of its media payments. The media would quickly go after the clients, who'd then pull the plug immediately on the Agency. Multiple lawsuits would be launched. The press would have a field day. And The Thomas Quirk Advertising Agency would almost overnight crash and burn!

Beyond that, Harley would be personally ruined…and not just in reputation. To get the loans he needed to massively renovate, refit and redesign the Agency's office complex, Harley had signed loan agreements that required personal guarantees… linking all of his other obligations. That meant that a single default on one loan would trigger a default on them all. This included the mortgages on his home, his Aspen lodge, and the condo in Martha's Vineyard.

Harley's wife had reluctantly co-signed that loan with him, after he reassured her that this was just standard banking red tape…and that there was zero risk of it ever becoming a problem.

Now there <u>was</u> a problem. A <u>huge</u> problem! And now absolutely everything was in jeopardy…the Agency, the houses, the cars, the kids' Ivy League College tuitions… possibly even his marriage. His whole life was now quickly going into 'the crapper'!

"What to do?" "What to do?" "I have no idea!"
"Please God, help me!"

And then 'the miracle' occurred.
It came by phone from a person named Jay Bickford…the owner of a company called 'Galileo Global Partners'.

9.

The Set-Up

INDIANAPOLIS--

AT PRECISELY 9:00AM the next morning, a very tall slender man dressed in expensive Western attire strode into the lobby of The Thomas Quirk Advertising Agency. Without pausing to glance at the elegant contemporary furnishings designed to impress, he moved directly to the reception desk, where an attentive blonde young woman smiled and asked—"How may I help you, sir?"

With a nod saying thank you, he smiled in return, and responded—"My name is Jay Bickford, ma'am. And I'm here to visit with Mr. Quirk. I believe he's expecting me. Would you be so kind as to let him know I've arrived?"

With a slight blush she answered—
"Of course, sir. I'll let him know you're here. Can I get you some coffee or water while you're waiting, sir?"

"Thank you. But I don't expect he'll be all that delayed because he was expecting me at 9:00...and we confirmed that again earlier this morning when he told me the best way to get here from my hotel. It's such a beautiful day, that I decided to stretch my legs a bit and walk over."

Less than two minutes after she rang him, Harley Quirk bounded into the reception room and extended his hand warmly to the visitor—

"Mr. Bickford? I'm Harley Quirk. It's a great pleasure to meet you and to have you visit our Agency!"

"Thank you, Harley. It's a real delight for me to be here in your beautiful city and to visit your wonderful advertising agency. I've heard great things about you!"

Then he added with a chuckle—
"But please don't call me Mr. Bickford. My first name is Jay…but my friends call me 'Tex'. Bet you can't guess why!"

Then acting like warm old friends, they went side-by-side through the Agency down to Harley's corner office.

Almost every head turned to watch this curious visitor as he passed through the Agency. So unlike the media reps dressed in suits and ties…and the clients and prospects in suits without ties…and the techno-geeks and Steve Job wannabes, dressed in black jeans and black T-shirts.

As soon as the door closed on Harley's office, the phone on the reception desk started ringing and the chatter began—

"Who is that guy? Is he a prospect or some aging male model?"

"Where's he from? Texas? My guess is he's probably really from Brooklyn!"

"If he's a prospect, I hope he's not from one of those polluting oil companies...or one of those freakin' fracking companies! Most of us in Creative would refuse to work on that kind of account!"

Sheila, the receptionist, whispered conspiratorially into her phone—"His name is Jay Bickford and he really is from Texas. I don't know why he's here. But I did get a good look at him while he was out here in the reception room talking to Harley.

"His boots looked like they were real python and they had this little signature logo on the side. I did a quick Google search and found they were made by a famous bootmaker in Houston, a guy named Rocky Carroll. He's dead now, but he's made boots for the first President Bush, Pope John Paul II, Liz Taylor, and lots of other celebs. His boots sell for thousands of dollars, and the python ones are probably the most expensive.

"I also checked out buckskin jackets. Those little fringe thingies along his jacket sleeves and on the yoke are apparently traditional in Western wear. Way back, they were functional...acting like little wicks to help shed off the rain so that the deerskin would dry faster. Now they're just decorative.

"And who knows about the hat? It looks just like the picture I saw on Google for a Stetson Diamante, which sells for $5,000. The same color. The same style. If it's a knock-off, I'd be surprised!

"Then there's his gold Rolex! Don't know if it's vintage, but apparently they go for over $20,000 dollars. This guy is something else! Plus he seems like a real gentleman. Reminds me a bit like that actor...what's his name? John something or other?"

With that, the buzz spread around the Agency. This could be a juicy new account!

Once seated in Harley's office, and after the usual pleasantries, 'Tex' Bickford got right to the point—

"As I mentioned on the phone, I'm screening ad agencies here in the Midwest to complete a syndicate of four independent ad agencies to service a major new account headquartered in Houston. The account…for strategic competitive reasons that I'll describe later… wishes to remain anonymous until we're ready to launch their truly revolutionary services coast-to-coast, with a marketing budget in excess of $300-million dollars.

"Rather than to go with a single big national ad agency, we believe that we'll have far greater marketing success with a syndicate of four smaller regional agencies who know their markets best. Agencies who can design campaigns specifically designed to maximize sales in each of their regional markets. This is a big and diverse country! Too big and too diverse a country for 'one-size-fits-all' advertising!

"My firm—'Galileo Global Partners'—will be the coordinator and will develop the advertising and marketing programs for the Southern States. We've already signed on agencies in the East Coast and the West Coast. And I'm screening agencies here in the Central States to complete the syndicate. To anticipate a possible question... yours is the only one I'm visiting here in Indianapolis. We picked you because of your creative work and reputation.

"So my first question is—would you be interested in being part of our syndicate?"

Harley quickly nodded yes and with a display of enthusiasm answered—

"By all means. Sounds like a great opportunity. But of course, I'd have to know more."

"Absolutely, Harley." Then 'Tex' Bickford added with a warm smile—
"But before we get into all those details, can you give me a little tour of your agency and let me know why you're the best shop here in the Midwest?"

Slipping into his practiced new business mode, Harley stood up and gesturing to 'Tex' said— "Let's get started!"

After the usual new-business-prospect tour around the Agency… with introductions and with well-rehearsed explanations by his key people in creative, account service, media, and market research… Harley led 'Tex' Bickford into the large central conference room, where the Quirk Advertising capabilities presentation was perpetually cued-up. The half hour presentation included case histories and testimonials, along with a segment on the Agency's history, work ethic, commitment to client success…and ending with a positioning statement that differentiated the Agency from all others in the business.

At the end of the presentation, Harley invited 'Tex' Bickford back to his office and asked—"Any questions or concerns?"

'Tex' shook his head and with a beaming smile said—
"Frankly, I'm blown away!"

Then…after a thoughtful pause of a few seconds…he added--
"Based on all that I've seen here today…and after having met you…I have really no need to look at any other agency here in the Midwest.

"Harley, I'm so impressed that I'd like to officially invite you to be part of our little group!

"Now, I know you have many questions, so let me leave this little background kit with you. You can check out our website, look through our full-disclosure financial documents, and read all the details of our proposed financial arrangement…plus lots more.

"Then, if you're still interested in joining us, I suggest you stop by my suite at the JW Marriott tomorrow morning. Make it around 10:00AM. I'd like to have our CFO, Lou Rhodes, and my Administrative VP, Harrison Smith, join us for the meeting. They're in Chicago right now, and I'll ask them to fly in tonight to join us."

The JW Marriott was just a 7-minute cab ride from the Agency's Lockerbie Square location on Fulton Street. But it was such a beautiful morning that Harley decided to walk the 1.7-miles, mostly along Maryland Street. That gave him time to think through how to handle the morning's meeting with 'Tex' Bickford and his people.

The materials 'Tex' left with him were certainly impressive, and the 'Galileo Global Partners' website was extraordinary. But the big questions were--Who was the client? How much income would it bring to the Agency? And how soon would that income materialize?

At the Marriott, Harley was directed to the penthouse level where 'Tex' Bickford greeted him warmly and led introductions all around.

Lou Rhodes looked very much the accountant…soft spoken and very conservatively dressed. About 50 or so, slightly balding, with wire-rimmed glasses and a dark brown three-piece suit. He had an open laptop on the coffee table before him. Harley guessed he was originally from New York.

Harrison Smith, the Administrative VP, was younger...probably in his late 30s. Very fit, maybe ex-military, close-cropped black hair, with a crimson tie and charcoal double -breasted pin-stripped suit. The pen next to his notepad was a Mont Blanc. He had no discernable accent, but he certainly wasn't a native Texan.

Once settled into the plush sofas and leather chairs in the suite's living room, 'Tex' began—

"I promised to tell you who the client was, once we decided to work together. As you'll soon see, the reason for all the secrecy is because their business plan is so bold, so enormous, and so revolutionary that for competitive market reasons they want nothing to leak out before the nationwide launch. That will assure them the greatest possible media impact and consumer excitement.

"To that end, they've asked that any agency we select for the syndicate be asked to sign a non-disclosure agreement before being made privy to their identity and plans. It's a pretty simple and fairly standard agreement…here's a copy…it just says that you won't disclose any of the specifics that I'm about to tell you with anyone outside your organization…and particularly no one in the media. "

After quickly scanning the one page agreement, Harley took out his own Mont Blanc and signed…anxious to know what this so-called revolutionary thing was all about.

'Tex' glanced at the signed document and handed it to Lou, who slipped it into a folder. Then 'Tex' began the big reveal—

"The client is 'Solar Winds Unlimited' and they intend to cut this country's CO_2 pollution down by a full 50-percent within the next 6 years. They'll obsolete the use of fossil fuels in our homes, cities and factories...while also making electric vehicles far less expensive to buy and to operate than even the automotive industry's most ambitious forecasts. They'll do all this...not by government regulations and subsidies...but by making electric power not only non-polluting...but also vastly less expensive than any other alternative...including nuclear.

"What's the secret? A patented new wind-capturing technology, along with an advanced new energy storage and transmission system...and a breakthrough economic concept that will incent both major investors and individual energy users to share in Solar Winds' success.

"While we're initially talking about the U.S. market, worldwide expansion will soon follow. The patents have already been secured.

"That in a nutshell is 'Solar Winds Unlimited'. Now, what about how you can share in its success.

"Rather than commissions, they have proposed a service fee arrangement...with $75,000 per month as your initial fee. Expenses incurred on their behalf would be rebilled at cost. As the program rolls out, your monthly fee can be negotiated upward to reflect growing manpower needs to service the account. Recognizing that you'd have to gear up in staffing for the account, your fees would begin immediately after the signing of an Agency Appointment letter.

"As I previously mentioned, four advertising agencies will be working on the account. One in Portland, Oregon...one in Baltimore, Maryland...you here in Indianapolis...and my firm in Dallas.

"For administrative purposes and financial control, Solar Winds has established an escrow account at 'El Paso Trust'...from which all of the various agency fees, media expenses, and out-of-pocket costs will be disbursed. The Assistant Manager and VP of the Bank...a Mrs. Georgina Morgan...is our primary financial liaison.

"So Harley...what do you think?"

Trying to stay cool and not appear overly hungry for this desperately needed added income...Harley reached out to shake hands with 'Tex'...saying—

"I'm 100-percent on board. This is truly exciting. I know we'll make history together!"

Then, with 'Tex' beaming on...Lou, Harrison and Harley dug into the details and specifics of establishing a working relationship.

10.

Despair

INDIANAPOLIS--

THREE MONTHS HAD passed since that fateful meeting with 'Tex' Bickford and his people at the Marriott. And Harley Quirk was now in an absolute panic. He was trapped in a nightmare with no waking-up and no apparent escape.

The first two weeks had gone brilliantly. The day after the meeting, Lou Rhodes had FedEx'd the Quirk Agency a check for $75,000… along with the counter-signed Agency Appointment letter from 'Solar Winds Unlimited'.

Harley's bookkeeper Dennis Conrad, hand carried the check to the Agency's bank to find out how long it would take to clear. Their Account Manager at the Bank phoned El Paso Trust and spoke directly with Georgina Morgan. She said the check should clear within five days…once endorsed, deposited, and run through the Federal Reserve clearing house.

She added that the whole process could probably be cut to minutes if Quirk Advertising ever decided to establish their own commercial account at El Paso Trust. Then, a transfer of funds could occur seamlessly within the same bank between 'Solar Winds' and 'Quirk Advertising'. This would give Quirk Advertising same-day access to the funds in their El Paso account. From there, Quirk Advertising could either wire the funds directly to Indianapolis....or disburse checks out of their El Paso Bank account, as they wished. She said that's what all the other agencies in the Solar Winds syndicate had decided to do.

This sounded like a smart idea to both Dennis and his Indianapolis bank manager. So they asked Georgina Morgan to fax them the forms to set up a Quirk Advertising corporate account at El Paso Trust, with funds-transfer provisions.

Later that same week, Harley called a meeting of the entire staff. With great fanfare, he announced that the Agency had just signed a major multi-million dollar account. He told them that they had been selected to introduce an exciting new product in all twelve of the Midwestern States. For competitive security reasons, the client would be temporarily code-named 'Powerhouse' and the launch itself would be dubbed 'Project Breakthrough'.

Harley told them that a 'client team' would be visiting the Agency within the next two weeks to brief the teams directly assigned to the account. But in the meantime, everyone should keep this news strictly under their hats.

He then introduced Lou Rhodes and Harrison Smith from 'Galileo Global Partners'. Both would have offices at the Agency. Lou, a CPA, would be in charge of the budgeting for 'Project Breakthrough'... and would be approving and processing all the invoices on the client's behalf.

Harrison would work directly with the Agency's media department to develop a comprehensive plan and budget for a dominant 3-month media blitz…print, broadcast, digital, and direct marketing. He'd also work directly with the research department to map prospect demographics and test alternate messaging strategies.

Harley himself would be the account supervisor, assisted by a team to be named after the client meeting here at the Agency.

Weeks progressed, and the client meeting kept being postponed… presumably because they were still at work with their other agencies in Texas, Portland and Baltimore.

Then there seemed to be a delay with the second month's fee. Somehow, it was miss-routed. Or there was a computer glitch. Or the client's CFO was out with the flu. Bottom line…it hadn't come through yet!

And when Harley went to Lou's office to ask about it, he found that a new digital lock had been installed on the door. Lou laughed it off as client paranoia, based on their demand for absolute secrecy. He apologized that he couldn't give Harley the combination without first getting client approval through 'Tex'.

Harley tried again and again to reach 'Tex'…who never returned his calls. That's when his worry turned to grave concern. "What's going on here?" "Am I being played?"

Then the full impact of the deception started to hit Harley full force… as the media began to call Harley complaining that the Agency was now more than 90 days late in paying their invoices.

Harley couldn't understand how this could be. His clients were always prompt in pre-paying the Agency for their media expenses. In fact, the Agency wouldn't even place an ad unless they had already received that pre-payment. Doing so would violate the long-standing regulation that an agency couldn't 'finance' a client's advertising without forfeiting their 'agent' status. Further, to avoid late charges, the Agency had a strict policy of paying all media invoices within 30 days. Even with the Agency's cash flow problems, Harley had told his people to honor this policy. Being 90 days late meant that someone had intentionally violated his instructions!

That's when Harley learned that Lou had transferred over $30-million dollars of the Agency's so-called client-escrow-account into the Agency's account at El Paso Trust. Lou had told the Agency's bookkeeper that he had made the transfer to earn a higher interest percentage in Texas than they were getting in Indiana. And Lou had assured the bookkeeper that all of the Agency's media bills would be paid on time out of that account.

Every Monday morning, Harley received a summary financial report from his bookkeeper. The latest report showed no overdue media bills…and showed a healthy cash balance in client pre-payments. This implied that being 90 days late was impossible. The bookkeeper nervously speculated that maybe there was a reporting lag from the El Paso Bank that affected the accuracy of his Monday morning report!

This didn't meet the smell test. So before interrogating Lou directly, Harley decided to call El Paso Trust to find out how much was actually in the Agency's account.

He was told that it was now just $102.68. That's because over the previous two weeks, the Quirk Agency had transferred $31,276,500 to their linked 'Solar Winds' account. Harley said that was totally unauthorized and that he wanted it transferred back immediately. The bank officer he spoke with said that unfortunately that wasn't possible, because the 'Solar Winds" account had been recently closed after a transfer of all their funds to various other accounts.

Breaking into a cold sweat, Harley demanded to talk to the VP and Assistant Bank Manager in charge of his account…Georgina Morgan. They apologized, saying that she had been out ill for the past week…which was totally unlike her because Georgina never takes sick days!

Harley pounded on Lou's door, and getting no answer called for a locksmith. Once opened, he found an empty office stripped of all computers, back-up hard drives, and files.

He then immediately rushed to Lou and Harrison's spacious 'City Way' apartment in the Wholesale District. That too was empty. The complex manager said that a van had arrived the night before and that they had vacated the place. The manager reminded Harley that Quirk Advertising had a 2-year lease on the apartment and asked how soon new occupants would arrive. Apparently, Lou had forged the lease agreement, too!

Proof that this was all an embezzlement scam was confirmed for Harley when his latest call to 'Tex' Bickford was greeted with a "this number is no longer in service" message. And when his search of both the 'Galileo' and 'Solar Winds' websites yielded the same message—"This website has been taken down for maintenance!"

Harley had no idea what to do. Angry that he had been made a fool. Fearful that life as he knew it had ended. In denial that he had absolutely no way to survive.

What would his father have said? What will his peers in the industry say? What will his wife and his kids say? Should he just take a dive off the roof here and escape it all?

What he did know was that he needed a lawyer. And that would be Brooks Gerard. Gerard was a former federal prosecutor and far more experienced in fraud and embezzlement cases than the Agency's long-standing law firm.

The next morning, Harley met with Brooks Gerard and laid it all out…the desperation he had felt in losing four big accounts…his total gullibility in viewing these fraudsters as potential white knights coming to his rescue…his stupidity in not realizing how these con men were setting him up to suck the Agency dry.

Brooks asked Harley many questions, making quick notes on his legal pad. He probed for facts about both 'Galileo Global Partners' and 'Solar Winds'. And he asked for details on El Paso Trust's apparent unorthodox role in all this. He asked for hard copies of everything that the Agency had ever received from these organizations…the kits, the agreements, the correspondence, screen shots from the original websites that Harley had fortunately made. And any photos Harley, or anyone else in the Agency, might have taken of 'Tex' Bickford, Lou Rhodes and Harrison Smith.

Brooks Gerard was particularly interested in hearing that three other advertising agencies were presumably also part of this so-called syndicate. If true, he theorized that they too might have been swindled.

Harley could name the cities where these agencies were supposedly located, but admitted that he had never asked for their names…all part of that need for secrecy that they kept talking about.

Brooks pointed out-- "If these other agencies have been victimized the same way...with embezzlement of funds they owe to the media...then the media could likely identify them for us. I'll have one of my associates get on that right away. We could have a far bigger conspiracy here!"

Trying to calm Harley, Brooks Gerard pointed out that while the $31-million dollars might be very difficult or even impossible to recover directly from the embezzlers, the Agency's fraud insurance policy would no doubt have to cover $10-million dollars of that amount. And if it could be proven that their bank officer had been complicit, then El Paso Trust would be required to repay the full amount. Certainly, the Agency's insurance carrier would very aggressively go after the Bank to shift full responsibility to them!

But Brooks couldn't avoid bringing up one admonition—
"You'll have to resign as an Officer and Board Member of 'The Thomas Quirk Advertising Agency' immediately. That won't personally protect you from corporate liability lawsuits, but it will help.

"We must also bring in the authorities immediately. We should file charges against 'Tex' Jay Bickford, his company, and his associates... or whatever all their real names are. And we should file charges against El Paso Trust for not only malpractice but participation in the fraud and embezzlement.

"I won't kid you. The Press will be all over this. Your life is going to be a nightmare. The Agency certainly won't survive. All we can hope for is that you emerge able to fight again another day!"

11.

The Target

NEW JERSEY--

George Trecott had been searching the internet to find someone in police custody that he could make Victim #2. Still feeling a bit guilty over upsetting the lives of Tilly and Howard Dixon in Boca Raton, George had decided that the target in his next little experiment should be someone who truly merited a little pain. A real bastard...if he could find one.

Thankfully, the world was full of such people. But one of them particularly caught his eye. It was some 'good-old-boy' Texas con man who had simultaneously defrauded a number of people in a number of States.

He especially liked targeting a Texan, because George's somewhat sleazy employer...'Ripper Publishing'...was based in Texas. Though all his contacts with them had been online and they had never actually met, he could find a little extra pleasure in picking someone who hailed from Texas!

The national media had provided only broad stroke summaries of the scam...the simultaneous embezzlement of over $100-million dollars from four advertising agencies in four different cities. All of this masterminded by a guy dressed like Buffalo Bill. A guy who was now sitting in the Marion County Jail in Indianapolis, Indiana.

George assumed that the local media in Indianapolis would have covered this story in great depth. And he was rewarded with a treasure-trove of detail that the local papers and TV stations had reported on over a several month period. All of this available online. The embezzlement. The scandal. The collapse of a respected local business. The anguish of its owner Harley Quirk. The reactions of his clients and staff. The nationwide search for the evil mastermind.

One paper called him-- "The Texas Bandit". And another dubbed him-- "The Texas Vampire"...so named because he had sucked the life blood out of one of Indianapolis's most prestigious companies.

The story still remained headline news in the local media week after week...providing details on the con man's identification and arrest, and on the full extent of his crimes. In addition to The Quirk Advertising Agency in Indianapolis, "The Texas Bandit" had looted major ad agencies in Portland, Baton Rouge, and Baltimore. His total take was reported to be in excess of $100-million dollars—almost all of which was client funds, purportedly being held in escrow by the agencies for the payment of their clients' media bills. Dozens of lawsuits had broken out...with both clients and the media and their respective insurance companies seeking redress.

Among the things George found detailed in the local Indianapolis media –

- The "Texas Bandit" was a career con man calling himself 'Tex' Jay Bickford who apparently assembled a team of grifters in a fictitious company called 'Galileo Global Partners'. All had disappeared immediately after the embezzlement, triggering an international search.

- Then just over a month ago, authorities announced that several arrests had been made in a series of coordinated raids.

- According to FBI Special Agent Sally Templeton in the Indianapolis FBI Field Office—"We followed the money!" All of the embezzled funds had flowed into and out of a number of business accounts at the Waco, Texas branch of 'El Paso Trust'. At the Bank, the VP-Assistant Branch Manager…a person named Georgina Morgan had personally managed all of these accounts.

- Ms. Morgan…also known as Ginger…was found in the Bahamas under an assumed name. With the help of local authorities, she was extradited to the U.S. and held as a person-of-interest as investigators determined the extent of her involvement in the crimes.

- The conspirators apparently used a modern variation of the old Ponzi Scheme in targeting four advertising agencies simultaneously. With the promise of lucrative new business from a Texas technology firm, the conspirators enticed each of these agencies into a formal business relationship. A key part of that enticement was pre-paying each of the agencies a generous monthly retainer fee. In actuality, these fees did not come from the new client…a purely fictitious firm… but came from funds embezzled from one or more of the participating agencies.

- The embezzlements were actually accomplished by persuading each of the participants to open business accounts at El Paso Trust…presumably to speed the collection of funds from the new client. But unknown to the embezzled agencies, these accounts had been structured to permit the flow of funds in the opposite direction…out of the agencies and into the El Paso Trust accounts. With full access to these accounts, the conspirators could then drain them at will.

- To execute the transfers, the conspirators had operatives at both ends…their resident financial person at the agencies… and Ms. Morgan at El Paso Trust.

- It was determined that Georgina Morgan was directly and personally involved in implementing all of these transfers. Faced with the potential of many years in prison, Ms. Morgan agreed to be a cooperating witness—providing information leading to the arrest of Mr. Bickford and two of his accomplices. Two others are still at large. And all of the embezzled funds are reported to be missing.

- As an interesting side-note, Ms. Morgan claimed to be the fiancé of Mr. Bickford and that he had manipulated her into participating unknowingly into an illegal scheme…simply following his directions, believing that he had full legal authority to establish and control all these accounts.

- Mr. Bickford in turn, had claimed that he had never personally met Ms. Morgan…and that she and others had conspired to pirate the legitimate bank accounts he had established for the benefit of four truly outstanding regional advertising agencies. Agencies that he had recruited into a syndicate to service a major new international account. He further claimed that this major account was owned by a foreign government; and that he could not reveal their names because he had signed a binding non-disclosure agreement to shield their identity. He characterizes himself as a scapegoat in the nefarious crimes of others whom he had foolishly trusted. And he has offered to aid the authorities in their pursuit of justice. And he further claims that he has no idea of where they had hidden all that money!

After digesting all this from the media, George Trecott was convinced that this guy… 'Tex' Bickford…was perfect for his next assassination attempt.

While George's goal, as always, was to gain real world knowledge of how to plan and execute a 'kill' without seriously injuring the target or being caught…he had to admit that this time he had the urge to really "hit" this slimy con man.

But it was not only the target himself that excited him. It was the fact that –

1. This guy was headline news in both the local and national media.
2. He was locked away in a high-security County Jail.
3. He was under the close scrutiny of Local, State and Federal prosecutors.
4. Reaching him would take a feat of supreme imagination and ingenuity.

This was the challenge! And George was very anxious to accept it!

12.

Options

NEW JERSEY--

George spent the next several weeks mapping out several strategies. They boiled down to two—

1. Hitting 'Tex' Bickford in his cell, with a substance that would put him into a health emergency. That meant finding a way around all the regulations and procedures designed to keep jailed prisoners isolated.

2. Hitting 'Tex' Bickford at, or on his way to, his court proceedings. Here, the security would perhaps be easier to penetrate, but it would put George in close proximity to the actual event. In other words, the chance of his being caught was much higher.

In mulling over the pluses and minuses of these options, George decided to implement both strategies. First, he'd try to hit 'Tex' in jail…if that failed, he'd use a back-up plan of hitting him in the courtroom.

13.

The Cell

INDIANAPOLIS--

AT 3:27PM ON Thursday October 26th, the guards in Block 2D of the Marion County Jail heard screaming and banging coming from one of the corridors. Rushing toward the sounds, they quickly zeroed in on cell #407 where an apparently deranged 'Tex' Bickford was in world-class panic mode...screeching incoherently and trying to pull apart the bars.

With wild eyes and foaming mouth, his high-pitched shouts ricocheted in the cell and down the corridor, unnerving both the usually stoic guards and the prisoners in nearby cells--

"Please, Jesus Lord, please!"
"Save me! Save me! Let me out! Please save me!"
"Don't let them get to me! Don't let them get to me!"
"They're demons sent straight from Hell to devour me!"
"Oh God, the pain! The unbearable pain!"

Not sure exactly how to handle this...and not sure if it was all just an act...the guards quickly called their superiors, who called the Warden and the Jail's On-Staff Doctor.

The consensus was that the prisoner had to be restrained and then tranquilized for his own protection. And then transported to the Prison Infirmary. There he would be kept restrained while a psychiatrist was brought in. At the same time, the Crime Lab was asked to screen blood and saliva samples to see if there was a chemical component involved.

By early evening, the prisoner...while still shaky...seemed to have returned to a rational state. He remembered all of the details of his terrifying experience, and claimed to have no idea why this had happened. He said he had no history of epilepsy, or panic attacks, or anything remotely like this.

Then he quickly added—
"Has someone here been paid off to poison me?
"Can't you see that I'm the one who is really the victim in all this?
"They're trying to stop me from proving my innocence because it implicates others in high places who are trying to make me the scapegoat for their crimes."

Hours later, the Crime Lab came back with the test results. 'Tex' Jay Bickford had traces of LSD in his system. The question is how he obtained it in the high-security Marion County Jail #1?

14.

Poisons

NEW JERSEY--

GEORGE HAD COMPILED an extensive file on poisons and their delivery systems. They ranged from naturally occurring substances to synthetics. They included poisons that were easy to acquire, to those almost impossible to obtain without leaving an evidence trail. They included poisons that left no trace in a victim's system, to those that left easy-to-identify markers for any experienced medical examiner or pathologist.

George's short list for 'Tex' Bickford included *Aconite* and *Nicotine.*

Aconite can trigger a heart attack…with no post-mortem signs other than those resembling natural asphyxia. Often dubbed the 'Queen of Poisons', *Aconite* occurs naturally in a number of botanicals. Over the centuries it has been called—monk's head, wolf's bane, leopard's bane, mouse bane, woman's bane, devil's helmet, and blue rocket. *Aconite* poisoning is not always fatal. Atropine, quickly administered, can be an effective antidote.

Nicotine is a deadly poison, once widely used as a pesticide in cultivating roses. Most commercial plant-care products no longer contain it, but it can be easily extracted and concentrated at home by boiling 5 or more cigarettes in a little water.

Few smokers realize the potency of *Nicotine*. They can enjoy and tolerate its effect in the smoking, chewing and vaping products they use, because the body only extracts a tiny percentage of the un-concentrated *Nicotine* into their systems. But if ingested in concentrated liquid form, *Nicotine* would prove fatal.

After devouring all the published online literature he could find on both *Aconite* and *Nicotine*, George recognized that he needed to do some primary research in the form of monitored experiments. While the literature was very clear about the fatal dose levels for humans, this information assumed pure *Aconite* and pure *Nicotine*. The question was how concentrated would these compounds actually be if George synthesized them at home?

So emulating Big Pharma, George embarked on a series of animal trials. For weeks, he visited animal shelters across New Jersey 'adopting' more than a dozen cats for his experiments. He administered various concentrations of the compounds that he synthesized, making detailed notes on the animals' reactions. His goal was to make them noticeably ill, but just short of dying.

George knew that humans would react differently than his small animal subjects, but he needed some empirical data to calculate his human dose levels. George felt badly when the last of the animals 'passed'. But research was research! Science was science!

The next question was how to deliver his concoctions into 'Tex' Bickford's cell and at his courtroom appearances. This took a different form of research. All possible again, thanks to the internet.

In Indiana like most States, there was a whole system set up to let family and friends send gifts and personal items to prisoners. George was surprised how many major firms provided online services to make prisoner gift-giving easy. One could pick from dozens of gift pack options…including not only food and personal grooming items…but also large food gift boxes to permit sharing with your jailhouse buddies. These packages flowed into the jails by the thousands, rivaling Amazon in convenience, if not in volume.

Obviously, every item sent to a prisoner was carefully inspected to make sure it contained no contraband or unapproved items such as cell phones or tobacco products. And at the Marion County Jail in Indianapolis, they even opened and inspected every personal letter sent to an inmate. But the gifts coming from one of the recognized 'Gift-Service' firms usually passed through without close inspection, since they were securely sealed in tamperproof packaging.

In its website, the Marion County Jail boldly stated that it encouraged friends and family to send letters and gifts to their "loved ones". And to facilitate that, they even provided an easy-to-navigate directory with each inmate's cell number. This made targeting 'Tex' Bickford easy. And it gave George the names and cell numbers of all of the other prisoners on Bickford's cellblock.

Combining all this information, George came up with a detailed operational plan to penetrate the system…and get his 'special little gifts' delivered directly to his target—'Tex' Bickford! This was his "Plan A".

Plan "B" was to hit Bickford in the courtroom…to be used only if things didn't work out at the jail. This would be far riskier for George, because implementing this plan would require him to be physically present at a site ringed with professional security. But his disguise had worked in Boca Raton, so he could use a disguise once again. Though penetrating the security of a fully-packed Courtroom in a large County Courthouse would be a far larger challenge than dodging a few cheap security cameras at the Boca Bean Coffee Shop.

To work out the details for "Plan B", George traveled to Indianapolis and sat-in on several hearings and trials in various courtrooms throughout the Courthouse. As in most jurisdictions, the prosecution always sat at the table on the right side, facing the Judge. The defense sat at the left side table…with the defendant farthest to the left.

Between larger hearings, the courtroom was usually cleared and a janitor gathered up any debris and discarded papers and empty water bottles at or near each table. He then set out fresh replacement bottles where needed. These small 8-ounce water bottles would be the perfect delivery vehicle in George's "Plan B"!

At the end of the last hearing that George attended, he pocketed one of the empty water bottles and three of the still full sealed bottles to take back to New Jersey with him. There he would use a hypodermic needle to practice adding the toxin without breaking the bottle cap seal. Piercing the bottle's bottom, then sealing the puncture hole with crazy glue worked perfectly.

He would repeat this process the night before the actual 'Tex' Bickford hearing, just in case the brand of bottled water being used had changed since his test run.

On the day of the 'Tex' Bickford hearing, he would make the switch right after the courtroom was emptied from an earlier hearing…and minutes before the janitor came in to clear things. Or if Bickford's was the first hearing of the day, he'd make the switch just after the janitor had finished setting out fresh bottles and pads at each position.

His choice of disguises this time? Possibly a member of the Press. With a rumpled jacket, slightly unkempt hair, and a facial prosthetic that would make him somewhat undistinguishable. But with credentials around his neck reading—"The Mojave Dessert Journal". His excuse, if challenged…"Just trying to filch a few free bottles of water. Last night sure gave me a powerful thirst!"

15.

Gift Pack

INDIANAPOLIS--

By the morning after the 'Tex' Bickford poisoning, the facts came quickly together.

The LSD had come from a powdery coating on sticks of 'Black Jack' chewing gum that Bickford had received in a gift pack the day before. The gift pack had been sent from an organization calling itself—"The Guardian Angel Missionary Society", based in Tulsa, Oklahoma. The gift pack also contained a still-sealed package of Gummy Bears and a pocketsize book of Prayers and Biblical quotations…along with an open letter to the recipient.

An analysis by the Crime Lab showed that the Gummy Bears had been laced with Aconite, and the pages of the book had been treated with a Nicotine solution.

The Warden demanded answers—"How the f… did this lethal package pass through our security system and be declared OK for delivery to 'Tex' Bickford?" Nervously, the Head of Security answered-- "Because this gift pack had been preceded by more than a dozen identical packages from this same organization, and we've never had a problem or an incident with them before. All the packages were received on separate days over the past two months… with each one addressed to a different inmate."

The Head of Security went on to explain—"When the initial two packages from this organization were first received, we checked them out for their legitimacy. It seemed to be a bona fide religious charity. And we carefully examined the sealed contents of each item in the packages before approving the boxes for delivery. After that initial screening, the approval of gift boxes from this organization became fairly routine, with only a cursory examination to make sure there was no tampering or restricted items added. That pretty much applies to how we've been handling all the gift boxes from the other organizations and internet gift services. And as you know, we receive hundreds of gift boxes each month."

It was agreed that there was a serious flaw in the Jail's security system…so corrective steps were immediately ordered.

The letters that came in each package were said to have been identical. The most recent one was scrutinized for clues about the sender —

THE GUARDIAN ANGEL MISSIONARY SOCIETY

An Outreach Ministry of the Evangelical Church of Tulsa

"I was naked and you clothed me. I was sick and you healed me. I was in prison and you came to me." Matthew 25:36

Dear Brother in Christ,

Be not discouraged. Be not afraid. Trust in the Lord. Let prayer be your comfort. And righteousness your resolve!

Please know that those of us in the Guardian Angel Missionary Society pray for you daily. We understand your ordeal. Hopefully, you can take a little comfort in knowing that you are not alone in your struggles.

And please do accept these little gifts that come from the heart. They're made possible thanks to a gift from a benefactor, who like you was himself once a prisoner too. He and we only wish we could send you more, but there are so many to serve!

You may remember 'Black Jack' gum from the time of your youth. And who doesn't like 'Gummy Bears'? They're both for your bodily enjoyment. And for your soul? A small book of Prayers and Biblical Quotations. Please read them and reflect, if you're so moved!

With all our sincere best wishes,

Brother Michael O'Rourke, SPJ
Outreach Chaplin

The Guardian Angel Missionary Society is an outreach ministry of the Evangelical Church of Tulsa.
317 Gordon Street East / Tulsa, Oklahoma, 74012 / 918-201-5700
www.GuardianAngelMinistry.org / www.EvangelicalChurchTulsa.org

---

After studying the letter, the Warden asked—"What do we know about this organization?"

"Sir-- When the first two packages came in, Prison Security went to the Guardian Angel's website to verify its legitimacy. They also checked the website for the Evangelical Church of Tulsa. All seemed in order. The contents were then carefully examined. Finding no problem, the gift packages were delivered to the two prisoners to whom they were addressed. Over the weeks, more packages arrived, identical in their contents, addressed to other prisoners. All were passed along to these prisoners without incident.

"However, in rechecking things this morning, it was found that while the Guardian Angel website is still active, there was no such phone number as the one shown in their letter. A phone call to the Administrator of the Evangelical Church of Tulsa found that they did not have, and had never heard of, The Guardian Angel Missionary Society. Obviously, this was all a carefully orchestrated plan to target 'Tex' Bickford."

With this recognition came a pivotal question that the Sheriff, the FBI, the prosecutors, and the defense attorney all wanted answered—

Who really did this and why?

The LSD dose level in the gum was enough to cause hallucinations, but not great enough to cause seizures. The Aconite level in the uneaten Gummy Bears was enough to trigger heart palpitations, but certainly not death. And the Nicotine coating on the book pages was barley enough to cause severe sickness, nothing more.

Even combined, they would not prove fatal to 'Tex' Bickford.

Considering all the careful planning and execution it took to get these toxic materials into 'Tex' Bickford's cell, it's hard to believe that the dose levels were all miss-calculated. They seem to have been intentionally set at levels to incapacitate but not kill!

To what end, one could only speculate.

Was 'Tex' Bickford…a lifelong con artist…the architect behind all this? Part of a scheme to use in his defense?

Was it one of his co-conspirators…or even a higher-up…warning him not to implicate them, and not to reveal where the embezzled $100-million dollars could be found?

Or was it one of his many victims seeking revenge, and seeking recovery of the monies he had stolen from them?

Or was it someone else, for reasons we do not know?

16.

George's Awakening

NEW JERSEY--

THE PRESS HAD a field day with the Second Act in the 'Tex' Bickford story.

"Texas Con Man Goes on 'Trip' While Still in Jail"

"Jail Security a Deadly Joke"

The Plot Sickens"

George Trecott read it all, immensely pleased over how things had played out. He had reached his target right inside a high-security jail cell. Had he wanted to actually assassinate Bickford, he certainly could have done so. But of course, that was not his aim. This was only research for his book. Or was there more?

At the outset, George had embarked upon his field tests to gain real-world knowledge of police procedurals and to learn how all those affected would react to an assassination attempt. He wanted to monitor the unpredictable mix of professionalism, emotions, and politics that might ensue. He also wanted to see the Press in action, to watch how they might report and spin the facts. But above all—he wanted to experience something of the life of a professional assassin. The detailed planning skills required. The nerves of steel when in the field. The suppression of all feelings of guilt. And the sheer talent it took to succeed without being caught.

All this was at the purely intellectual level. Just research for his novel. Or at least that was the intended goal. But almost without realizing it, George now found something new welling up inside himself. A half-formed set of emotions that George had never felt before. An awakening! It was the feeling of control…and of POWER.

George was a naturally shy person, always drawing back from interactions with others. Some would call George a loner. Behind his back, others might call him a loser. But for most of his life, people would simply ignore him. And it had always been that way as far back as he could remember.

As an overweight semi-asthmatic kid…with a single mother who worked a series of low paid jobs and moved them to different towns every few years…George had never made any real friends. No dad was around to play catch or shoot hoops. So he was so inept in sports that none of the other kids wanted him on their teams. He was also the favorite target of bullies in the neighborhood, giving the other guys and girls in his class a good laugh at his expense.

His mother was always too tired…or maybe just too 'cold'…to do much more than give him a safe place to live. Hugs and kisses definitely weren't her thing. And if he reflected back upon it, he'd realize that he had never had a meaningful conversation with his mother…a conversation about his feelings or concerns. It was all just…"Remember to do…*this or that.*" "No, we don't have the money to waste on…*that or this.*" Or…"Not now, I've got to do… *this or that.*"

Some say that we humans are social animals, thriving only when we interact and interrelate with others. But George knew little of that on a personal level. As a kid he had certainly read about close relationships in books and seen them dramatized on TV…but 9-times-out-of-10 those stories ended with one person disappointing or even harming the other. Not something George wanted to ever experience himself. So he was happy to be what he liked to call— "A private person, very content within myself."

Of course, that was really just a defense mechanism. Just a way of protecting himself from being hurt by others. But remarkably now, for the first time in all his life, he was experiencing what it was like to be <u>the one actually doing the hurting</u>. And it was a remarkably thrilling and fulfilling experience!

Though he still might have some qualms about Howard and Tilly, he now almost wished that he had delivered a fatal dose to 'Tex' Bickford. He had the power to do so. And certainly justice truly demanded it!

And he particularly marveled over the power he could exercise over the authorities. Getting them to run around in circles. That was indeed a heady new experience. An experience he craved to expand upon even more. All of which told him that for his next experiment he needed something truly extraordinary. Extraordinary in both challenge and scale!

LOOSE ENDS—

17.

Target #1 – The Young Wife

More than four months had passed since George Trecott in his granny disguise had 'spiked' Tilly Dixon's latte at the Boca Bean Coffee Shop. But even though he was busy with his other experiments, he had kept a watchful eye on Tilly and her husband Howard, on their lawyer Doug Sullivan, and on Lieutenant R.C. Nichols of the Palm Beach Sheriff's Office. All possible thanks to the spyware he had installed on Tilly's and Howard's computers. Not only could he read all their emails and attachments, he could also access all their saved documents and other files. And what fascinating insights he had gained!

First of all, he had to admire the diligence of Lieutenant Nichols in pursuing the case...and in fulfilling his promise to keep the Dixons fully informed. George had read more than his fair share of police procedural novels over the years, many written by ex-cops, but he learned more here than all of them combined.

From the emails that Lieutenant Nichols sent to the Dixons, George learned how alternate theories were formulated and pursued. He saw the power...but also the limitations...of the database and internet searches by the authorities... the inner workings of the Crime

Lab and CSI…and how APB-All-Point-Bulletins really worked. All valuable information for George, the author!

But the fact that Lieutenant Nichols and the PBSO had not yet broken the case…had no idea who the "mystery woman" was…and still had absolutely no idea why Tilly was even targeted…all that gave George a feeling of great accomplishment. Even in this, his very first venture, he had outwitted the PBSO…one of the most accomplished law enforcement agencies in the Nation. And considering that the FBI had also played an advisory role…George gave himself an A+ for the planning and execution of this one!

But George felt he deserved only a C when it came to Howard and Tilly. Yes, they had performed pretty much as planned up through the Coffee Shop incident. Marionettes to his Puppet Master role. But the after-effects on them were a tad disturbing. Tilly had become withdrawn and fearful. George learned this in Howard's email exchange with Doug Sullivan, where both men expressed their concern.

Howard too had changed. There was a noticeable pull back in both his business and social life. He seemed far less active in attempting to expand his real estate holdings, passing up showings and auctions. And he declined far more invitations to events at the Club and elsewhere than he accepted. Clearly, Howard was feeling guilt in not having protected Tilly. Guilt in mishandling the whole affair. And with no explanations as to the "who" and the "why", there was no resolution to the problem…no way to put all this behind them.

Their marriage still seemed solid, but it too had changed. The event had apparently drawn a pall over their lives, screening out much of the light and the joy. Once a cheerful and optimistic duo, they were now cautious survivors.

George had done this to them, and for that he felt a small twinge of regret.
So…in an effort to erase any feeling of guilt, he decided to write another letter to Howard.

Talk about a jolt! There in his home mailbox, Howard Dixon found a letter addressed exactly as the first one. The one that had destroyed his life. Carefully wrapping the envelope in his handkerchief…he placed it on the dining room table. Then after calling upstairs to Tilly, he went for the phone. He wanted Lieutenant Nichols and Doug Sullivan their lawyer to be there with them before the letter was opened.

It would take more than two hours until all could convene. These were the most excruciating hours in Howard and Tilly's lives! Their thoughts ran to wild possibilities. Another demand? Another threat? An explanation of some sorts?

They paced, then sat, then leapt up and paced again. They tried to steady their nerves with some brandy. That didn't help. Finally, the doorbell rang… Lieutenant Nichols and Doug Sullivan had finally arrived!

Circling the table, all agreed that the Lieutenant should be the one to open the letter. Wearing crime scene gloves, he carefully picked up the envelope and slit open the flap. Then, withdrawing and unfolding the letter, he read aloud—

Mr. Dixon,

I owe you an apology. The letter I previously sent you was sent to you in error.
It was another couple, not you and Mrs. Dixon, that I had been asked to deal with.
I sincerely hope my blunder has not caused you undo worry or concern.

And there's another matter—I've seen in the newspapers that Mrs. Dixon suffered a bad reaction to something she ate or drank at a Boca Raton coffee shop. Please know that I have had absolutely nothing to do with this unhappy event and have no knowledge of the identity of the woman they suspect. This unrelated incident was a pure coincidence.

With sincere apologies,
Your Guardian Angel

Howard spoke first—

"So, what do you all think? Is this legit? Are we safe? Can we now put all this behind us?"

Their lawyer, Doug Sullivan, answered first—

"I sure hope so. But I worry a little that this guy is still trying to mess with us. I don't think we can take what he says at face value…that he sent you that first letter in error. However, I do see this letter as his way of declaring a truce of some kind…and possibly trying to get us to call off the cops. He probably wishes he had never started this whole thing with his dumb letter! So, yes…Howard and Tilly…I think this seals it. I think there's no real threat out there for you anymore. Try, if you can, to put this sicko and his shenanigans behind you!"

"And Lieutenant? What do you think?"—asked Tilly.

"Well, Doug makes a good point. But I can't call off the investigation just yet. I have to run things past my team and bosses at the PBSO. I'll take this letter with me, if I may, and have forensics match it up with the first letter.

"Doug has also given you some great advice. I know it's hard, but try to get back to your old lives. Over the months, I've seen just how much this whole thing has taken out of you. Easier said than done, I know. But get away, take a trip, maybe a second honeymoon. I really like you folks, and I don't want to let this bastard and his stupid letters permanently affect you. Don't let him!"

With handshakes and hugs all around, Lieutenant R.C. Nichols drove back to the PBSO in West Palm. What he didn't tell Howard, Tilly and Doug was his real reaction to the letter.

In his letter, this guy had claimed to have… "no knowledge of the identity of the woman" at the coffee shop who spiked Tilly's latte. The only problem was this—the Sheriff's office had never released the fact that it was a woman. Ergo—this guy was clearly behind the whole thing. Time to renew our efforts. This ain't over yet!

18.

Target #2 – The Con Man

It was four months since George Trecott had sent 'Tex' Bickford on an LSD trip in his cell at the Marion County Jail in Indianapolis. And even while George was finalizing plans for his next...and greatest... assassination experiment, he kept checking for news about Bickford's comeuppance with the Law.

It appeared that Bickford's talents as a master deceiver had not been enough to completely save him this time. The sheer magnitude of his crime...$100-million dollars...and the fact that four States were involved, pretty much assured that dozens of prosecutors would give Bickford's conviction their top priority.

It was more than 'justice being served'. The 'Tex' Bickford case would be a major career builder for anyone who brought him down. And the case could be Pulitzer material for a fame-hungry journalist.

Bickford and his lawyer knew all this very well. And they played it to the fullest. They could delay a trial for years by encouraging a jurisdictional war between competing States. And they could feed the Press diversionary tidbits to keep reshaping the narrative.

Bickford asked to be released to house arrest until the jurisdictional issue was settled. He argued that it could take years, and that keeping a presumed-innocent man in jail for that long would be inhumane and unnecessary. The question of flight-risk was countered when a $1,000,000 bond was posted by a major studio that had purchased rights to the story and was already casting the key roles. 'Tex' Bickford asked if he could play himself in the film, but his lawyer persuaded him that this was going too far and could hurt his sympathy with a jury!

In the meantime, possible plea deals were being offered and rejected. A reduced sentence for a return of all the money. Shorter jail time if he signed a full confession.

Throughout it all, 'Tex' Bickford claimed his innocence...arguing that he was just a foolish and unwitting participant in an illegal conspiracy. He pointed the finger at Ginger Morgan, who he said pulled all the strings from her luxury home in Waco, Texas. It was <u>she</u> who had made all the Bank wire transfers that looted the accounts of all four ad agencies. <u>She</u> who had enlisted Lou Rhodes and Harrison Smith into her embezzlement scheme!

'Tex' Bickford's lawyer pointed out that there was absolutely no documentation of his client's role in anything illegal. Yes, he had met with all four ad agencies at the outset. Yes, he had discussed with them the opportunity to join a syndicate to service a large new account. Yes, he had introduced both Lou Rhodes and Harrison Smith to them. But that was it! He had no further involvement whatsoever! In fact, he had totally abandoned the whole project once he learned that the client he represented had canceled all their plans. He had passed that bad news along to Mr. Rhodes and Mr. Smith, asking them to inform the ad agencies and to thank them for their interest. He had also informed Ms. Morgan at El Paso Trust that he wanted the bank accounts he had opened for the syndicate to be closed, because the project was now dead.

'Tex' Bickford's lawyer went on to speculate that Ms. Georgina Morgan had then hatched a plot. Knowing that Rhodes and Smith were extremely upset over their loss of potential income, she proposed a scheme that would make them all very rich. A scheme where the mystery client would still exit, and 'Tex' Bickford would be set up to take the fall!

'Tex' Bickford's lawyer underscored the fact that <u>every</u> document, <u>every</u> financial authorization, and <u>every</u> transfer of funds bore the personal signatures of Georgina Morgan or Lou Rhodes. And that it was Harrison Smith, and not his client, who had <u>direct involvement</u> with these agencies. Yes, Mr. Bickford had met with the owners of these agencies…but that was only twice, and that was <u>before</u> those agencies signed-on to any agreements!

Of course, 'Tex' Bickford's claim of innocent naivety was severely undercut once his life-long history of fraudulent dealings was discovered. Seeing his very-distinctive photo in the news, more and more people came foreword with stories of how he had bamboozled them. All his old aliases came flowing forth!

Of all the many people who wanted to see 'Tex' Jay Bickford get the max, Harley Quirk was near the top. His reputation, business, wealth and marriage had all been destroyed. The owners of the other three embezzled ad agencies felt the same.

And they were not alone—

- The President of El Paso Trust and the Manager of their Waco Branch were both fired for "negligence" and their futures in banking and business were gone for good. They both hungered for Bickford's punishment!

- All of Bickford's co-conspirators would like to see him drawn and quartered. He had betrayed them all to save his skin!

- Then there were those caught up in what was now being called-- "The Jailhouse Package Caper". As a direct result of the 'Tex' Bickford incident, the Marion County Sheriff had replaced the Warden, the Head of Security, and three others at the Jail. Were it not for Bickford, they'd still all have had their jobs. Without doubt, they'd like to see Bickford put away for life!

- If somehow...in a total failure of justice...'Tex' Bickford managed to escape serious jail time, all of the above would 'not be very pleased'. In fact, one or more of them might even be moved to resort to a little violence!

Of course, all those 'who and why' questions about 'Tex' Bickford's jail cell attack still remained open! Yet only one person seemed fixated on finding the answers. That was FBI Special Agent Sally Templeton.

It wasn't just that her childhood home was in Tulsa...where the fictional 'Guardian Angel Society' was supposed to be located...it was because no one else involved in the case was objectively investigating the matter. They were all so absorbed in protecting their own reputations that they had no appetite for seeing the 'who and why' aspects of the case take center stage. They all wanted 'Tex' Bickford brought to justice, with no distractions for the defense to wiggle through.

Surely, Sally Templeton had other cases and assignments to pursue, but finding the 'who and why' for this one remained a personal priority. She vowed to solve what she now called…"My Guardian Angel Case" no matter how long it might take!

TARGET # 3—

The Queen

19.

The Queen Mary 2
-- Test Run --

NEW JERSEY TO BROOKLYN--

George Trecott loaded two black suitcases and a zippered tote bag into his car for the 40-minute drive to the Park & Ride lot at the Vince Lombardi Service Area on the New Jersey Turnpike. The tags on his luggage matched the name and address on his forged documents—Roger S. Sayles of 53 Arch Street, Ramapo, NY 10974. This was the address of a one-room office space he had rented for cash, but visited only once a week to pick up any mail.

Over the past few months George had grown a short gray beard to cover his receding chin line. With the addition of a wavy center-parted wig and dark-rimmed glasses, the 'new' George was now a perfect match to the photos in his fake passport and fake driver's license.

Parking in the long-term lot at the Park & Ride, George made his way to the central terminal building, where using his 'Roger Sayles' cell phone and credit card, he booked an Uber trip to the Brooklyn Cruise Terminal. There he would board Cunard's Queen Mary 2 for a 7-day transatlantic crossing to Southampton, England.

This trip would be a test run. The real event wouldn't occur for another 3-months. But because of the size and audacity of his plan, George knew that careful pre-planning was an absolute necessity!

On the Uber drive to the Brooklyn Cruise Terminal, George went through a mental checklist of each phase of the operation. His ultimate goal? To successfully 'kill' hundreds of VIP passengers while at sea, even though the authorities had been pre-warned that an international terrorist was aboard. And to accomplish this without being stopped or apprehended.

As they entered the Lincoln Tunnel into Manhattan, George zeroed in on his first challenge—the issue of Passport Control. In booking his Queen Mary 2 cruise on the internet, George had entered his Roger Sayles' passport specifics. These were accepted without question and he was issued a passenger confirmation number and cabin assignment. But the actual passport itself would be inspected at the Brooklyn Cruise Terminal before check-in and boarding. However, this would be by a Cunard employee and not a Federal Immigration Officer. George's fake passport was of excellent quality and would hopefully pass without a problem.

Over the past year, George had learned a lot about securing fake documents. Those shady neighborhood guys were basically scam artists, selling crude, easily detected driver's licenses and credit cards, and selling stolen or out-of-date passports. To a pro, they would be flagged immediately as bogus!

Amazingly, an internet search for "fake passports" brought up links to many vendor sites. And the search title "novelty passports" delivered even more, with some even claiming to access official government sites to record your new identity. Of course, they all had the disclaimer—"Not to be used for any illegal purpose, etc., etc."

But it was the 'dark web' that provided the most authentic documents, with some actually issued by operatives in government agencies. These were the gold standard in fake documents. And were priced accordingly.

Once he had the fake documents, with an authentic social security number, opening local bank accounts and securing credit cards in the name of Roger Sayles was easy.

Of course, the real challenge would be overcoming the hidden security elements found in many official documents today. The holograms, color-changes under UV light, the embedded microchips, instrument sensitive papers, etc. To the naked eye, a passport or driver's license might look authentic, but to a Security Professional it would be immediately flagged as counterfeit.

Some sources on the 'dark web' claimed to offer totally undetectable custom documents. By utilizing the same type of encoding equipment used by the government agencies, they guaranteed absolute authenticity. Most of these firms were in Eastern Europe or Asia. But a few were far closer to home.

Though the price was far higher, George had chosen a 'dark web' source. And this transatlantic voyage on the Queen Mary 2 would be a test of its value.

Coming home from London by air was another matter. Recognizing that he'd have to go through Passport Control at both Heathrow and JFK, George planned to travel home under his real name with his real passport. He'd keep his beard, but loose the wig and glasses. However, after landing in the U.S. he'd first test out the Roger Sayles passport in one of the automated passport reading kiosks at JFK. If the kiosk printout came out with a big "X" across it, and the message "See Immigration Agent", he'd know there was a problem. He'd then move to another kiosk to run through his real George Trecott passport.

After leaving the Lincoln Tunnel, the Uber driver headed south on 12th Avenue along Manhattan Island's West Side. They were too far south to see much of the two cruise ships docked at the Manhattan Cruise Terminal—the 'Viking Star' at Pier 90 and the 'Norwegian Breakaway' at Pier 88. But straining a bit to look out of the car's rear window, George could see the bridge and flight deck of the aircraft carrier 'USS Intrepid'--docked at its permanent home at Pier 86 as an Air & Space Museum.

For many decades, all of the luxury cruise ships sailing out of New York docked at one of the four Hudson River piers. But as the size and number of cruise ships increased, only 2 Manhattan piers could accommodate them. That led to the 2004 opening of the Cape Liberty Cruise Port in Bayonne, New Jersey—now used by the Royal Caribbean Cruise Line, Celebrity Cruises and Azamara Cruises. And the 2006 opening of the Brooklyn Cruise Terminal, now used by Cunard's Queen Mary 2 and the Princess Cruise ships.

Driving past the Hudson Yards and past the Chelsea Piers to Manhattan's southern tip, George's thoughts zeroed in on the Queen Mary 2. And why this ship? And why these dates?

In this, his third and most challenging experiment as a would-be assassin, he wanted to attempt a spectacular mass killing of a high-visibility VIP target group—perhaps an international delegation of business or government leaders, or sports figures, or film stars, or politicians, or the media, or the socially prominent 'one-percenters'.

There were many events each year that brought VIP groups like these together, but there was little challenge in just planting a bomb in a hotel ballroom. And as always, he wanted to use his signature speciality—a potentially undetectable toxin. And even more, to make this a true 'Thriller', he wanted to create a cat-and-mouse scenario… where the authorities would be forewarned but have no way of dispersing the target group before he struck. What better place than the confines of a cruise ship far out to sea!

And as for cruise ships, what better than the famous Queen Mary 2. She was indeed the only true ocean liner afloat—specially built for transatlantic crossings. Her sharp prow, sleek design, thick steel hull and powerful engines let her cut through the roughest of seas to keep to her schedule. While conventional cruise ships would be forced to turn back or linger in port during a storm, the QM2 would valiantly sail on!

When built in 2004, the QM2 was the largest, longest, tallest, fastest, and most expensive passenger ship in history. And regular refits kept her arguably the most luxurious—with an uncompromising dress code that included several black tie evenings, classic afternoon teas, and gala dress-up balls. If a VIP group wished to sponsor a weeklong get-away cruise, the Queen Mary 2 would be their venue of choice!

George's initial choice of the QM2 was more than confirmed when he saw the special events planned for her October 8th crossing from New York-to-Southampton. On this particular voyage, 'The Greylord Project'—a Davos-like think tank—would be hosting its annual invitation-only conference, with an anticipated attendance of over 350 opinion leaders. And equally exciting, George saw that the QM2's headline guest speaker for that crossing would be none other than Sir Cecil Jenkins-Doyle, the retired head of New Scotland Yard. Taunting and then outwitting the famous Sir Jenkins-Doyle and his frantic attempts to stop him would prove especially instructive to George. This would be true 'Thriller' material!

As George's Uber rounded the bottom tip of Manhattan, it plunged into the Brooklyn Battery Tunnel for a quick run to Brooklyn's Red Hook Neighborhood. Then a sequence of complex turns to the Brooklyn Cruise Terminal and the awaiting Queen Mary 2.

On this final car leg, George replayed his plan to hopefully outwit the Ship's boarding control system. For this test voyage, George had booked a single cabin in the name of Roger S. Sayles. But for his October 8th sailing, he had booked a double—in the names of Roger S. Sayles and his fictitious cousin, Peter L. Brown. He reasoned that this would significantly reduce the odds of his being caught. Passengers traveling alone would be prime suspects. Particularly male passengers under 60 traveling alone. They were far far fewer in number and their motives for traveling alone would possibly be open to question.

For the October 8th crossing, George would attempt to check-in and board twice—once as Roger Sayles and again as Peter Brown. If successful, the ship's manifest would show his stateroom with double occupancy. Just one of more than 1,200 occupied staterooms, blending him into a massively large crowd of travelers on holiday. In just a few minutes he'd find out if that was doable!

20.

QM2 - Embarkation

DAY 1 --

As George Trecott's Uber ride pulled into the Brooklyn Cruise Terminal, his jaw dropped at his first glimpse of the Queen Mary 2. He knew she was big, but all the brochure photos and online images had not prepared him for seeing the real thing.

To say that she was mammoth was an understatement. Rising 200-feet above the waterline...the height of a 23-story building...and extending almost four football fields in length, she was simply dazzling in her brilliant and historic white, red and black color scheme. If you could lower the Empire State Building onto its side, you'd have a clear understanding of the Queen Mary 2's enormous size!

George's immediate reaction was one of near panic and overwhelming anxiety. On paper, his plan seemed so straightforward and achievable. But seeing the actual ship gave him true concerns that this venture was far too ambitious and perhaps doomed to failure. Perhaps he should scale things back? Perhaps moving his experiment to another venue? But NO. That can be decided later! He was booked for this sailing and it was merely a test run. Move ahead. If his plan proved unworkable, he could always revise it or select another venue. A bomb in a hotel meeting room would be an easy alternative.

As he exited the car, a Cunard agent unloaded his bags, checked their QM2-supplied luggage tags, and before loading them onto a rolling cart said with a smile… "Welcome to the Queen Mary 2, Mr. Sayles. We're honored to have you with us."

Then upon receiving and graciously acknowledging his tip, the agent added… "Mr. Sayles, you may proceed directly to the Arrivals Hall for your check-in. I'll see that your luggage is delivered right to your stateroom."

Inside the Arrivals Hall, George saw the long check-in counter with nearly a dozen Cunard agents. He had arrived a full hour early for his assigned check-in time. With more than 2,500 passengers to process, guests were given various check-in times based on their stateroom locations, to spare them long lines and to optimize boarding operations. George took one of the hundreds of empty seats in the Hall to observe the whole check-in process.

Prior to going to the check-in counters, passengers were asked to complete an information form at one of the many stand-up stations arrayed around the Hall. George did so, taking a few extra forms for later use. He then inspected each of the Hall's several Men's Rooms to gauge their relative appropriateness for a future unobserved switch of disguises.

At his scheduled time, George—now as *Roger Sayles*—proceeded to the check-in counter. The very cordial agent welcomed him, took his completed form, asked for his passport and preferred credit card, gave them all a cursory look, and then scanned them.

The agent then explained to *Mr. Sayles* that he would be given a personalized QM2 'Embarkation Card' that would serve as his all-purpose identification card throughout the voyage. It would be his stateroom key, could be used for all his onboard purchases, and would be his boarding pass whenever disembarking or returning to the ship. The agent volunteered that this was a security feature to make certain that everyone was back on board before sailing. That was of particular importance when visiting multiple ports during a vacation cruise. But as the agent explained..."For today's transatlantic crossing, this feature will be used only during embarkation here in New York, and when leaving the ship in Southampton."

The agent then asked *Mr. Sayles* to smile for his official photo that would be electronically linked to his card. This was an important security feature, she explained, that would allow the QM2 Security Officers to verify his identity while scanning his card during embarkation and disembarkation. It was a vital safeguard against permitting any unauthorized persons to come aboard using a stolen or lost Embarkation Card.

George, as *Roger Sayles*, then complied, adopting a broad smile for his photo.

Then after a moment or two, *Roger S. Sayles* was presented with his official 'QM2 Embarkation Card' along with an information folder containing the Ship's Deck Plans and other information.

So far, so good. The *Roger Sayles* passport and credit card were accepted without question, and would not be required again. Next step? To see if it was possible for the same person to check in twice, as two different people. That would require his ability to go on board, then come off, and then re-board again before leaving New York. This he'd test out today.

Assuming that this would be possible, then his plan for his next voyage...3-months later...would proceed as follows—

The procedure at check-in would be fairly straightforward. George would arrive with two suitcases going to the <u>same</u> double stateroom—one with the *Roger Sayles* QM2 luggage tag, the other with the *Peter Brown* QM2 luggage tag. If asked, he'd say that his cousin Mr. Brown had gone directly to the Arrivals Hall to meet up with their other cousins who had already checked-in.

Inside the Arrivals Hall, George, as *Roger Sayles*, would check-in several minutes early and get his Queen Mary 2 Embarkation Card. He'd then go to the Men's Room, where he would switch disguises to become *Peter Brown*. The transformation would be as easy as removing the wig, widening his nose with cotton ball inserts, and clipping in a set of prosthetic teeth. His reversible jacket and adding a noticeable limp would complete the process.

As *Peter Brown*, he would then check-in with his own fake documents and proceed to his stateroom aboard ship. There, he'd quickly switch his disguise back to become *Roger Sayles*--and using the Roger Sayles ID Card make a quick trip off...and then back onto... the Ship.

Net effect? If it all worked, the QM2 security system would show that both *Peter Brown* and *Roger Sayles* were aboard at the time of sailing. Throughout the voyage, George might or might not choose to alternate personalities. But he would use both cards to run up minor incidental charges at the gift shop or at one or more of the QM2's many bars.

This scheme, of course, required that George be allowed to get on and then off the Ship before it left New York. And it assumed that the Ship's security system...while primarily designed to prevent unauthorized individuals from coming aboard...was also designed to identify passengers who had still not come back on board after visiting a local port. A 'logged off' indication paired with a 'logged on' indication would hopefully cancel each other out in the system. At least that was George's fairly safe assumption, based on his online reading of several commercial security system manuals.

In England, upon disembarkation, the process would work in reverse. *Peter Brown* would go ashore, quickly change his appearance, and as *Roger Sayles* ask permission to come back aboard for a few minutes to retrieve the briefcase he had forgotten in the nearby Men's Room. With a sigh of relief and thanks to the whole security team, he'd 'again' disembark the ship. Net effect—the QM2's security system would show that both *Peter Brown* and *Roger Sayles* had left the ship. That is, if it all worked!

But today, only George as *Roger Sayles* would be boarding to test out the system.

After checking-in at the Arrivals Hall, George as *Roger Sayles* walked up the enclosed switchback passenger-way to enter the ship at the Grand Lobby level, midships on Deck 3. His QM2 card was scanned and his carryon was run through the X-ray scanner. A Ships Officer with a proper British accent welcomed him aboard and assigned a uniformed steward to escort him to Stateroom 3008...his single Ocean-View Stateroom on the Port side.

Pausing in his stateroom for less than 5-minutes, George retraced his steps to the Grand Lobby and the embarkation station. Feigning great anxiety, George told the Ships Officer that he had left his favorite tweed hat in the Arrivals Hall Men's Room and asked if he could possibly go back ashore to retrieve it. The Officer assured him that he was more than welcome to leave the Ship for whatever time needed, just as long as he was back on board before the Ship's 5:30PM sailing.

With a warm smile and a little chuckle, the Ship Officer tried to comfort *Mr. Sayles* by confiding that such a thing happens all the time. "On our last voyage, one of our passengers had forgotten to give something of importance to the friend who had dropped him off at the Terminal. And another found he had walked off with the car keys, and his less-than-happy wife had just phoned him from the Arrivals Hall."

Once back in his stateroom, George breathed a long sigh of relief and collapsed onto the room's small but comfortable couch to settle his nerves. It took more than a half hour before he could bring himself to unpack. By then it was nearing 5:00PM, and he was finally ready to start exploring the ship.

The QM2 was so huge that it would probably take him most of the voyage to cover it all…to find answers to his two priority questions—

1. Where in all likelihood would the 'Greylord Project' be holding their various sessions?

2. How would he best penetrate those areas undetected to achieve his goals with maximum effectiveness?

George was well aware that without doubt the QM2 had extensive security systems. Hundreds of concealed cameras, password protected doors and devices, monitoring sensors, and dozens of highly trained personnel. To his knowledge, the QM2 never had a successful breach of their security systems. And finding a way to avoid and bypass them would pose a great challenge. But that's exactly what George was here for! And it was now time to begin!

For this first night at sea, the QM2 dress code for men was 'informal'...which meant jacket with no tie required. To remain fairly inconspicuous, George chose the 'standard upscale man's uniform' of dark gray woolen slacks, navy blue blazer, and white button-down shirt...in this case open at the neck.

The QM2's main dining room was the spectacular *Britannia Restaurant*, with pre-assigned dinner seatings at 6:00PM and 8:00PM. More than 1,200 passengers were served at each seating by a large staff of waiters, sommeliers, and dining room captains. George had not signed up for either of these seatings, because that would have placed him at the same table with the same group of chatty fellow-passengers for each and every night of the voyage. He would choose the *Britannia* for breakfast and lunch during the daytime, when it was always open seating.

Tonight, and probably for every night during the crossing, he'd eat at the *Kings Court* on Deck 7. This was the Ship's huge buffet-dining venue. Open 24-hours a day, with numerous hot and cold food stations, it was staffed by dozens of toque-wearing chefs and servers. Unlike the *Britannia Restaurant*, the *Kings Court* provided ample opportunity for solitary dining. Its hundreds of 2-person tables were spread out into several carpeted dining areas, each tastefully appointed with paintings and artwork. While the tables could be pulled together to accommodate four or more people, most were occupied by couples or a few solo diners. There were also smaller tables in ten window bays that overlooked the ship's *Promenade Deck*. George would avoid these areas because they seemed the most popular and quickly filled up with passengers anxious to chat and make friends with the couples at neighboring tables.

Almost three-quarters of Deck 7's thousand-foot interior space was devoted to food service, with the *Kings Court* amidships occupying the largest area. But before eating there, George decided to quickly explore all the other food service areas on Deck 7.

Forward of the *Kings Court* was the much smaller *Carinthia Lounge*, open for lighter dining and relaxation during the day, and musical entertainment afternoons and evenings. The *Carinthia Lounge* offered bar service for itself and for the *Kings Court*.

Aft of the *Kings Court* were the two exclusive dining areas reserved for the 300 or so guests occupying the ship's luxury staterooms, suites and duplexes on Decks 8 and above. There was the *Queens Grill* to starboard and the *Princess Grill* to port, with the adjoining *Grill Lounge* and its Grill Bar servicing both. There was a strong possibility that the VIP attendees of the 'Greylord Project' would be drinking and dining in this area. As such, it would deserve closer inspection during the week ahead.

Deck 7 was also the site of two major 'wellness centers'. Far forward near the bow of the Ship, passageways led to the elegant *Canyon Ranch SpaClub*...a professionally staffed 20,000-sq.ft. complex, with 24 private treatment rooms, saunas, steam rooms, a therapy pool, whirlpool bath, and a spacious dimly lit relaxation lounge. George didn't enter it, but he could see that it was predominately used by women.

And just forward of the *Canyon Ranch* was the QM2's *Fitness Center*, with a full array of the latest exercise equipment and the assistance of several personal trainers. Both men and women used these facilities, but the majority right now were men.

Completely encircling Deck 7 was the *Promenade Deck*. More than one-third-of-a-mile long and surfaced entirely with expensive hand-caulked teak planking, it replicated the ambiance of luxury ocean liners of the past. While many cruise ships had promenade decks, they used a vinyl decking material to simulate the appearance of caulked teak. Only the Queen Mary 2 had the real thing!

The QM2's *Promenade Deck* is where the Ship's passengers would take their morning walks and evening strolls, or lounge in a deck-chair with a good book or cup of broth…or gaze out taking in the sea air and the mesmerizing attraction of the vast ocean.

All that was fine, but to George the most significant aspect of the *Promenade Deck* was that it allowed quick entry and exit to every venue on Deck 7—and that it permitted movement from bow to stern without passing through any interior passageways. Passageways that were certainly closely monitored with security cameras.

It was nearing 5:30PM, and the scheduled time for the Ship's sailing. To see how all that was accomplished, George cut through the *Kings Court* to the Ship's dockside. He expected to see motorized equipment pulling away boarding ramps and burly crewmen moving heavy hawsers, with the Ship's Captain issuing commands from the extended landside bridge wing.

All that was there, but it was the sight ashore that literally took his breath away. Just to his right, and brilliantly lit by the late afternoon sun, the entire southern end of Manhattan Island was arrayed before him—with the 1776-foot high Freedom Tower and its surrounding skyscrapers in crystal clarity. Directly across from him was historic

Governor's Island. And just off to his left at some distance was the Statue of Liberty with her golden torch.

Three blasts from the QM2's massive whistles, signaling that the ship was about to sail, brought George back to his senses and reminded him of his mission. No time for daydreaming. This was not a pleasure trip; he was here for serious business!

Inside the *Kings Court* for his dinner, George carefully observed the movement of passengers in both the buffet areas and the dining areas, looking for vulnerable spots to possibly 'wreak his toxic magic' on a large targeted group. The hot and cold buffet stations were out. They offered far too many food choices to achieve anything more than randomized results. Plus everything was overseen by large teams of chefs, servers, and uniformed restaurant managers.

The *Kings Court* seating areas were just as heavily staffed. Dozens of waiters assisting diners, refilling glasses and cups, clearing away plates and utensils, responding to every guest request. And numerous supervisors hovering over everything to make sure all the guests were well served.

One possibility was spiking a few of the four centralized beverage-dispensing stations where guests could fill their own glasses and cups with juices, coffee, tea or chilled water. Many did so, but far more were filled by waiters and delivered right to the tables. So again a 'no'.

George concluded that the only area in the *Kings Court* that did show promise was the soft-serve ice cream dispensers. There were two of them, one on the port side and one on the starboard side in the main buffet section. Here, passengers filled their own bowls or cones with a choice of vanilla or chocolate ice cream. But fewer than a third of the diners did so, opting instead for a plate full of the tempting pastries that were arrayed on the buffet counters.

Before returning to his stateroom, George decided to take one of the several elevators down to the *Grand Lobby* to get a more comprehensive feel for the typical QM2 passenger. With its atrium rising from Deck 2 all the way up to Deck 7, the *Grand Lobby* was the midpoint between the *Britannia Restaurant* toward the stern and the *Royal Court Theatre* toward the prow. At both the Deck 2 and Deck 3 levels, very broad richly-decorated passageways connected the two venues.

When he arrived at Deck 2, George found a gathering of people grouped around a string quartet playing Mozart—framed by the *Grand Lobby's* two sweeping curved stairways that led up to the Deck 3 Lobby level. He quickly recognized that this upper level would give him a far better vantage point—allowing him to unobtrusively peer down on Deck 2, presumably to enjoy the music, while also casually observing everyone passing by him on Deck 3 as well.

When the quartet completed their set, George wandered through a few of the several high-end shops radiating off the *Grand Lobby* at the Deck 3 level. Here, from their overheard accents and speech patterns, he could tell that the large majority of his fellow passengers were from various parts of Great Britain. Maybe 15-percent more were Asian. And no more than 30-percent were Americans. The average age was mid-60s. All were conservatively dressed, refined and soft spoken. Clearly, the Queen Mary 2 was no 'Love Boat'!

As he entered his stateroom, George noted that the cabin steward had turned down his bed and left some chocolates on top of the 'QM2 Daily Briefing Packet' that previewed their next day at sea. He also noted that fresh ice had been added to the wine bucket holding the bottle of sparkling wine that had been placed earlier in his stateroom, with a note from the Captain welcoming his arrival. Also, his partially consumed liter bottle of Avian water had been replaced on the stateroom desktop.

With his iPhone, George took close up photos of both the chocolates and the wine bottle. Injecting a toxin into either one of them, or into the bottled water, would not pose an insurmountable problem. But doing so on a mass basis certainly would. But still, that was a possibility.

For the next hour, George made comprehensive notes on everything he had learned and observed that day—and listed his priorities for tomorrow. One item on his list was to find out where, and how securely, the complimentary chocolates and the wine and water bottles were stored. Another was to do the same for the gallon cartons of ice cream mix that he had seen being poured into the *Kings Court* soft serve machines.

But his top priority for the next few days at sea would be to make a close-up inspection of all the Ship's many group meeting areas… and to take a deep dive into the Ship's entire food delivery and air handling systems.

21.

QM2 – Public Spaces

DAY 2 --

BEFORE HEADING OFF for his breakfast in the *Britannia Restaurant*, George reviewed his planned schedule for the day. There were three major entertainment centers on the Ship where very large groups could convene. All three of these locations offered events today. And George planned to attend them all.

The *Royal Court Theatre* would have a 10:30AM lecture by a distinguished EU statesman. And then at 8:30PM, an hour-long Broadway-style musical production. That same show would be repeated again at 10:30PM for second-seating diners. George would attend the lecture this morning and the early show later in the week.

At 2:30PM, *Illuminations* would feature a spectacular planetarium show, and would then show first-run movies at various times throughout the late afternoon and at night. He'd do the planetarium show, but skip the movies.

At 5:00PM today, one hour prior to the first seating in the *Britannia Restaurant*, the huge *Queens Room* ballroom would be the site of the Captain's Welcoming Reception. A black tie event, with champagne and hors d'oeuvres, this largely stand-up cocktail party would give George the opportunity to roam around the room and inspect all the entrances. Not today, but on all future days at sea, the *Queens Room* would be home to the QM2's traditional 3:30PM 'High Tea'. With finger sandwiches, scones with jam and clotted cream, pastries, and of course steaming hot tea. All served by a large roaming staff of attentive waiters. And after dinner every night, the *Queens Room* would be transformed again into a themed Big-Band-Ballroom. This crossing would feature a formal 'Black & White Ball', a 'Masquerade Ball', and a 'Royal Ascot Ball'. Throughout the week, George would attend a High Tea and monitor one of the dances.

But immediately after breakfast today, before scouting these three principal entertainment areas, George would head directly to the *Ship Library* and the *Ship Book Shop* on Deck 8. Here he would try to find engineering drawings of the Ship's construction and outfitting. He particularly wanted details on the HVAC air handling systems, the potable water storage and distribution systems, the desalinization plant to convert salt water to fresh, the food storage and food preparation areas, and the layout and workings of the crew decks and work areas…all of which were below the lowest passenger decks.

Accomplishing all this would keep George very much on the go during this, his first full day at sea. But the challenge made it all the more exciting! And to stoke up his energy for the big day ahead, he'd start with a full English Breakfast and lots of coffee!

Just before 8:30AM, George strode into the *Britannia Restaurant* through the main entrance on Deck 2. The maître d' welcomed him and asked if he'd like to be seated alone or with other guests. When he said, "Alone", the maître d' nodded to one of the more than a dozen waiters lined-up in pristine white-jackets, who then came forward to escort George to a private table in the center of the vast space.

After pulling back the chair for George, plumping up and presenting the crisp white napkin and today's breakfast menu folder, the waiter asked if George would prefer coffee or tea or something else before ordering? Returning with a pot of steaming coffee and a small pitcher of cream, the waiter indicated that he'd be standing by for whenever George was ready to indicate his breakfast selections.

While waiting for his order to arrive, George carefully studied the enormity of the space. Inspired by the grand dining rooms of the 1930s golden era, the 1,347-seat *Britannia Restaurant* was two decks high and crowned by a massive stained glass skylight, with backlighting that subtly changed to match the time of day. At the far end of the spectacular room there was a 20-foot-high Gobelin tapestry portraying a stylized Queen Mary 2 with the New York skyline.

Guests could choose to dine in the spacious central court on Deck 2, or in one of the several tiered-dining-areas that ringed it. Or they could ascend one of the paired sweeping grand staircases to the Deck 3 level, where they could dine while overlooking the full sweep of the Restaurant below. Because the Deck 3 level had its own main entrance, it also allowed guests dining on Deck 2 to make a dramatic appearance by strolling down one of the grand staircases to their table.

Without doubt, the 350 or so attendees of the October 8th 'Gaylord Project Cruise' would dine here in the *Britannia Restaurant*, probably in the larger tiered section on the port side of Deck 2. But even if they all chose the same early or late seating, they'd represent only about one-quarter of the Restaurant's diners at that seating. It would be very difficult to target just them through their food, especially considering that a typical dinner menu offered many many choices of starters, entrées and desserts. Therefore the only practical way to deliver a toxin was in the wine served to their group…either injected into the bottles or through clear droplets placed in their yet-to-be-filled wine glasses.

A further complication was the large number of entrances and exits to the *Britannia Restaurant*. At least ten that George could easily see, plus what appeared to be four more for food and beverage delivery. Clearly, there was no way for a single person to lock everyone into the massive room. That would make the use of a toxic gas impractical.

As the waiter poured George his second cup of coffee, George asked why there were so few passengers at breakfast this morning? The waiter told him that the busiest time for breakfast in the *Britannia* was usually between 9:30 and 10:30 each morning, but that even then most guests preferred to breakfast at the *Kings Court* buffet. With that opening, George probed further with a series of seemingly casual questions. Where did his waiter call home? Indonesia was the answer. How long was the usual contract period before going home? Six months was the answer. Where did the crew actually live aboard ship? On Decks A and B, which were below Deck 1 at the very bottom of the Ship. Why do we never see any crewmembers in the elevators and stairways? Because we have our own service elevators was the answer.

With different waiters at different breakfasts and lunches throughout the week, and through a series of short innocuous chats with some junior ship officers and crewmembers, George would compile a comprehensive dossier on the inner workings of Queen Mary 2.

Immediately after breakfast, George rode up to Deck 8 and walked the long starboard passageway past over 50 staterooms to reach the *Ship Library* at the prow. Beautifully appointed with rich wooden paneling, glass-fronted bookcases, large leather chairs and a few writing desks, it housed thousands of volumes, maps and periodicals. Here George had great success, quickly finding even more than he had hoped for in the Ship's reference section. Making sure no one was watching, he snapped dozens of photos of schematics, drawings and lists with his iPhone.

Adjacent to the *Ship Library* was the *Ship Book Shop*. In addition to the expected selection of 'best-sellers', the Shop featured a fairly large collection of Cunard and Queen Mary 2 books, brochures and souvenirs. And it was here, in the corner of an upper shelf, that George found a single copy of an amazing volume... "*The QM2 Owner's Workshop Manual*"...a 180-page oversize book, with comprehensive details of the ship's design, construction and operation, along with hundreds of photos. George immediately bought this copy. It would be his prime study material for late tonight and into early tomorrow morning!

After dropping off the book in his stateroom, George raced to the *Royal Court Theatre*, just in time to make the 10:30AM lecture. Indeed, the space was very much like a modern Broadway theatre, with a thrust stage and over 1,000 seats split between a wrap-around orchestra level and a wrap-around mezzanine.

During the day, the *Royal Court Theatre* was the venue used by the QM2 for its premiere lecturers. Most likely, this is where the Greylord Project's principal speakers would appear...and attendance would be strictly limited to the Conferences' delegates, almost all of whom would certainly attend. This made the *Royal Court Theatre* an ideal location for George's purposes.

But how to 'poison' them was the question? A ricin gas or something similar could do the trick. But the area was so large that several cylinders might be required. At two decks high, the *Royal Court Theatre* spanned the width of the entire ship. People would have to be trapped inside for some time for a gas to be fully effective. And again, all the many exits posed a problem. Without help, they couldn't be properly sealed off.

Still, the *Royal Court Theatre* in most cases was ideal. With a little more study, he might find a way. Then something caught his attention. Looking down at the stage from his first row seat in the side-mezzanine, he noticed some nozzles along the edges of the thrust stage.

The stage was equipped with all the latest in theatrical-effect equipment…a turntable, floor lift, LED digital backdrop, advanced lighting and sound systems, and what looked very much like a stage-smoke generating system. It was this last item with its nozzles that caught George's attention. If that indeed was what he thought, perhaps he could find a way to add a little something special to the smoke mix and redirect the nozzles to automatically dose the entire audience. Hopefully, during the week's several musical productions they'd use this equipment and he'd see if it was indeed a smoke-generating system!

The QM2's second theatre was *Illuminations*, designed primarily as a planetarium, movie theatre and lecture hall. With 493 seats, this could well be the place the Greylord Project would hold most of their group meetings and general lectures. Its smaller size was ideal for a group of their size. And its single-level amphitheater-style seating provided truly excellent sight lines between speaker and audience. Two main aisles flowed smoothly downward to focus directly on the large raised stage. The stage itself appeared to have first-rate sound and lighting systems, but none of the theatrical equipment for large-scale musical productions.

For planetarium shows, a 60-foot-wide motorized dome descended over the mid-section of the theatre, where 150 seats were designated for viewers. Upholstered in red, these seats could be tilted far back to provide a panoramic view of the projected heavens above. While attendance for each planetarium show was limited to just 150 passengers with advanced reservations, multiple shows were offered each day to eventually accommodate everyone interested.

Of course there was no way of knowing where the Gaylord Project general meetings would be held. But certainly for a group this large and important, the choice would be between the *Royal Court Theatre* and *Illuminations*. As such, George had to develop a workable plan for both.

The problem to be overcome with the *Royal Court Theatre* was not only its great size but also its multiple exits—with the orchestra section exiting at two places on Deck 2 and the mezzanine section exiting at two places on Deck 3. But in its favor, it did have that stage-smoke system going for it.

Illuminations, at half the size and all on one level, would be much easier to effectively rig. But gaining undetected access could prove difficult because it was kept securely locked between scheduled events. And its two separate entrance lobbies, one on each side of the Ship, were almost always fully staffed before and after an event. Further, immediately after an event, staff members would quickly clear everyone from the theatre, making sure that no one remained.

Presumably, this was to protect the sensitive and extremely valuable synchronized planetarium projectors, which were precisely positioned at floor level in all four quadrants of the room.

At 5:00PM precisely, George lined up outside the regal entrance to the *Queens Room* on Deck 3 for the "Captain's Welcoming Reception". For this event, everyone was arrayed in their finest. The ladies in gowns and glittering jewels, the men in tuxedos or formal military uniforms. A few of the older men had their campaign medals proudly on display. And two Scotsmen were wearing their formal kilt outfits.

After passing through the receiving line and exchanging pleasantries with the Captain and Cruise Director, George was offered a choice of champagne or juice as he entered the domed *Queens Room*, with its 1,048-sq. ft. dance floor beneath two huge crystal chandeliers. On raised levels around the dance floor, small cocktail tables accommodated 562 guests. At the far end of the ballroom, a Hollywood Bowl-style arch framed the bandstand, where a ten-piece Big Band orchestra often performed. But for this reception, a small combo played cocktail music.

Once the room had filled, the Captain made a brief welcoming speech and introduced his key officers for each of the Ship's main departments—including engineering, hotel, food and beverage, and entertainment. Before and after these formalities, smartly attired waiters roamed the area, serving canapés and refilling champagne and juice glasses.

At 6:00PM precisely, a gong was sounded, telling attendees that the *Britannia*'s first dinner seating was about to begin. The room quickly cleared. But the entire event would be repeated a second time, just one hour later for a whole new group of attendees—those scheduled for the 8:00PM *Britannia* seating.

During the brief time he had in the *Queens Room*, George made a beeline to a select few of the Ship's junior officers who were also in attendance. One could tell their areas of responsibility from the stripes and color bands on their epaulettes, as illustrated in the small foldout Ship Map that every passenger had been given.

Introducing himself as a retired engineer, or chef, or meeting planner, or naval officer, he quickly determined that---

- He could join a small group scheduled to tour the Ship's Bridge at 2:30PM tomorrow.

- For safety reasons, it was <u>not</u> possible for him to tour the ship's engine room or see the water treatment plant.

- There would be a kitchen tour for everyone the day after tomorrow.

- For large conference or affinity groups, the *Queens Room* was where their evening cocktail parties were most frequently held. But the ballroom was almost never used for group banquets, although there had been a very few exceptions.

This was all useful information. But above all, it confirmed George's initial impression, formed as he first entered the *Queens Room*, that this could well be the best place to target the Greylord Project attendees. A private gala cocktail party in the *Queens Room* would assure maximum turn out in a confined space!

22.

QM2 – Below Decks

DAY 3 --

GEORGE HAD THREE objectives today. There was the small group tour of the Ship's bridge at 2:30PM...and by appealing to the concierge he had managed to get added to the list. Second was finding a way to get below decks to inspect the Ship's food storage areas and the water and air-handling systems. These decks were off-limits to passengers, but after studying the materials he had gathered in the *Ship Library* and *Ship Book Shop*, George had perhaps found a way to gain entry. And lastly was a top-to-bottom exploration of the Ship—every passenger deck, every lounge, every bar and entertainment area, every elevator bank, and every stairwell. Today, he'd just do a fast walkthrough of these areas. Then on future days, he'd go back for a closer inspection of key locations.

All passengers were given a small foldout map showing the QM2's deck plans. And illustrated plaques throughout the Ship repeated this information to help passengers find their way around easily, without getting lost or confused. But the lowest deck shown on all these maps was Deck 2. Not shown were the <u>four decks</u> below that. These were the 'behind-the-curtain' work areas that kept the Ship operating. But George had detailed schematics of those areas on his iPhone...thanks to materials he had photographed in the *Ship Library*.

Deck 1 was called the Ship's 'Main Artery' by crewmembers. With its steel bulkheads painted bright white and its wide center passageway devoid of decoration, it was all 'strictly business' and 'pure function'.

Far forward were cabins for the QM2's officers and senior staff members.
Aft were the Ship's extensive medical facilities, which as George learned, did have a separate entrance for ill passengers.

Still further aft were the Ship's food storage areas, with lifts to the kitchens above. And beyond the food storage areas was the garbage handling and processing plant...with incinerators for combustibles, compactors for recyclables, and a refrigerated containment area for other refuse.

Deck 1 was also the site of the QM2's 'Engine Control Room', where all the Ship's propulsion and mechanical functions were monitored—including both the air-handling systems and the fresh water production and distribution systems. Though not specifically mentioned in any of the reference materials, George strongly suspected that the QM2 had a major 'Security Command Center' on this level too, with a large staff monitoring video and sensor feeds from thousands of points throughout the Ship.

At midships was the luggage handling area, and the embarkation point for the Ship tenders that were used to transfer passengers ashore when the QM2 was at anchor in a port.

And completing the picture for Deck 1 was a large mess hall and canteen for the crew...and the crew bar, *The Pig & Whistle.* With over 1,000 crewmembers working different shifts, these areas were almost always busy.

Next level down was Deck A—devoted almost entirely to high-density crew quarters. But it also housed the Ship's bakery, fruit and vegetable bulk storage, and the ice cream and frozen food lockers. All well worth a look, if George could find a way to gain entry.

Down lower still was Deck B—which housed the crew gym, library, cinema, photo lab, and print pressroom. But of special interest to George were the 4 potable water storage tanks with a combined capacity of over one million gallons. For this seven day crossing, the QM2's potable water consumption would exceed two million gallons, much of which would be generated right aboard ship by the desalinization of seawater. If George wanted to make the entire ship population his target, adding a little something 'special' to these water tanks could well do the trick. But even though that was not at all in his plans, figuring out how to do so would still prove instructive, as a little bonus research!

Also on Deck B was the Ship's laundry and linen storage. This area George definitely wanted to visit. Because, if his reference materials were correct, all the new and freshly cleaned crew uniforms were stored here, in a room right next to the laundry.

Like any good hotel, overnight laundry and dry cleaning services were available to the Ship's passengers via room service. And it was on Deck B that all that work was done. But the Deck B laundry also had an adjacent laundromat section primarily for use by crewmembers, but with a separate entrance for passengers. By loading up a bag with wet laundry, George could claim that he couldn't wait for the usual overnight service and that he needed to use the Ship's laundromat. His real goal was to filch a few QM2 uniform jackets so that he could pose as a waiter or room steward. Not only would that let him more freely explore areas below decks, but also enter the main entertainment areas between events, as a crewmember straightening up.

Below Deck B was the QM2's "Double Bottom"—a 2-meter-high 'inner-skin' deck running most of the Ship's length. In this space, separate tanks held the Ship's water ballast, the grey water collected from showers and baths, and both the heavy fuel oil and marine gas oil. And importantly, the Double Bottom was the location of some of the Ship's major machinery installations—four diesel generators for electricity, the desalinization plant for potable water, four chillers for the air conditioning, steam generators for heat, and the sewage treatment plant.

George hoped he could sidestep security to visit this lowest QM2 level, not so much for his current project but just to see if it could be done!

So, to summarize his below-deck priorities—

1. He'd start with a feigned illness this morning to visit the infirmary on Deck 1. Then wander around, acting lost, to see all that he could see.

2. During the dinner hour, while many crewmembers were above decks, he'd visit the laundromat on Deck 2 with a bag of wet laundry. Then attempt to collect a few crew uniform jackets from the adjacent storeroom. If he couldn't get through any locked doors, he'd see what he could find tumbling around in one of the dryers.

3. Then the day after next, wearing a crewmember jacket and carrying a clipboard, he'd go below decks to do a closer inspection of the food storage and prep areas on both Deck 1 and Deck A. Then also the potable water storage areas on Deck B. And if possible the air-handling equipment in the "Double Bottom". But this last one he'd skip if there appeared any chance at all of his being challenged.

In truth, from the materials he had gathered and studied, George already had fairly comprehensive information on the Ship's important air-handling systems. With over 3,000 passengers and crewmembers effectively sealed within a multi-sectioned giant steel tube, circulating purified fresh air at the right temperature was absolutely critical for both health and comfort. And the QM2 had a state-of-the-art system to accomplish that.

Giant fans drew in <u>fresh air</u> through huge ducts on Decks 7 and 8. <u>Stale air</u>… along with fumes from the Ship's engines, kitchens and incinerators…was expelled through the Ship's massive 'Red Funnel' and 2 white exhaust masts on the upper deck.

The drawn in fresh air was distributed to nine individual air-handling systems located within each of the Ship's nine separate fire zones There it was filtered and cooled or heated as needed…using cold water and hot water piped directly from the giant chillers and the steam generators in the Ship's "Double Bottom".

For the Public Spaces and Event Rooms, the pre-conditioned air was delivered through their large ceiling diffusers, with return ducts in both the deck and the bulkheads. Within each space, the rate of airflow could be adjusted, but not the temperature.

Every passenger stateroom was equipped with its own controls for both temperature and rate of airflow. Return ducts in the bathrooms expelled the stale air.

So, if one wanted to take out the entire Ship with a toxic gas or airborne organism, the obvious way to do it would be to release it through the unguarded air intake ducts on Decks 7 and 8. However, that assumes that it would make it through the filters in the nine separate fire zones. It might take a special toxin or organism to achieve that.

But if you wanted to target just a few passengers, rigging their stateroom vents would be the best way to go.

And for a large target group like attendees of the Greylord Project, you'd place the toxin release mechanisms directly inside the air diffusers in the meeting rooms they'd be using. This would bypass all the filters, which are well upstream from these rooms.

George recorded all these observations in his notebooks.

The 2:30PM Bridge Tour, while interesting, proved not very useful. When asking about the Ship's security systems, the only response George could glean was…"It's extensive. Not to worry!" They wouldn't even comment on where the Security Command Center was located, or if the QM2 even had one. The entire Bridge tour lasted just 20-minutes.

23.

QM2 – Above Decks

DAY 4 --

Pleased with yesterday's progress, George set out right after an early breakfast in the *Kings Court* to more closely explore all the passenger decks of the Ship. But he would also include four events—a Kitchen Tour at 10:15AM and the afternoon High Tea at 3:30PM in the *Queens Room*. Then tonight, he'd attend the 8:30PM show in the *Royal Court Theatre* and the Masquerade Ball at 9:30PM in the *Queens Room*.

The QM2's public areas spanned 13 decks…7 of them largely devoted to passenger staterooms. The less-expensive staterooms were located on Decks 4, 5 and 6. There were no meeting or entertainment venues on any of these three levels, with the exception of a play area and small pool for kids at the aft end of Deck 6. So George could safely bypass them for now.

The QM2's premium staterooms…and most of the luxury suites…were located higher up, on Decks 8-thru-11. Combined, they accounted for about one-third of all the Ship's staterooms. And importantly, with the sole exception of Deck 10, there were a number of special meeting places and entertainment areas at both the bow and stern ends of these levels.

Decks 12 and 13 were mainly open-air decks, though they did have a limited number of high-end staterooms. A major feature of Deck 12 was the *Pavilion Pool & Bar*, with a retractable glass roof that in good weather was opened to Deck 13.

To assess all these areas, George would start at the very top of the Ship…and work his way down. And that meant finding his way up to Deck 13.

The QM2 has four public access elevator banks running from Deck 2 to Deck 11. But only three of them continue on to Deck 12. And only the forward elevator bank continues on to open-air Deck 13. From there, one can climb a metal stairway to *The Lookout* atop the Ship's bridge. Though it provided a commanding view of the QM2's sharp-pointed prow, *The Lookout* proved of only general interest to George.

Back down on Deck 13, George saw that this is where 30 of the Ship's most desirable balcony staterooms were located. Moving aft past them, George entered *The Sun Deck*, which was both very large and totally unoccupied. As were two nearby *Sports Centers*--one for shooting baskets, the other for driving golf balls. And beyond all that was the large sliding glass roof that covered the Ship's swimming pool on the level below. Though the day was sunny, today the roof was closed.

Other than the VIP staterooms, there was not much to interest George on Deck 13. But as he looked up to scan the Ship's top superstructure, the two giant white satellite communication domes caught his eye. Taking them out would certainly add a little spice!

Then it was down to Deck 12. Moving aft, George passed 56 more premium staterooms before coming to the *Pavilion Pool & Bar*. This area was abuzz with activity. But frankly, seeing so many wrinkled old people in their swimsuits was more than a bit off-putting. Quite a contrast from last night's glamorous gowns and tuxedos.

Farther aft was another sun deck. This one being set up for luncheon, served from the adjoining *Boardwalk Café*. And beyond that, to George's somewhat surprise, there was a sizeable kennel. At the moment, he saw only 5 little dogs, none of which looked like bomb sniffers!

Things started to become more interesting on Deck 11. A number of stewards were busy cleaning the 142 staterooms on this level, four of which were *Queen Suites*. Without seeming at all obvious, George could see where all the supplies were stored and where the internal elevators and passageways used by the crew were located.

At the bow end of Deck 11, there was a large *Observation Deck*. And immediately behind it was the *Atlantic Room*—a semi-circular room with spectacular views used for cards and private parties. Almost certainly, the Greylord Project would hold one of their VIP functions here!

At the far aft end of Deck 11 was the open air *Grill Terrace* with its chaise lounges and whirlpool bath. This area was for the exclusive use of passengers occupying the Suites, Penthouses, Duplexes, and Club staterooms. Another target of opportunity?

Deck 10 was almost entirely Luxury Suites...135 in number. These included 2 Penthouses, 4 Suites, and the upper levels of 5 two-story Duplexes. No doubt, this would be preferred lodging for the Greylord Project's most important VIPs.

From his upper deck tour, George could see that all it would require to 'take out' virtually all of the Greylord Project attendees would be a little doctored water, or wine, or snacks, or a bit of powder sprinkled on the towels or bedding of the staterooms on Decks 10 and 11. This was getting exciting!!

On Deck 9 there were four public gathering places worth exploring and seriously considering. At the bow end was the posh *Commodore Club*, an intimate 100-seat cocktail lounge with entertainment at night and light meals during the day. Connecting to it on the port side was *The Boardroom*, a meeting room and venue for small private parties of up to 15 guests. And connecting to it on the starboard side was the *Churchill Cigar Lounge*. Beautifully paneled and with welcoming leather chairs, it was the only place aboard Ship to permit smoking.

And then further along, at midships, was the *Concierge Lounge*, a large private lounge for Grill-level passengers to relax and meet, with full concierge services and refreshments. The Greylord Project crowd would certainly congregate here and in all three of the other Deck 9 gathering places—to exchange ideas and cement personal contacts. In fact, it was the opportunity to informally network with one's peers that was the conference's big attraction, far more important to most attendees than the formal meetings and presentations.

After a break for his 10:15AM Kitchen Tour, followed by an early lunch in the *Kings Court*, George resumed his tour with a quick visit to Deck 8.

Forward toward the bow were the *Ship Library* and the *Ship Book Shop*, both of which George had already spent considerable time in. And on the port side, the upper level of the *Canyon Ranch SpaClub*, with an entrance directly into its *Beauty Salon*.

But aft on Deck 8 was the *Verandah Restaurant*, a specialty 'up-charge' restaurant serving lunch and dinner either inside or al fresco near the open-air *Terrace Pool*. This being a beautiful June day, the *Terrace Pool* and its surrounding area were extremely popular. But come October in mid-Atlantic, George doubted it would still be open. Bathers would most certainly use the *Pavilion Pool* four levels above.

George bypassed Deck 7, because he had completely toured it on his first day aboard. And after a quick look at the *Kid Zone* on Deck 6, he proceeded directly to the major entertainment areas on Deck 3.

Midships on Deck 3 he visited The *Chart Room*...said to be the preferred place for pre-diner cocktails, with its large circular bar, fine furnishings, and etched glass panels featuring stylized nautical charts of the Atlantic crossing. The original Queen Mary had inspired its decor.

Next to the *Chart Room* was the smaller and very elegant *Champagne Bar*, a sophisticated alternative for pre- and post- dinner imbibing.

And across the way was *Sir Samuel's*, a small cocktail and wine bar seating just 66. It also offered specialty coffees and Godiva chocolate treats throughout the day.

All three were interesting, but didn't fit into George's plan.

However, the fourth site on Deck 3 had enormous potential. Tucked away at the far end of the Ship, and entered through the *Queens Room,* was a place mysteriously called *G-32.* After hours, *G-32* was a 2-level 251-seat disco. And during the daytime it was used for private parties. This was just the kind of place the Greylord Project planners would definitely want on their schedule.

Another real find was on Deck 2, a place called *Cunard Connexions.* In addition to a large computer room with dozens of internet-connected workstations available for use by the QM2's passengers, it had 7 meeting rooms that could be sectioned-off as needed to accommodate various size groups. It was almost a certainty that the Greylord Project would use these rooms for their break-out sessions. *Cunard Connexions* was far forward, beneath *Illuminations.*

Midships on Deck 2 were two other places yet to be visited. The *QM2 Casino*, with its banks of slots, gaming tables and dedicated bar. And the *Golden Lion Pub*, which offered lunch, dinner and snacks throughout the day, plus all the traditional pub brews and whiskeys. Musical entertainment was provided nightly.

Though of no 'professional use' to him, George found the *Golden Lion Pub* particularly inviting. Maybe for the next few evenings he'd take a break there. He deserved it!

Completing his Deck Tour, George returned to the *Queens Room* for his 3:30PM 'High Tea'.

It was even more elegant than he expected, as squadrons of waiters sortied into the grand ballroom—first with pots of steaming English tea, next with finger sandwiches, then with scones along with jam and clotted cream. They circled again and again until everyone had their fill. While musicians played light classical music on the bandstand.

Almost every one of the *Queen Room's* 562 seats was taken for this classic but fast-paced tradition. George's bottom-line assessment? A not to be missed experience. But far too difficult to do anything during the 'High Tea'. It's a "No".

Back in his cabin, George began to make notes on what he had learned during his morning Kitchen Tour, which was held in the massive galley directly behind the *Britannia* restaurant. While this was by far the Ship's largest galley, George was surprised to learn that there were also nine other galleys throughout the Ship. Each was fully staffed, had differing menus, and did their own food prep and cooking. However, there were a few items that were centrally prepared, baked goods among them.

Each galley drew its provisions throughout the day from the storerooms on Decks 1, A, and B, where there were 21 refrigerated rooms in addition to bulk storage. Frozen items were pre-thawed below decks as needed, then transferred to refrigerated holding rooms where they stayed until called for by the independent galley kitchens above. Large tubs of ice cream and sorbets, of course, remained frozen until called for.

In all, almost 16,000 meals were served on board each day, including the meals prepared in the Crew Galley for officers, crew and ship staff. In addition, over 9,500 canapés were prepared each day for the Captain's cocktail parties. And each afternoon, 700 scones were baked for the *Queens Room* High Tea.

To prepare all this food, the QM2 had over 160 chefs and a large number of support workers. And the volume of food consumed was staggering. During the Kitchen Tour, George snapped a picture of a placard providing a few statistics.

On a typical 7-day transatlantic crossing, these quantities of food were consumed—

- 58-tons of fresh fruits and vegetables.
- 14-tons of red meat.
- 9-tons of chicken, duck and turkey.
- 15-tons of fish and seafood.
- 2.5-tons of dairy and cheese products.
- 24,000-liters of fresh milk.
- 2.5-tons of sugar.
- 37,000 eggs.
- 5-tons of flour.
- 2.5-tons of rice.
- Plus 120-miles of cling wrap.

Consuming that much food during all those meals required an equally massive cleanup operation. Even with automated equipment, the Ship needed a staff of 85 dishwashers and dozens of laundry workers. Each day of the voyage, they washed over 87,000 pieces of china and glassware. And they washed and ironed over 8,000 linen napkins.

During his Kitchen Tour, George could plainly see that intervention here was almost impossible. A senior chef closely supervised each of the numerous gleaming, stainless steel workstations. And the long stainless steel counters where waiters could pick-up individual course items—like soups, or appetizers, or entrées, or salads, or desserts—were also fully supervised. George had to assume that all the other galleys throughout the Ship were similarly supervised.

There was no possible way for him to put anything into the food in the central galley kitchens. His only option would be dosing the food, or the glasses, inside the restaurants, bars, or party sites. In other words, at the point of actual consumption.

Of course, spiking the booze was still an option, and perhaps probably easier. But drink orders varied widely, so functions pouring pre-set choices of wines, waters and juices rose to the top of George's possibles!

24.

QM2 – Master Plans

DAYS 5 & 6 --

ON DAY 5, George slept in, not setting his alarm until 9:00AM. After last night's *Royal Court* show and the *Queens Room* Masquerade Ball, he had worked until 3:00AM rating each area on the Ship for its vulnerability… and detailing exactly how he could circumvent its security. With his research behind him, he now knew precisely how to accomplish his October mission—'killing' most of the attendees of the Greylord Project conference…in a non-lethal way, without getting caught.

After treating himself to a full English breakfast in the *Britannia*, he returned to his stateroom cabin to finalize his step-by-step plan. In fact, he developed a Plan A, a Plan B, and a Plan C for fail-safe reasons. And then he wrote "The Letter"…the singular document that would set his whole "thriller" into motion. Because first-and-foremost, he wanted his novel to be acclaimed as the world's greatest 'Thriller'.

The hallmark of every good 'thriller' is a frantic attempt by the good guys to stop some catastrophic event from happening. And that means that the good guys have to be forewarned of the impending disaster…and that the clock has to be ticking.

Watching this all happen in the real world was the whole point of this little Queen Mary 2 exercise. And this time, George would be right there watching it all unfolding. Observing their valiant attempts to stop the inevitable.

He'd see how real-world professionals met the challenge—how they organized and operated. The smart things they did and their failures. All the little and big stuff that a fiction writer could only guess at. Nothing made up. Nothing that doesn't really happen.

A conventional 'thriller' almost always has a hero. An often-underappreciated maverick who against all odds stops the clock with just seconds to spare. Or kills the evil mastermind just moments before he can press the destroy-the-world button. George's 'thriller' wouldn't be like that. In George's novel, the bad guy would be the hero. And the excitement would come from how he outwitted even the best and brightest in law enforcement, counter-terrorism, the military, the intelligence community, the administration, and what have you.

And this wouldn't be made-up stuff. It would come from George's own real-world experiences, carefully planned and executed by him personally over these past many months!

Satisfied with his progress, George decided to do several test runs of Plans A, B, and C. Not actually delivering the payload, but running through all the steps required to put it in place. He knew unforeseen complications could always arise, so these run-throughs would help him factor in the unpredictable. Help him keep flexible and avoid over-confidence.

And that's how he spent Days 5 and 6. Along with more time observing other passengers and members of the crew. He'd try imitating the carefree attitude and walk of vacationers. The reserved manner of the more experienced travelers. The deferential courtesy of the waiters and stewards. The friendly authority of the QM2 senior officers. Because on his October cruise he in no way wanted to stand out!

He did all that during these final two days, along with some enjoyable evenings in the *Golden Lion Pub*.

25.

QM2 – Homeward Bound

DAY 7--

DISEMBARKATION IN SOUTHAMPTON. No problem with Passport Control.
Two nights in London at the *Tower Hotel.*
A non-stop flight to Newark Airport. No problem with Passport Control.
Uber to the New Jersey Park-and-Ride.
Pick up the car and drive home.

Now it was getting ready for the real thing in October!

THREE MONTHS LATER

Terror on The Queen

26.

Sir Cecil

SUNDAY, OCTOBER 8 --

AT JUST AFTER 3:00PM, Sir Cecil Jenkins-Doyle boarded the Queen Mary 2 at her berth in Brooklyn for her 7-day crossing to Southampton. Once there he would be met by his driver for the 2-hour journey along the M3 and M25 to his townhouse on St. James Place in London.

Sir Cecil Jenkins-Doyle was the retired Head of New Scotland Yard. He had flown into JFK ten days earlier to participate in the 'Joint International Terrorism Task Force'. He was one of the 16 people worldwide considered to be a true expert in this field, and was the official UK delegate.

Knowing that he'd be in New York just prior to the October 8th sailing, Sir Cecil accepted the Cunard invitation to be their featured guest speaker on this particular QM2 transatlantic crossing. He had sailed on the QM2 and the other Queens several times over the past 20 years, and always found them most enjoyable. Of course then he was traveling with his wife, Lady Anne, but now as a widower he would be traveling alone. Doing this series of 3 lectures would keep him happily involved, erasing any sense of loneliness or boredom.

As he entered the Grand Lobby of the Queen Mary 2, Sir Cecil drew curious glances from a number of the other passengers. Immaculately dressed in a bespoke dark-grey pinstriped suite, with a starched white collar, french cuffs, and crimson red tie, he stood in stark contrast to the very casually dressed fellow passengers boarding the Ship.

Yet his attire seemed somehow right for a man with so otherwise distinguished an appearance. In fact, if he were casually dressed, something would seem a bit off.

One could only guess at his age. While he had a full head of snowy-white hair, his skin was free of wrinkles, and he had the bearing of a man still in his prime. At slightly over 6-foot and about 160-pounds in weight, he seemed extremely fit. By conventional standards, he was not a handsome man, but then again not unattractive. His most striking feature was the brilliant color of his eyes, an intense blue almost as deep as lapis lazuli.

From his courteous manner and genial smile, one could sense that he was a man of some breeding and accomplishment. That he was carrying a well-worn Peal & Company leather attaché case cemented that impression for those who know of such things.

Sir Cecil was one of those rare individuals in public life whom everyone seemed to like. He was a genuinely nice person, without artifice or guile. To dine with him was always a delight, an evening filled with self-deprecating good humor and lively insightful discussion.

What made this particularly remarkable with Sir Cecil was that along with his good fellowship was an astonishingly brilliant mind. He possessed almost total recall and could analyze a complex issue with laser-like precision. Most people are linear thinkers, moving step-by-step from point A to point B to point C to reach a final conclusion. Sir Cecil had the uncanny ability to see the ultimate answer before others had even begun. Little wonder that he had graduated from St. John's at Oxford University with top honors while just barely 18. And that soon after he embarked on a brilliant career holding various posts in the British Home Office. That led to his appointment as Director of the CID, and then Head of New Scotland Yard twelve years ago.

As Sir Cecil glanced around the Grand Lobby, he too drew some conclusions. Most of his fellow travelers were holiday seekers, almost all of them clearly British. They were no doubt on the return leg of a 30-day QM2 vacation holiday that had originated in Southampton…made the crossing to New York, sailed on to New England and Canada, then back to New York before heading home to England this evening.

But many others seemed to be boarding for the first time…just for the New York-to-Southampton 7-day crossing. And most of these newly arriving travelers were lining up at the welcoming desk of the Greylord Project.

Sir Cecil was familiar with the Greylord Project, though he had never attended one of their annual conferences. It was an invitation-only gathering of so-called "world opinion leaders", coming together to address and find solutions to the world's most vexing problems. Sort of a low-budget Davos. But it did attract a VIP attendance, usually from the financial and business community, with a few government leaders often in attendance. But unlike some other think-tank conferences, the Greylord Project almost never brought in guest speakers. Its staff presented a well-defined critique of a world problem, and the attendees worked collaboratively in teams to pose solutions.

Out of curiosity, Sir Cecil went up to the Greylord Project welcoming desk, where attendees were being registered and given information kits. Acknowledging that he was not an attendee, but that he was a QM2 guest speaker for the overall voyage, he asked if he might have a copy of their agenda. They graciously gave him one and told him that their first function would not begin until tomorrow morning. And that today was free time.

When he asked who would be attending this year, they apologized and explained that the attendee list was always kept confidential. He thanked them and then went along to his stateroom--#8032 on Deck 8.

Cunard was particularly excited to have Sir Cecil as their featured guest speaker for this QM2 October 8th crossing, and they had promoted his planned appearance heavily. He'd be delivering a series of three lectures entitled—"Scotland Yard in Fact & Fiction". And in all the announcements they billed him as "The Retired Head of New Scotland Yard".

Of course that was incorrect. Scotland Yard and New Scotland Yard don't really exist as organizations. They're simply the names of the buildings in London where the Metropolitan Police Service (or MPS) and its famous Criminal Investigation Department (or CID) were once located. These are the organizations that Sir Cecil had headed before retirement a little over a year ago.

Most Americans assume that Scotland Yard is the British equivalent of the FBI. But for most criminal matters, its staff of over 30,000 focuses almost exclusively on law enforcement in the Greater London Area. The important exceptions are terrorism, where it is the UK's lead agency, and its nationwide role in guarding Royals, statesmen and visiting dignitaries. Here it acts much like the US Secret Service. In addition, New Scotland Yard maintains extensive files on all known criminals in the UK, and is responsible for links between UK law enforcement and Interpol. It is the clearinghouse for fingerprints, DNA and other forms of identification in the UK.

When called upon, Scotland Yard also assists the two major British Intelligence Agencies—'MI5' responsible for domestic counterintelligence and security, and 'MI6' responsible for covert overseas intelligence operations in support of UK's national security.

And at the highest levels, Scotland Yard enjoys informal relationships with its American and EU law enforcement counterparts. Sir Cecil's recent participation in the New York meeting of the 'Joint International Terrorism Task Force' is just the latest example.

When Sir Cecil entered his stateroom, he saw that his luggage had already been delivered and that an envelope was sitting atop the bed, along with a folder of informative materials on the Ship and its scheduled events for today and tomorrow. Setting his jacket aside, he sat on the room's small sofa to open the envelope and read its letter inside.

It was a welcoming message from the QM2's Events & Facilities Director, Marcus O'Toole, saying how thrilled and honored they all were to have Sir Cecil Jenkins-Doyle as their featured guest lecturer for the crossing. And it contained an invitation to join O'Toole for dinner at 7:00PM in the *Verandah Restaurant* on Deck 8, where they could confirm all the details of Sir Cecil's three lectures during the week.

"*How nice*", thought Sir Cecil. Nailing things down today was exactly as he hoped.

On the sofa table was a chilled bottle of sparkling wine and a basket of fruit, along with a handwritten note from Captain Jeremy Cornwall. In his note, the Captain welcomed him aboard and said he was looking forward to visiting with him in the days ahead. It explained that joining him tonight for dinner would be sadly impossible, because he'd be on duty at the helm...sailing this proud Queen out through New York Harbor and under the Verrazano Bridge to then enter what some Yanks liked to call "The Pond".

Sir Cecil smiled at the Captain's droll humor. It would be a pleasure to meet him.

After unpacking, Sir Cecil still had a few hours before dinner, time he used to write a summary report of his New York Joint Task Force meetings and his suggestions for follow-up actions and future meetings. Then he freshened up and dressed for his 7:00PM dinner with Director Marcus O'Toole.

The *Verandah Restaurant* was at the stern end of the Ship, on the same Deck level as Sir Cecil's stateroom. As he entered the restaurant, a young well-groomed Ship's officer wearing a crisp white uniform and a broad warm smile came forward to greet him--

"Sir Jenkins-Doyle?
"I'm Marcus O'Toole. And indeed Sir, it is a great honor to meet you. All of us are so eagerly awaiting your lectures. And if I may add a personal note, as a boy I always fancied myself as one day becoming a super sleuth in Scotland Yard. I was always Inspector

O'Toole to the other kids' kidnappers and robbers. But alas, fighting crime was not to be my career destiny. Oh well!

"Our table Sir is right over here, where we can chat without being rushed or disturbed."

"Thank you, Mr. O'Toole. May I call you Marcus? And please do call me Cecil."

After looking over the menu and the wine list, placing their orders and exchanging some pleasantries, Sir Cecil asked about the times and locations for his lectures. Marcus replied--

"All your lectures will be in the *Royal Court Theatre*. The first is at 2:00PM tomorrow, our first full day at sea. Then we skip a day. And on Wednesday and Thursday you're scheduled for 11:00AM. I'm sure we'll have a very large audience for all three lectures.

"Typically, our featured guest speaker lectures run about 45-minutes, with an extra 15-minutes for Q&A. But you can extend that time as you see fit, because the *Royal Court Theatre* is free for a full hour more.

"I understand that you have visuals and film clips to project. We can do a technical run-through tomorrow morning, if you'd like, Sir Cecil. Even though our AV team is Grade A, a run through is always a good idea, especially if you wish to control your own projections."

"Yes, I would like a technical run-through, so that I can get comfortable with the room and sound system, as well as the projector controls. Would 8:00AM tomorrow morning be possible?"

"Absolutely, Sir Cecil. I'll have everything set up for you then and meet you in the Royal Court Theatre at 8:00AM.

"Now I know your 3-part lecture is titled 'Scotland Yard in Fact & Fiction'. If I may ask, can you give me a little preview of what each of the three sections covers?"

"In Part I, tomorrow, I'll describe what really happens inside the Yard. How, from its humble beginnings with very little authority back in 1829, four major cases led to its transformation into today's legendary law enforcement agency, with over 30,000 people working to solve more than 1,000,000 crimes a year.

"In Part II, on Wednesday, I'll delve into some of our most famous cases and how we solved them. From the 'Railway Murder Case' in 1864, which shocked the nation because it was the first time someone had ever been murdered on a train. To the 'Stratton Brothers Killings' in 1905, the first use of fingerprints to get a murder conviction. To the Inspector Fabian 'Cat Burglar Case' in 1920, a model for deductive sleuthing. To the 1963 'Great Train Robbery', where forensic science came into its own. To the 'Millennium Diamond Heist' in 2000, bringing high-tech to crime fighting. Plus two cases we never solved—'Jack the Ripper' in 1888—and also around the same time, the so-called 'Napoleon of Crime', a 5-foot tall American named Adam Worth who was the inspiration for Sherlock Holmes' nemesis Professor Moriarty.

"In Part III, I'll show and comment upon the portrayal of 'Scotland Yard Detectives in Fiction'—in print, but mainly in film and on TV. There are literally hundreds of instances. But I'll show clips of some of the most popular. Starting with the somewhat dim Inspector Lestrade, of Sherlock Holmes fame. P.D. James' coolly aloof Inspector Adam Dagliesh. Charles Dickens' shrewd but colourless Inspector Bucket from Bleak House. The always-charming Inspector Lynley in the Elizabeth George thrillers. And from several long-running TV series—Inspectors John Morely, Michael Jericho, Roderick Alleyn, George Gently, Allan Grant, Sir James Blake, and many more—each with their own special quirks and peculiarities. What an odd lot we seem to be!

"I'm always intrigued by the audience reaction when they see one of their favorite fictional Scotland Yard Detectives. The applause, or laughter, or nods of recognition. It tells me a lot about the age and temperament of the audience. Kind of a Rorschach Test, if you will!"

"Sounds like a wonderful series. People will love it. Personally, I can't wait"

After a cognac and a hearty good night, Sir Cecil Jenkins-Doyle went to his stateroom, with absolutely no inkling of the challenge tomorrow would bring.

27.

The Threat

MONDAY, OCTOBER 9 --

-- 3:30 PM --

IT WAS JUST after 3:30PM when Sir Cecil Jenkins-Doyle returned to his stateroom after his very well received first lecture. He was quite pleased with the size and engagement of the audience and the quality of the informed questions that were asked.

As he went to unlock his door, he noticed a thin white envelope in the information rack to the right of the entry. Perhaps a question or comment about his lecture? Or possibly an invitation of some sort?

Entering his room, Sir Cecil dropped his briefcase on the bed. But then hesitated and thought: *'I should probably check to see if any new messages have come in.'* He removed his laptop from the briefcase and went straight to the desk to boot it up. And while waiting, decided to see what this letter was all about.

As he unfolded and read the single sheet inside, a chill raced through him. Only one word could describe the letter—"Alarming".

CUNARD

Dear Sir Cecil,

On the fifth day of this crossing, more than 300 passengers will meet their maker. They'll be leaving the Ship in body bags in Southampton. That is, unless you're clever enough to thwart my already in-place plans for their demise.

It's only fair that I give them a champion and protector. And who better than you, Sir Cecil—the former Head of New Scotland Yard- -to come to their rescue?

You have three days to counter my plans and block my efforts. And as a gentleman, I assure you that if you succeed, absolutely no harm will come to a single passenger.

Are you up for the challenge? Their fate is now solely in your hands!

Sincerely yours,
Michael A.

PS- If the Ship alters its routing and attempts to return to New York I will accelerate my timetable to one day—and make a general announcement to create panic among the passengers and crew.

Sir Cecil read and reread the letter three times. And a series of quick conclusions raced through his mind. These were the professional reactions of a person who had spent his long career in solving crimes.

- The writer of this letter is an American in his 60s. The American spelling of 'routeing' and the bold script penmanship are clear indicators.

- It's no doubt a bluff. He's toying with us, or maybe me, and has no intention of actually following through. This type of advanced warning is atypical of any terrorist, or extortionist, or revenge-seeker we've ever seen. Secrecy and surprise is essential to their success. It's actually a parody of a "stop-me-if-you-can" letter written by a serial killer. But we've never seen a serial killer threaten mass murder. Their pleasure or compulsion comes from individual one-by-one slayings. A series, if you will. That's what defines a serial killer!

All this led Sir Cecil to these conflicting thoughts:
"While my initial assessment is to ignore this letter as some twisted-mind prank and just toss it away, I know I can't really do that. There's far too much at stake here!

"He may have anticipated and factored in my reactions to his letter. Intentionally used the American spelling, knowing that it would stand out to my eye. Penned the letter in bold longhand script to seem older and male. Why else not type it on a hard-to-trace keyboard before coming aboard ship? And he may have mimicked the style of a serial killer letter to get me to conclude that it's all just a hoax.

"But then why? To get me to ignore the warning or take halfway measures, so that when he actually strikes in even a far scaled back way, Cunard, Scotland Yard and I would be charged with and guilty

of negligence. That's a real possibility. Some sort of payback for a wrong the writer perceives to have happened.

"But there's another possibility. That the letter is intended to make me conclude that we could have a truly dangerous psychopath aboard. A person who threatens to kill 300 human beings without reason or remorse, as part of some sick game designed to show his intellectual superiority. Under this scenario, I'd be forced to initiate a panic-causing top-to-bottom search effort on the Ship—unleashing the uncontrollable fears and unpredictable actions of over 3,000 passengers and crewmembers who would rightly feel trapped aboard a death ship.

"There may even be a third possibility, not yet apparent to me!"

Without further hesitation, Sir Cecil picked up his room phone and asked to speak directly with the Captain. When connected, he stated the issue in the most explicit terms—

"Captain Cornwall, I've just received a letter from someone who threatens to kill 300 passengers before we reach Southampton. It could be a hoax, the work of a madman, or perhaps an extortionist. But we must take this threat seriously. Can we meet as soon as possible?"

After a three second pause while he took it all in, Captain Cornwall said: "Sir Cecil, come to my quarters just aft of the Bridge on Deck 12. I'll ask my Head of Security, First Officer Jonathan Blakely, to join us."

-- 5:00 PM –

The three had met for nearly an hour before scoping out a broad stroke strategy to achieve these dual objectives—

1. Foil any and every attempt to harm even a single passenger or crewmember throughout the voyage.
2. Achieve this in a way that does not cause disruption or panic among the passengers and crewmembers.

As part of their discussions, Sir Cecil had asked the Captain and First Officer if they had ever seen this type of threat before? The Captain answered--

"Nowhere on this scale. On one of our sister ships, a few years ago, an individual asked for £100,000 or he would set off a bomb. He was apprehended when he tried to collect the payoff. There was no bomb, incidentally.

"Another time, we had a killing aboard. Even before docking we had a confession from the murderer. The motive here was a mix of revenge and future inheritance. But we had received no advance warning like here."

Sir Cecil asked another question, this one to First Officer Blakely--

"What procedures do you have in place to deal with a threat like this one? How would you normally handle it?"

"We have well rehearsed procedures to deal with a full range of crimes and threats aboard, but frankly, none anywhere near this scale. This goes far beyond anything we've seen before or are prepared to counter.

"With 3,000 people aboard, we're like a small city at sea. And just as any city has its occasional law-enforcement problems, so do we. But considering that our passengers are typically older and in a holiday mood, and that our crew has been fully vetted and under long-term contracts, our crime rate is extraordinarily low. Altercations, attempted suicides, crimes of passion, theft…these are the issues we sometimes encounter. So to be frank, we're flying a bit blind to deal with an issue like this!"

At this point, Captain Cornwall asked Sir Cecil and First Officer Blakely to work together to structure a plan of action. He said he'd return at 6:30PM after his mandatory appearance as host of the Welcoming Cocktail Reception for the Greylord Project in the *Queens Room.*

He asked Blakely to have some food and a large urn of coffee sent up, so that they could work for as long as it took this evening and into the night

-- 5:30 PM --

While dressing for the reception, Captain Cornwall made a series of decisions, all of which he would have to clear with his boss in London, Sir Oliver Walters, the CEO of Cunard Lines.

- First, he planned to put Sir Cecil Jenkins-Doyle in full charge of the entire effort.

- Second, he planned to call in extra resources from the U.S., probably the FBI. The QM2 was too far from the UK to make calling in a British team possible.

- Third, he planned to sever passenger and crew communications with the mainland in order to head-off panic incited by wild rumors and speculation in the press and on social media.

Captain Cornwall didn't come to these decisions rashly. A man of studied discipline and logic, he was trained to weigh the implications of every choice before him. As such, he looked beyond the immediate threat posed by the letter to the possible ultimate outcomes under a range of scenarios.

As Ship Master, he was without question the person in singular control of everything aboard ship, both at sea and when in port. But it was not that simple. When a criminal act occurs aboard ship, almost always government authorities will swoop in just as soon as the ship makes land, to take charge of both the investigation and any prosecutions that follow. That's why getting ahead of the game with the authorities was absolutely critical!

In five days, the Queen Mary 2 will dock in Southampton. And even if the letter was just a hoax, a number of crimes under British law would still have been committed. Which means, the authorities will be waiting. Hopefully by then the threat will be over, with the perpetrator in custody. But even then, there is a strong possibility that the authorities will order the passengers and crew kept aboard, and that the QM2 would be forced to cancel its planned same-day departure to Hamburg. Thousands of travel plans would be disrupted. Angry passengers would demand compensation, some threatening lawsuits. Press coverage would be disastrous, not only tarnishing Cunard's reputation but also scaring away future travelers, perhaps for years. And untold millions would be lost.

The matter would be made even more complex, because multiple countries could rightly claim jurisdiction. Under both international and UK law, Great Britain should have primary jurisdiction and prosecutorial authority. But for an incident like this one, it was almost a certainty that the United States would also claim jurisdiction.

Captain Cornwall was well versed in maritime law, including UNCLOS (the 'United Nations Convention on the Law of the Sea'), MSA (the UK 'Merchant Shipping Act'), and the CVSSA (the U.S. 'Cruise Vessel Security and Safety Act').

> UNCLOS clearly states that when a crime has been committed aboard ship on the high seas, "the flag state has exclusive jurisdiction". Since the QM2 is registered in the British territory of Bermuda, that means the UK has exclusive jurisdiction. But... UNCLOS does provide a few potential exceptions, including: the ship's previous and next ports, and the citizenship of the accused and the victim. That opens the door to U.S. jurisdiction.
>
> MSA clearly states that the United Kingdom has jurisdiction for "Criminal acts committed on British Ships on the 'high seas'"
>
> CVSSA clearly states that the United States has jurisdiction... "Over any foreign vessel during a voyage having a scheduled departure from or arrival in the U.S., with respect to an offense committed by or against a national of the U.S." Further, it should be noted that the U.S. has refused to sign the United Nations UNCLOS agreement, arguing that it favored the economic systems of communist states.

Taking all this into account, Captain Cornwall concluded that both the UK and the U.S. would want...and ultimately get...jurisdiction.

And that as such, it was important that the authorities in both countries be fully briefed, consulted, and involved immediately. Not only did both countries have critical resources that the QM2 needed to avert the threat and identify the perpetrator, but also getting them to work together as a team from the beginning would lessen the chance that the QM2 would be held up in port.

Captain Cornwall knew there was only one person aboard with the experience and contacts to accomplish this feat, and that was Sir Cecil Jenkins-Doyle. Which is why he decided to officially appoint him as his 'Deputy in Charge of the Investigation'. Under this arrangement, the QM2's Head of Security and all the other Ship Officers directly involved in stopping the threat would report directly to Sir Cecil.

Not only was Sir Cecil Jenkins-Doyle eminently qualified due to his vast experience and professional accomplishments as head of New Scotland Yard, but he had long and well-established personal relationships with the Prime Minister, the heads of MI5 and MI6, as well as the Director of Great Britain's 'National Counter-Terrorism Security Office'. And he could tap into the full resources of New Scotland Yard, with its extensive files on all known criminals in the UK. He was also well known to his law-enforcement colleagues in the U.S. He was on a first-name basis with the Directors of the FBI, the Secret Service, and the CIA. And he had just met the Directors of the Federal, State and Metropolitan anti-terrorism task forces in New York City. All these he could muster while still at sea via satellite phone and secure internet connections!

Captain Cornwall concluded that putting Sir Cecil Jenkins-Doyle in charge of the investigation was not only the surest way to disarm the threat and identify the culprit, but also the surest way to reduce the likelihood that the authorities would order the QM2 kept in port with all its passengers aboard.

-- 6:30 PM --

When Captain Cornwall rejoined Sir Cecil and First Officer Blakely in his quarters, he informed them that he had spoken to the Cunard CEO, Sir Oliver Walters in London. And he informed them of their joint decision— That Sir Cecil should be appointed as the Captain's 'Deputy in Charge of the Investigation' with complete authority over all QM2 resources. And that if Sir Cecil deemed it necessary, he had full authority to bring in additional U.S. and UK resources. And that until they reached Southampton, the Ship's Wi-Fi connection to the internet would be "under maintenance" and be unavailable to passengers and crewmembers. The Ship's secure satellite phone and direct internet connections would remain operative for authorized personnel only. Sir Oliver was particularly concerned about leaks from the Ship that would result in a worldwide speculative media frenzy, which when seen in turn by the passengers would create and accelerate panic among them.

With that, Captain Cornwall asked Sir Cecil if he would accept. And he did.

The Captain then asked: "So what's our plan?"

-- 8:00 PM --

With the Captain and First Officer Blakely in full agreement, Sir Cecil's detailed plan was ready to implement. A team of Ship Officers had been selected to execute parts of the plan. Scotland Yard and the FBI would be asked for support. MI5 and MI6 would be briefed. And Sir Cecil would record a special message for the passengers and crew tonight, for broadcast throughout the Ship in the morning. This broadcast would be the first step in an ongoing 'information campaign' to head-off any concerns among the passengers and crew.

Sir Cecil had explained the logic behind the "information campaign"—

"The steps we'll necessarily be taking to prevent any harm to people or property during this voyage will be highly visible to both passengers and crew. They're smart and observant and will start questioning what's going on. Rumors will spread and concerns will grow. And before long we'll have a hard-to-control panic that will actually aid our culprit in carrying out his threats.

"So at the outset, we must give everyone a credible alternate scenario; one that they can not only believe and understand, but one that makes it seem like an entertaining adventure that they are all involved in. I'll lead it off in a broadcast address, follow it up at each of my lectures, publish updates in our daily Ship's Bulletin, and all three of us will exude confidence and good cheer as we walk around the Ship and participate in our regularly-scheduled events.

"And absolutely critical to all this is that only the three of us in this room are to see and know about this letter and its threats. Even the Ship Officers that we bring onto our team should be given the alternate scenario. In this, we must absolutely agree! Inadvertent leaks will otherwise occur!"

He then gave them a copy of the script he had written for his broadcast announcement—and read it to them in his best Oxford-honed voice—

-- An Important Announcement --

"Good day to you all—

"Those of you who have attended my lecture know that I am Cecil Jenkins-Doyle, the former head of New Scotland Yard. It's my great pleasure to be with you here on the magnificent Queen Mary 2 for our transatlantic crossing.

"I'm here speaking to you today for a very special reason. It's because I have something quite important to confess. My being on the Ship as your guest lecturer is really something of a subterfuge. I'm actually here to supervise a 'classified mission'…a mission that I can only reveal to you now, while we're all far out to sea.

"This voyage of the QM2 has been specifically chosen to test-out one aspect of the Cruise Industry's anti-terrorism effectiveness. While this Ship, and all other major passenger ships, are now well-prepared and well-trained to thwart all known terrorist threats on board, only one seemingly unlikely threat remains. That threat is the hijacking of an entire cruise ship at sea!

"While some small cargo ships and large tankers have been hijacked along the coastline in the Middle East, there's never been an attempt to hijack a giant passenger ship on the high seas. But because it's never happened doesn't mean we should not be prepared. That's the conclusion of our 'Joint International Terrorism Task Force'. And it's why this, the most important passenger ship in the World...The Queen Mary 2…has been selected as the site for our latest test.

" To be specific, the planners of this test have placed a well-trained group of would-be hijackers aboard our Ship. They're on loan from various security agencies and are a wilily lot indeed. And a crack team of FBI agents has been flown in to supplement the QM2's own security force. If you observe one or more individuals being arrested or detained during the days ahead, do not be alarmed. That means the "good guys" are winning and doing their job.

"We're also temporarily taking the Ship's Wi-Fi system offline, to prevent the would-be hijackers from communicating with each other, or with any boarding vessels that may be part of their plot. And you'll see other security measures being taken throughout the voyage.

"If you notice anything you deem suspicious, please call our 'hot line' on your room phone. As you'll see on the screen below, our 'hot line' number is…5173. But please, no crank calls! This is serious business and we want this security exercise to be very seriously taken.

"Now, as you'd expect, if we had any inkling of a real threat, you would normally not have been informed. But at the 'Joint Task Force' meeting that I just left in New York, the consensus decision was that you should be briefed, just as I have done today.

"If the threat was real, canceling events, or putting you through lockdowns, or implementing other severe security measures would be more than justified. And more than likely, we'd now be steaming back to New York. But those kinds of disruptions during your cruise for a simulated hijacking attempt could not be justified. That was our consensus decision. The drill will be run around you. And hopefully not infringe on your relaxation and enjoyment!

"So now you know why I'm really here…and know what will really happen in the days ahead.

"And now...as that old friend of Scotland Yard always liked to say—

"The game's afoot!!"

Captain Cornwall shook his head in amazement at Sir Cecil's script.

"If I didn't know better, I'd totally believe you. Are you sure you're with Scotland Yard and not MI6?"

And First Officer Blakely added--

"I can see now that we couldn't contain things if we tried to do a proper search of the Ship in secret. Rumors and misinformation would go viral. And while it concerns me that we have to keep our fellow Ship Officers in the dark, I have to agree that if we didn't it's more than likely that something would leak out."

28.

War Room

TUESDAY, OCTOBER 10 –

-- 7:00 AM --

Alerted to a special meeting by the Captain, five senior Ship Officers reported to Queens Suite #8130, aft on Deck 8. To their surprise, it had been converted into a conference room, with a large table and 10 chairs replacing the bed. Three desktop computers were on folding tables along one bulkhead. And a large coffee urn and tray of breakfast rolls stood on the credenza. Obviously, something important was going on.

Awaiting them in the suite was Captain Jeremy Cornwall and Head of Security, First Officer Jonathan Blakely, along with Sir Cecil Jenkins-Doyle. The Captain introduced everyone to Sir Jenkins-Doyle, telling them that Sir Cecil would be conducting this briefing and would be in direct charge of all the actions to follow.

Sir Cecil began by showing them the video he had recorded last night, telling them that it would be shown throughout the Ship on every channel of every stateroom TV. He then elaborated on the reasons the Joint Task Force had selected the QM2, and the thinking behind the decision to inform the passengers and crew that a simulated attempt to hijack the Ship would occur—a full scale hijacking attempt designed to measure the ability of the response team to firmly nip the plot in the bud.

He then went on to say that everyone in this room would play a key role in this effort. And he then detailed how—

"Priority number one is identifying the 'hijackers' and taking them into custody before they can execute their plan. We haven't been told who they are, or how many they are. That's for us to discover. And with over 3,000 people aboard, this could be quite a challenge. But we can hopefully narrow it down by analyzing the data we have on file for every passenger and crewmember on board. And we can run that against the files of both Scotland Yard and the FBI to identify anyone with a criminal past or on a terrorist watch list. It's more than likely that one or more of our undercover hijackers are traveling under the names of someone on these lists to test our ability to ferret them out by data analysis.

"First Officer Van Zillen, you'll be in charge of this effort. May I call you Donald? As the Ship's 'Passenger & Crew Administrator', I'd like you to put together and analyze a database of everyone onboard. Can you get back to me with your findings by 2:30PM today?"

"Yes Sir. You can count on it!"

"Simultaneous with our efforts to identify the hijackers, we need to immediately put in place a stem-to-stern upgrade of our security systems. There are at least three ways that the hijackers might try to take over the Ship. First, is a frontal attack on the Bridge and the Engine Control Room below decks. Second, is taking passengers hostage in one or more of our large public areas. And third, is by immobilizing almost everyone on board by injecting some substance into our water or air-handling systems, or into our food supply.

"Our Head of Security, First Officer Jonathan Blakely, will have armed personnel posted 24-7 outside both the Bridge and the Engine Control Room. He'll also have the Ship's metal detectors moved from the boarding areas to the entrances of the *Britannia Restaurant* and the entrances of all our large meeting rooms—the *Royal Court Theatre*, *Illuminations*, and the *Queens Room*. And he'll double the number of personnel monitoring the Ship's hundreds of security cameras, to watch for any and all suspicious people or actions. He'll also post guards at the entrances to our below-deck levels, to make certain that only authorized personnel are allowed to enter. Jonathan will also be working with me, and with the FBI team that we're bringing in to support our efforts. I'll tell you more about the FBI team in a few minutes.

"Chief Engineer Conrad Schmidt, we're counting on you to do whatever it takes to make absolutely certain that no one can tamper with the Ship's water or air-handling systems. And that no one can sabotage the Ship's power, navigation or communication systems. Please report back here by 11:00AM this morning to let us know the details of your plan.

"Senior Hotel Manager Perry York...In your role as the Ship's 'Food & Beverage & Staterooms Director', you'll know best where our potential vulnerabilities lay in all three areas. Think like a terrorist or hijacker, and put-in-place a plan to absolutely block any nefarious actions. Later today, please brief us on your actions.

"And Marcus O'Toole...As our 'Chief Entertainment Director' you're in charge of all the QM2's entertainment events and the venues where they take place. Please begin immediately to have all these areas swept for bombs, gas canisters, or stashed weapons. And have these procedures repeated more than once daily. Our FBI partners are bringing in 2 bomb-sniffing dogs that will help you clear all of our venues both before and after each planned session. In between, they'll cover the Grand Lobby and Grand Passageways.

"And perhaps most important of all--our need to launch a comprehensive communications program designed to maintain absolute calm among the passengers and crew. Ivy Witcomb, our Chief Purser, will head up this program. This effort is absolutely critical because the hijackers will exploit to the fullest any unrest or panic among the passengers or crew. And here, I think we need to be very proactive. Perhaps adding another few lectures on how Scotland Yard has foiled would-be hijackers in the past...by combining intelligence and surveillance with science...to nip threats in the bud. And how the FBI has perfected 'profiling' techniques to zero in on prime suspects. In the Ship's daily newsletter, perhaps an article on how drug-sniffing and bomb-sniffing dogs are trained...the best breeds, etc. And perhaps on the Ship's TV and on the *Illuminations* big screen, a range of spy movies...particularly those with a lighter or comedic twist.

"Ivy, go all out to make the passengers and crew feel like they're on a grand adventure. Something to tell their kids and friends about when they return home. Something to actually enjoy. Something that makes the voyage extra special, not scary! You'll also have to find a way to soothe all those with complaints and demands about disrupted Wi-Fi and internet service. I know it's a tall order, but can you get back to me with your plan by 1:00PM today?

"Now, what about the FBI? Within the hour, a vertical takeoff Boeing V-22 Osprey will land on our Sun Deck with 6 Special Agents and 2 K9 dogs and their handlers. They'll help us identify and interview suspects, guard key locations, disarm the hijackers, and disable their devices if it comes to that. They too will be graded on their effectiveness, so we can expect them to be super aggressive.

"And speaking of being 'graded', this entire team will be graded on our professionalism and effectiveness. In that regard, 'this is definitely not a drill'. How well or poorly we do will be permanently noted in our career files. Need I say more?

"So, that's it for now. Those of you I've asked to report back to us with your plan know what's required. And as a full group, we'll reconvene right here at 7:00AM each morning. We've set up a series of secure internal phone lines so that you can communicate individually or together as a group. Here's a sheet with those numbers.

"I'm sure that none of you expected this crossing would be quite as exciting and challenging. But I'm supremely confident that we'll show the planners of this little exercise that we're at the top of our game and ready to defeat any devious plot they've concocted to deceive us.

"Let's get at it!

"And oh, one last thing. Along with placing the hijackers aboard, the planners have also inserted a few Director-level officials to observe our response to the threat. They'll be recording the things we do right, and the things that we miss, so that training for future threats can be perfected."

-- 7:45 AM --

After a few questions, five of the Ship Officers left the meeting… with only Captain Cornwall, Head of Security Blakely, and Sir Cecil remaining. Sir Cecil restarted the session by reporting—

"Last night I spoke with FBI Director Jack Kilpatrick, after getting agreement from New Scotland Yard Director Sir Kim

Farley-Thomas. And also agreements from the heads of MI5 and MI6, Sir Kevin Chatsworth and Sir Thaddeus Long. I read all of them into the threat we received, and detailed our plans to counter it—including our 'false flag' scenario to keep the passengers and crew in the dark regarding our true threat. They're in total agreement with our strategy on that! And all agreed that considering our current location at sea, we should bring in help from our American cousins at the FBI. That help will be here within the hour!

"This morning I told everyone that we're flying in 6 FBI Special Agents, plus two dog handlers with their K9s. That's true. But there will also be 5 additional undercover FBI Agents who'll be playing the role of our hijackers. One will be a waiter, the other four will be passengers. During the week, they'll move around the Ship and at times appear suspiciously nervous or overly curious. And for show, one or more of them will be confronted and taken into custody, after an attempt to break free.

"But of course, all the FBI Agents and their dogs are really here to help us find and stop just one person…our letter-writing friend who calls himself 'Michael A'. So the FBI team knows our true challenge!

"At the Yard, we usually assign a working code name to an unidentified perpetrator to make communications clearer and more precise. So let's start calling our guy 'The Author'. And we'll call our undercover hijackers from the FBI—'The Five Amigos'. And we'll call our fictional hijackers that we're presumably searching for 'The Bad Guys'. That way, we'll have no confusion as to which group we're talking about.

"Jonathan, any progress yet on your end?"

"Yes, Sir Cecil. Let me bring you up to date. Last night I reviewed the security camera footage from the passageway outside your stateroom to see who put the letter in your message holder. It was your regularly assigned cabin steward. He had a number of envelopes to deliver in his section and nothing seemed out of the ordinary in his delivery. Nothing to suggest he considered this letter anything but routine. I then traced the letter back to its source, which proved to be the mail basket on the Pursers Desk in the Grand Lobby. At 11:47AM, a staffer from the Greylord Project added a large stack of envelopes to that basket for delivery to their meeting attendees. Over the next half hour, eight other passengers added envelopes to the basket. Only one of all the letters was similar in size to the one ultimately delivered to you. And our security camera footage confirmed that this was indeed the letter sorted out for delivery on Deck 8.

"Unfortunately, we were unable to identify the male passenger who dropped off your letter at the Pursers Desk, because he worked very effectively to conceal his face. He wore dark glasses, had on a black cap, and wore a black windbreaker with the collar up. And when facing the security camera, he held a white handkerchief up to his nose and mouth, as if trying to stifle a sneeze. He appeared to be of average height and weight, and had no distinctive gait. He appeared to be right handed and wore no distinctive watch or rings. He entered the Grand Lobby from the stern, and returned that same way after dropping off the envelope. That, of course, could be an attempt to deceive us. We've printed out the images of the person that we believe to be 'The Author', but I fear they won't be of much help."

At that very moment, the Captain received a call from the Bridge that the Osprey had just radioed the Ship for permission to land. The Captain gave his approval and then he, Blakely and Sir Cecil headed to the Sun Deck to greet the arriving FBI Team.

-- 11:00 AM --

Chief Engineer Conrad Schmidt arrived precisely on time to what was now called 'The War Room'. In addition to Sir Cecil Jenkins-Doyle, Captain Jeremy Cornwall and First Officer Jonathan Blakely, there were six men wearing identical blue windbreakers seated around the table. Sir Cecil introduced them to Conrad Schmidt—

"Meet the FBI team that's here to help us…Special Agent in Charge Larry Gregg, and Special Agents Gil Cooper, Jason Eldridge, Mitch Pearson, Tony Casale and Sal Price. Our two FBI dog handlers are up in the kennels and you'll meet them later.

"So Conrad, fill us in on our plans to protect our mechanical and electrical systems."

"Yes Sir. First of all you should know that all our systems are remotely monitored 24-7 to make sure they're operating properly, and to detect early signs of any performance problems. They're almost all below decks, in areas restricted to authorized personnel only.

"But obviously, that doesn't go far enough in a situation like this; one where we are trying to head off potential seizure or sabotage. So we're installing dozens of additional surveillance cameras and motion detectors to protect all key systems. These include—our generators, our propulsion systems, our air handling systems, our desalinization plant, and our communication systems. We're now also monitoring the satellite and radar equipment topside, and the air intake vents above decks, along with their air filtration units.

"We're double-staffing our monitoring personnel in the Control Rooms. And we're stationing armed personnel in all our below deck and upper deck equipment locations. Plus we've set-up procedures to coordinate with First Officer Blakely's Security Team, which will be in charge of keeping all entrances to the below-deck crew areas free from intruders,"

"Excellent, Conrad. Does anyone have any questions or suggestions?"

Larry Gregg of the FBI spoke up—

"Chief Engineer Schmidt, our team will be moving all across the Ship to nab these guys before they can get to you. But if they do get through, signal us and we'll be there in force. Just tell your guys to go easy on the firearms. We wouldn't like to have any friendly-fire accidents."

"Point taken. But all the men I'm assigning are ex-military and don't panic. We have to assume that the hijackers will be armed, so we have to be armed too, in order to hold them in custody until your team arrives. But I do suggest we use a password to let us know who's a friendly. How about *Churchill*?"

"Couldn't be a better choice."

After Chief Engineer Schmidt left the meeting, the group reviewed the strengthened security actions being taken throughout the Ship, particularly in the large meeting places. Their focus, of course, was on preventing 'The Author' from implementing his death threats. But at the same time, in order to support their hijacker ruse, some minor but highly visible activities would have to be staged throughout the Ship over the next three days.

One pivotal question before the group was…<u>who</u> precisely was 'The Author' targeting? The logical answer was the Greylord Project attendees. 'The Author' said he would kill "more than 300" passengers, and that was approximately the number attending the Greylord Project conference.

Sir Cecil then asked that copies of the Greylord Project's agenda be distributed to the group. After carefully studying it, they agreed on an action plan to intensify security at every one of their many functions.

THE GREYLORD PROJECT

The Enlightenment 3.0

"Achieving the Incompatible"

Sunday -- **Arrival & Sign-in** .... Grand Lobby
Afternoon & Evening at Leisure

Monday -- ***"Growth vs. Sustainability"***
9:00AM – General Session – "The Challenge" ....*Royal Court (Deck 2)*
10:00AM – Small Group Discussions ....*Break-Out Rooms - A-K**
12:00 Noon – Buffet Luncheon .... *Kings Court (Deck 7)*
2:00PM – General Session – "Our Best Options"....... *Illuminations (Deck 3)*
6:00PM – Cocktail Reception (Black Tie)..............*Queens Room (Deck 3)*
7:30PM – Group Dinner (Black Tie)....................*Queens Grill* (Deck 7)*

Tuesday -- ***"Capitalism vs. Central Planning"***
9:00AM – General Session – "The Challenge" .... *Illuminations (Deck 3)*
10:00AM – Small Group Discussions ....*Break-Out Rooms - A-K**
12:00 Noon – Luncheon .... *Queens & Princess Grill* (Deck 7)*
2:00PM – General Session – "Our Best Options" .... *Illuminations (Deck 3)*
6:00PM – Cocktails Reception .. *G-32 (Deck 3) & Commodore Lounge* (Deck 9)*
7:30PM – Group Dinner .... *Britannia Restaurant (Deck 2)*

Wednesday -- ***"Equal Opportunity vs. Equal Outcomes"***
9:00AM – General Session – "The Challenge" .... *Royal Court Theatre (Deck 2)*
10:00AM – Small Group Discussions ....*Break-Out Rooms - A-K**
12:00 Noon – Luncheon .... *Britannia Restaurant (Deck 2)*
2:00PM – General Session – "Our Best Options" .... *Illuminations (Deck 3)*
6:00PM – Cocktail Reception (Black Tie)...............*Queens Room (Deck 3)*
7:30PM – Group Dinner (Black Tie)........ *Queens & Princess Grills* (Deck 7)*

Thursday -- ***"The Common Good vs. Personal Freedom"***
9:00AM – General Session – "The Challenge" .... *Illuminations (Deck 3)*
10:00AM – Small Group Discussions ....*Break-Out Rooms - A-K**
12:00 Noon – Buffet Luncheon .... *Kings Court (Deck 7)*
2:00PM – General Session – "Our Best Options" .... *Illuminations (Deck 3)*
6:00PM – Cocktail Reception .*Concierge Lounge & Commodore Club* (Deck9)*
7:30PM – Group Dinner ....*Britannia Restaurant (Deck 2)*

Friday -- ***"Achieving the Incompatible"***
10:00AM – General Session – "Meeting The Challenge".. *Royal Court (Deck 2)*
An Action Plan by Team Leaders
12:00 Noon –Group Luncheon .... *Queens & Princess Grills* (Deck 7)*
6:00PM – Gala Reception & Dinner (Black Tie)........*Queens Room (Deck 3)*

*See welcoming packet for Break-Out Room and Dinner Room assignments

Along with the question of who…was the question of how. If the Greylord Project attendees were indeed the target, how exactly would 'The Author' attempt to kill them? For a group that large, only a bomb or lethal gas in the meeting areas seemed likely. Both would require bringing in fairly large devices, easily detectable by the dogs and the metal detectors. Unless of course, they had already been placed well in advance, concealed in a way to preclude detection. That meant that all the air vents and all the wall, ceiling and floor compartments in these rooms should be opened and inspected. The areas beneath the stages and in the wings should be meticulously examined. This includes not only all the equipment and movable platforms and scenery, but even inside the pianos, the instrument cases, and the drum sets. The grills on all the speakers should be opened and the lighting equipment examined. Even the rows of upholstered seating should be individually inspected.

They also agreed that another possibility was poison. Poison in the food or beverages served at the receptions and cocktail parties, or even in the restaurants. Or while less likely, even in the staterooms. Senior Hotel Manager Perry York was in charge of all those areas, and was due to report in with his plans at 1:00PM. They decided that they should ask Events & Facilities Director Marcus O'Toole to attend that briefing too.

-- 1:00 PM --

Hotel Manager Perry York didn't have to tell them the scope of the challenge. With 16,000 meals and tens of thousands of canapés and snacks prepared each day, and with oceans of wine, juices and various other beverages poured daily, an absolutely foolproof way to screen for poisons in all that food and drink was impossible. However, the risks of poisoning at the source could be reduced to a minimum by enhanced surveillance to make sure no unauthorized persons entered the many galleys or the food and beverage storage areas. This was already being put in place.

Perry then went on to tell them that the most vulnerable spots were those areas between the kitchens and the actual diners. All these service areas are heavily supervised to assure both efficiency and professionalism. But now an extra mandate has been added to preclude any food or beverage tampering.

As an added safety measure, food and beverage room service was being suspended and the usual room amenities like complimentary wine and bottled water were being eliminated for the duration of the voyage…as was the chocolate treat, usually given as part of the bed turndown service.

A few questions for Perry York were asked and answered. Then Events & Facilities Director Marcus O'Toole took over. He reported that 'as-we-speak' all the entertainment venues were being thoroughly swept for bombs, weapons or other devices, and that the K9 dogs are clearing the areas, one-by-one. And whenever food and beverages were served in these areas, his team would be closely monitoring any and all buffets and bars. He raised the question of complimentary bottled water and the extra demand that would occur if in-room service were eliminated. All agreed that the distribution of bottled water was a necessity and that supervised distribution stations should be set up around the Ship. Shrink-wrapped cases of 8-ounce bottles would be delivered directly to each station, and then unwrapped only as needed.

-- 2:15 PM --

Prior to their scheduled 2:30PM meeting with the QM2 Passenger & Crew Administrator, Donald Van Zilen, the core group…Sir Cecil, the Captain, Jonathan Blakely, and the 6 FBI Agents…met to assess the strength of the security measures currently being put in place throughout the Ship. They agreed on their completeness and saw no weaknesses or needed additions. But all that was defense. Still to be tackled was the vastly more difficult job of identifying and apprehending 'The Author' before he could strike. He was one-in-three-thousand! And finding him quickly would take intensive and perhaps rule-breaking detective work to succeed. And all were in total agreement that being here on the high seas gave them the leeway to do whatever it would take!

Shortly, Van Zilen would join them with a database profiling everyone on board. They agreed that Van Zilen's role should end there… to keep him unaware that they were really searching for 'The Author' and not the hijackers. The Head of Security, Jonathan Blakely, would take over the search—beginning by requesting that the FBI and Scotland Yard scan their files for matches. Since the Directors of both agencies had already given it A-Level priority, that response could be expected within hours. And Cunard Headquarters was already running a search through the employee records of all the crewmembers on board to see if anything of concern stood out.

-- 2:30 PM --

First Officer Van Zilen entered the War Room carrying a stack of thick folders and an envelope with three thumb drives. Before distributing the folders to each of the nine present, Van Zilen gave them this summary—

"We've set up three databases. One for passengers. Another for the crew. And a third for authorized subcontractors and various other temporary workers aboard. This last category includes the musicians and performers, the people who work in the leased shops and in the *Canyon Ranch Spa*, our guest speakers, our dance escorts, etc.

"For each individual, we've entered a full range of demographic information. And we've run subsets by nationality, age, single travelers vs. couples, number of trips previously taken with Cunard, and any large group they're traveling with, such as The Greylord Project. And importantly, if they just boarded the Ship in New York."

Van Zilen then distributed the folders, and continued— "Inside you'll find the full database sets, along with a one-page summary analysis. Please look over that analysis to see if anything important stands out to you."

QM2 Passengers & Crew -- October 8th

Passengers	Total	Boarded in NYC	First Time on Cunard	Greylord Project	Single Rooms
British	969	212	388	57	25
EU Other	287	51	176	38	12
American	652	506	420	206	48
Asian	23	7	16	8	0
Other	51	12	32	3	0
	1982	788	1032	312	85

Crew	Total	Boarded in NYC	New to Crew
British	68	2	2
EU Other	69	4	4
American	64	2	2
Asian	816	8	8
Other	8	0	0
	1025	16	16

Sub-Contractors	Total	Boarded in NYC	New to Ship
British	46	1	0
EU Other	15	0	0
American	1	1	1
Asian	3	0	0
Other	0	0	0
	65	2	1

Among Crew-- 16 new to the Ship / All 16 boarded in NYC

American Passengers-- 33% of all passengers / 64% of all boarding in NYC

56% of all Single Room passengers

After giving them a few minutes to study the analysis, Van Zilen pointed out—

"As you'll see…even though less than one-third of our passengers are American, they make up two-thirds of the passengers who joined the Ship in New York. They're also the largest group of our first-time travelers …and 56-percent of the passengers in our single staterooms. While it's likely that the hijackers have come aboard in pairs, they might have split up in single rooms to appear non-connected. I'd be very surprised if some of our hijackers aren't in that group.

"As you'll also see, almost the entire crew has sailed with us for several months. Only 16 out of 1,025 are new to the crew, and all 16 joined us in New York. These 16 deserve closer scrutiny in my judgment.

"Only one of the subcontractors is new to the Ship, having just joined us in New York.

"Of course, this is only a first step. We can run crosstabs to narrow down our search by any parameters you wish. All the data is on these thumb drives, so you can also run your own analyses if you'd like."

Sir Cecil thanked Van Zilen for his great efforts, telling him that after running a crosscheck against both the FBI and Scotland Yard files, the FBI Agents would begin interrogating all likely suspects. He took the thumb drives and added that if they needed any help in identifying the hijackers, he would let him know. First Officer Van Zilen then left the meeting.

As soon as the core group was alone, Sir Cecil restarted the discussion—"I'd agree with Van Zilen that Americans traveling alone is a logical subgroup to investigate. But I caution that we not make any premature assumptions. 'The Author' could be any of one of the more than 3,000 people aboard. At this point in time, we have no solid reason to believe that our protagonist is American…and not British, or European, or Asian, or something else. No solid reason to believe he or she has never traveled with us before, or that he or she waited until New York to join us. Our odds of predicting who 'The Author' is remain at 3,000-to-1 until we get the FBI and Scotland Yard scans. At that point we can possibly narrow down our suspect list considerably. I'm also anxious to see if any persons-of-interest turn up in Cunard's employee record files.

-- 8:45 PM --

The core group reconvened immediately after Head of Security Blakely called to say he was ready with the second phase of the passenger and crew screening.

After distributing a single page report and giving everyone time to review it, he pointed out the key findings—

Past Criminal Charges-QM2 Passengers & Crew-

All	Total	Theft	Fraud	Political	Violence
British	37	6	23	0	8
EU Other	16	3	5	4	4
American	18	0	13	0	5
Asian	2	0	0	2	0
Other	4	1	1	1	1
	77	10	42	7	18

All	Total	Theft	Fraud	Political	Violence
Passengers	73	10	42	5	16
Crew	4	0	0	2	2
Other	0	0	0	0	0
	77	10	42	7	18

Passengers in	Total	Theft	Fraud	Political	Violence
Single Rooms	11	3	6	0	2
Doubles	62	7	36	5	14
	73	10	42	5	16

Among Crew-
4 have criminal records

Among Passengers-
73 have criminal records
53 are from Britain or the EU
37 charged with financial crimes
9 of these in single rooms

"Combining the FBI, Scotland Yard and Interpol results, we have 77 people aboard who have had criminal charges filed against them. Only a relatively few of them resulted in convictions, and even those few occurred more than 10 years ago.

"Now, we don't know the motive of 'The Author'...whether it's terrorism, extortion, revenge, psychotic, or something else...so we can't out-of-hand dismiss any category of his prior crimes. I say 'his', because none of the matches showed a female.

"Let's start with the crew. As you'll note, only 4 of the 1,025 crewmembers have had a prior criminal charge or arrest. There are probably many more, considering that arrests in most Asian countries are not included in the Scotland Yard, FBI, and Interpol databases. But it's worth noting that all 4 of these crewmembers came aboard the QM2 in New York, all are new to the crew, and all are European. Their criminal charges? The German, who is now one of our cooks, was a student member of the militant far-left Baader-Meinhof Gang. The Italian, also as a student, was a member of the equally radical Red Brigade. He is now one of our sous-chefs! Of the two others who are new to the crew? One is a Polish national who is now a deckhand. He was charged with felony assault in a bar brawl some years ago. And the fourth is a cabin steward from Romania, where he was charged with assault and resisting arrest in a domestic disturbance. So we have two with political crimes and two with crimes of violence. I'm sure you'd agree that we need to keep a close eye on all four of these crewmembers!

"Now for the passengers. Here's what stands out to me. Among the 73 of them with criminal charges, 53 of them are from Britain or the EU, far outnumbering the Americans. Of these, 37 were charged with theft, fraud or embezzlement. That's almost 70-percent. Incidentally, the 4 charged with political crimes were all for corruption while in office. And the 12 charged with violent crimes were mainly for spousal abuse.

"As for those in our single staterooms, passengers with a criminal record occupy 11 out of our 85 single staterooms…with 9 of them charged with financial crimes.

"As you say, we don't yet know the motive. But the threat letter doesn't sound like classic terrorism or revenge. So I'd speculate that 'The Author' is one of the 37 British or EU passengers with a past history of financial crime. But I'd also include the 4 new crewmembers with criminal records. They're not new to violence and could well be inclined to use violence for financial gain.

"But that said, we can't really eliminate anyone. I'd just call this group a good place to start. Agree?"

There were nods all around. Then Sir Cecil asked— "So, how do we most effectively surveil these potential suspects?"

Jonathan Blakely, glancing first to the Captain, spoke up—"This is not common knowledge, in fact it's highly confidential, but there is a way. While on land, it would require a court order from a judge. But it can be employed here at sea with the authorization of our Captain. And Captain Sir, I recommend that you give it.

"We can not only search all of their staterooms, including the contents of their safes, but we can also listen to and watch everything going on in their staterooms. Again, this is highly confidential, but all of the stateroom TVs have hidden cameras and microphones built into them. When activated, they give the TVs a capability similar to Facetime on a computer. This feature was included purely for emergency safety reasons. We value our passengers' privacy and would never infringe upon it unless absolutely necessary for the safety of the passenger or the Ship. But if a sensor detects a fire or smoke or water leak in a stateroom, we can immediately activate the camera and microphone to assess the situation in order to dispatch the right team to solve it. Equally important, we can even speak with the passengers to give them proper advice and assure them that help is on the way."

Sir Cecil asked—"How many staterooms can you monitor at the same time? And can you record everything you see and hear?"

"While we've never had to use the system for more than 2 or 3 staterooms at the same time, we have the capability to activate and record up to 120 simultaneously. The software will let us start and stop the recording based on any motion in the room. Or the presence of sound or room brightness.

"Clearly, this would be an enormous invasion of privacy and we could face massive lawsuits and a gigantic reputational loss if any of this ever came out. That's why, if we do go ahead with this type of surveillance, I'd strongly recommend that we only do the recordings very selectively."

After a moment of contemplation, Sir Cecil gave his decision—"For now, let's immediately do a thorough search of the 37 staterooms on our list, including the contents of the safes. If that produces anything suspicious, then we'll do the video surveillance on just those rooms that have given us 'just cause'. The FBI should do the searches of these staterooms.

"Additionally, we should go ahead with personal interviews of all 73 passengers with a record of past criminal charges. Our cover story should be that we've had a theft aboard. Bearer bonds have been stolen from the stateroom safe of one of the passengers. And that when we did a search of Scotland Yard and FBI files in conjunction with identifying the hijackers, your name came up as having a criminal record. As such, you've been flagged for screening.

"We can ask if they know anything about the theft? Ask where they were between 11:00AM and 4:00PM on Monday? Ask why they have chosen this particular cruise? And their plans after disembarking the Ship in Southampton?

"Obviously, they'll all claim absolute innocence. But as FBI Agents, you know how to watch for any 'tells' that suggest they might be 'The Author'. Nervousness or over-confidence, jocularity or feigned outrage. You know what to look for. And based on our room search and your professional intuition, we may narrow down our suspect list to a handful for TV monitoring.

"OK, that's it for now. Let's get moving. We only have two more days. Keep me posted."

When the FBI Agents had left, Sir Cecil confided to the Captain and Jonathan Blakely—"I'm not optimistic that their efforts will turn up anything solid, but we have to pursue this on all fronts. And if 'The Author' just happens to be one of the 73 passengers they interrogate, he may feel enough pressure to convince him to abandon his plans because we're closing in on him."

29.

Diversion

WEDNESDAY, OCTOBER 11 -

-- 7:00 AM --

WITH EVERYTHING IN place, the day began with the 7:00AM Group Meeting. Sir Cecil Jenkins-Doyle opened by asking Chief Purser Ivy Witcomb to report on the reactions of the passengers and crew over the announcement that a hijacking practice-drill was in progress.

"Most everyone seems to be energized, seeing this as a fascinating topic of discussion. Your lectures, Sir, and the items in our newsletter have added to the intrigue. I've overheard passengers relating their observations of the security measures we've put in place and how impressed they are with their thoroughness. I've overheard more than a few men placing wagers on how long it will take to apprehend the hijackers. There are also rumors that a betting pool is being set up. And of course, everywhere you see passengers eyeing others who appear a bit suspicious. Sadly, that's directed mainly at those of a different nationality or social class. And the universal assumption seems to be that all the hijackers are men. If one or more proves to be a woman, that would enliven all the banter significantly.

Here, as elsewhere, stereotypes are ingrained. And particularly here perhaps, where the average age of our passengers exceeds 65.

"To date, we've received only 7 calls on our 'hijacker-watch' hot line. Nothing specific, only broad generalizations with no commonality other than a hint of mild paranoia.

"I don't really know much about the reactions of the crew. First Officer Van Zillen is closer to them than I am. Don, what are you seeing?"

"With the crew, it's pretty much business as usual. They're used to our routinely running all kinds of safety and security drills, though nothing of this magnitude. Also, many come from countries where crime and uprisings are widespread and the authorities are quick to put down unrest. They've learned that the best policy is to just keep your head down and quietly do your work. So to date, we have seen nothing to suggest that the crew is especially nervous or concerned. As I said, they're used to routine security drills and special exercises. This is just the latest for them, as I see it from their reactions."

Sir Cecil asked the others to report. One-by-one, they confirmed that all their security procedures were in place and that as of yet nothing significant had turned up. With that, the meeting was adjourned. But before they left, Sir Cecil underscored the importance of letting him know the moment anything out-of-the-ordinary came to their attention.

By prior agreement, the Captain, Head of Security Jonathan Blakely, and the FBI Agent in Charge Larry Gregg remained in the War Room with Sir Cecil. After asking for any comments, Sir Cecil said—

"It looks like our cover story of a hijacking exercise is working... keeping the passengers and crew settled down...while allowing us to take maximum precautions to keep 'The Author' from planting one or more devices around the Ship. That's fine, as a good first step. Now we must go further to flush him out. Ideas?"

FBI Agent Gregg responded— "Let's make a visible arrest of one of our plant undercover hijackers. Not only will this energize the passengers...keeping them on their toes and keeping their eyes open, but it may spook 'The Author' into doing something erratic."

"Go ahead. Good idea. Let's do it today.

"Jonathan, I want to ask you about our stateroom searches. But first, are we spotting anything unusual from our security cameras throughout the Ship?"

"Yes, a few things. But nothing definitive just yet. We're monitoring the movement of 3,000 plus people as they roam constantly around the Ship. Most of them follow a highly predictable pattern...restaurants, entertainment venues, lounges, the outer decks, etcetera. It's the unusual that we're trying to focus on. Specifically, those who wander the Ship at night, long after most have retired. And those who seem curious about the meeting rooms and entertainment areas at times when they are not in use.

"Using those criteria, we have nearly 50 passengers and 6 crewmembers worth closer scrutiny. Identifying the specific crewmembers was easy, because we could simply focus in on their name badges. For passengers, we used our AI facial-recognition software and the digitized ID photos that we had from when everyone first boarded the Ship. Of course, that's not 100-percent reliable because a number of people look alike and our guy could be wearing a disguise. So to confirm their identity, we followed each of their paths to their staterooms. This has given us a short-list of potential suspects to monitor. This morning we'll be following their moves all day from the very moment they leave their staterooms. No doubt 'The Five Amigos'...our FBI hijack imposters...are in this group, but it's more than likely that 'The Author" is in there too!"

"Excellent. Now, what about the 37 stateroom searches we agreed upon yesterday?"

"Obviously, we had to conduct them while the staterooms were unoccupied. And that meant during the dinner hour last night, disguised as part of the normal bed turndown service. We used two teams. With my assistant, two FBI agents and me doing the searches. We completed 35 of the 37. The other 2 had 'do not disturb' cards hanging from their door handles. We'll try them again at lunchtime. So far, we've found nothing suspicious or out of the ordinary."

"OK! Agent Gregg? How are the interviews progressing?"

There are 73 passengers on my list of people with past criminal charges. We've completed interviews with 41 of them so far, using our cover story of stolen bearer bonds. We've provisionally cleared 34 of the 41. That leaves 7 worth further scrutiny. Plus we still have 32 more interviews to conduct. Most of these will be completed by early evening. To date, no single individual has raised our red flags. But you know us, everyone is still a suspect until the real perp is tried and convicted!

"Here's a list of the 7 worth further scrutiny. Sir Cecil, do you want Jonathan to turn on the surveillance cameras in their rooms?"

"Not yet. I want us to pull things together a bit more before taking that step! And lest I remind you, keep me posted!"

-- 1:55 PM --

The Greylord Project attendees had pretty well settled down for their afternoon General Session in *Illuminations* when all hell broke loose.

On the stage, with hardly anyone noticing, a female QM2 waiter had been quietly distributing chilled water bottles to the six places along the panelist table. Bottles she had taken them from a large cooler, which she had wheeled onto the stage and left next to the speaker's podium.

Suddenly, loud shouts riveted everyone's attention to the stage. Two blazer-clad men rushed out…one from stage left, one from stage right…shouting—"Stay where you are! Don't move! FBI! You're under arrest!"—as they converged on the woman.

Freezing for no more than a second, the female waitress leapt from the stage, with all the speed and agility of a gymnast. She darted up the starboard-side aisle attempting to reach the Exit.

But there, two awaiting FBI agents suddenly appeared, blocking her escape. She then attempted to reverse course, but the agents from the stage were fast coming up the aisle to seize her. Without hesitation, she then leapt over the right-side aisle seats in an attempt to actually run across the seat tops to reach safety. But there she stumbled, and two seated Greylord Project attendees grabbed onto her and held her thrashing arms and legs for the few seconds it took for the four FBI agents to converge and pull her back into the aisle.

As one agent held her fast, another bound her hands behind her back using plastic ties. And without a word led her away to who knows where.

Almost all eyes were on the capture, totally oblivious to what was simultaneously taking place on the stage. Two QM2 Ship Officers were gingerly wheeling the cooler off the stage.

For what seemed like minutes but was only seconds, everyone in the giant room was stunned into total silence. But then a cacophony of disbelief and amazement reverberated throughout the room.

"Can you believe this?"
"She must be one of the hijackers."
"A woman, I never would have guessed it!"
"Where are the others?"
"How soon will it take to get her to turn them all in?"
"Was she trying to plant a bomb?"
"Wow, that was fast. It all seemed like a blur!"
"Those FBI guys don't fool around!"

As the buzz of random conversations continued and everyone kept looking around, a series of loud knocks came over the sound system. Then a voice— "Please take your seats! And please settle down!" It was the program director of the Greylord Project trying to restore order.

"Wow! Wasn't that something? Pretty exciting! But let me assure you that we were never in any danger, and the FBI tells me that everything is fully under control. Remember that this was all part of a simulated test of the Ship's readiness to thwart an attempted hijacking at sea. It's all a drill. Merely a drill!

"And with that, let us get on with our planned program for this afternoon. Please welcome to the stage our six panelists. And I'll ask each of them to come up and introduce themselves before reporting the consensus recommendations of the discussion groups they chaired this morning."

With that said, the afternoon session began. But few were as attentive as they might have been under normal circumstances. The image of that woman leaping from the stage and her dramatic apprehension played over and over again in their minds.

-- 3:15 PM --

In the War Room, Special Agent Gregg gave Sir Cecil and Jonathan Blakely a detailed description of the staged drama that had played out a little over an hour ago in the *Illuminations* lecture hall...the public apprehension of hijacker #1, portrayed by FBI Agent Harriet Tyler. He predicted that news of her arrest would spread quickly throughout the Ship. This would soon be followed by the announced arrest of hijackers #2 and #3 in their stateroom, a fictitious event that wouldn't actually need to be staged. He added that Agent Tyler was now joining the team to search for 'The Author'—having discarded the black wig and sallow middle-aged makeup she wore in *Illuminations,* to once again become a young blonde.

The men then speculated how 'The Author' might react to the whole hijacking scenario. Almost certainly, he would see it as a charade designed to mask their intensive search to find him and to block him. But it did checkmate any attempt he might make to panic the passengers. And it did narrow his opportunities to find a vulnerable place to accomplish a mass killing. With security so tight in all the major venues, he might be forced into finding one or more alternative sites. All of which could mean that he had to be out of his cabin actively scouting targets throughout the Ship. But then again, he may have already developed a Plan B and Plan C?

One could hope that seeing all the obstacles now in place, 'The Author' would simply abandon his threats and settle for the massive disruption he had caused. But it would be foolish and derelict to expect that of him. If anything, 'The Author' may now be more dangerous, feeling less in control and therefore more likely to deal recklessly.

Bottom line? All their defensive efforts, though strong, were definitely not enough. It was absolutely essential that they now double-down on their efforts to find him. The unequivocal goal—to have 'The Author' in custody by day's end tomorrow!

Even before the meeting broke up, 'The Author' effectively poked his finger in their eyes, in the form of three messages that he had placed around the Ship. As each was found, members of the QM2 Security Staff quickly phoned in to report them. The time between calls? Less than 5-minutes!

The first call came from *Illuminations*, where in clearing the room after the afternoon Greylord Project session, the staff found…sitting atop of one of the seats…a sheet of white paper with a handwritten message in bold marker pen. The front side said— "**SIR CECIL… BRAVO!**" The reverse side said…"**B O O M !!!**"

The second call came from outside the *Royal Court Theatre*. Taped to the mirror in the Men's Room was a similar handwritten page. This message— "**DON'T DRINK THE WATER**".

The third call came from the *Britannia Restaurant*, where the hand-written message was left on the Maître d's podium. It read— "**TICK, TICK, TICK**".

Clearly, 'The Author' had no intention of retreating and quietly fading away! Instead, he was gleefully displaying his delight in pursuing the bizarre and deadly game he was playing!

30.

The Arrest

THURSDAY, OCTOBER 12 –

-- 6:15 AM --

"We've got him!" Blakely exclaimed.

"As you know, we've been closely tracking those passengers we've seen wandering the Ship in the middle of the night. One of them began to stand out, so we began following his movements. Yesterday afternoon he made several back and forth passes by the *Concierge Lounge* and the *Commodore Club*, where the Greylord Project will be holding their cocktail receptions tonight. Then around 2:15AM this morning he repeated the process, actually trying all the doors, which of course were locked.

"When he went to the *Kings Court* for coffee at 2:45AM, we entered and quickly searched his stateroom. His booking showed that he was traveling with another man, but the cabin steward told us that only one of the twin beds had ever been used. A knock on the door confirmed that the room was empty, so we went in.

"A quick search revealed the following— a locked suitcase under the bed that contained two wigs and three false moustaches, a professional stage makeup kit, rubber gloves, a number of eyeglasses in various styles, and a full face balaclava ski mask. A locked briefcase under the couch contained detailed plans of the Ship, the event schedule and attendee list for the Greylord Project, along with everyone's stateroom numbers. And most tellingly, a comprehensive file on both you, Sir Cecil, and on Captain Cornwall.

"The room safe contained cash, several pieces of ladies jewelry, two cell phones, and 3 passports, only one in the name of the room occupant. A wallet of credit cards in various names was also in the safe. We've photographed them all for further follow-up.

"In the closet, inside a zippered suit bag, we found a QM2 waiters jacket. The rest of the clothes and toiletry items in the bathroom suggested that there was only one stateroom occupant. We did not find any weapons or bomb-making devices, however. That doesn't mean there are none. They could have already been stashed elsewhere."

"Describe the guy." asked Sir Cecil.

"An American. Average height and weight. Mid-50s. Full head of greying hair. Clean-shaven. Pleasant looking, I'd say, with Anglo-Saxon or Celtic features. Very much fits in with our usual travelers.

"He doesn't appear on the lists we received back from the FBI and Scotland Yard. So as far as we know, he has had no criminal charges filed against him. He boarded the Ship in New York and is scheduled to disembark the QM2 in Hamburg, Germany, our second stop on this voyage. He has never traveled with us before, at least not under the name he's using. But with all those passports, who knows who he really is!"

"Excellent work, Jonathan. Let me call Special Agent Larry Gregg. The three of us will then have a little chat with our friend 'The Author' in his stateroom, before he can head off to breakfast!"

-- 6:47 AM --

It took five knocks on the stateroom door by First Officer Blakely before it was opened. Blakely pushed into the room, followed by FBI Agent Gregg and then Sir Cecil.

The startled occupant blurted out--"Who are you and what do you want?"

Then in rapid fire questioning, FBI Agent Gregg took the lead—

"Where's your roommate?"

"Why, has something happened to him?"

"Just answer our question."

"He didn't come home last night. That's not uncommon with him. He's quite the ladies man and is probably spending the night elsewhere. Has something happened to him?"

"Why were you roaming the Ship late last night?"

"I'm not a good sleeper. So sometimes I take a walk to tire me out a bit."

"Coffee in the *Kings Court* at 2:45AM doesn't seem like a good way to get back to sleep!"

"How do you know that? Have you been tailing me?"

"We have a few questions for you. What's with all the disguises, waiter's jacket, and the multiple passports? Who are you really? And what are you up to?"

"I'm not answering any of your questions. I want a lawyer!"

"You're certainly entitled to one once we reach the UK. But here in the mid-Atlantic, the rules of the sea apply. So answer our questions."

"Do you think I'm one of those hijackers? Is that what this is all about?"

"Are you one of the hijackers?"

"I thought they were supposed to be undercover agents just playing the role of hijackers in some sort of security drill. Do you mean there are real hijackers aboard? Either way, I'm definitely not one of them!"

"We'll let our military team at Guantanamo Bay determine that! Our folks at Camp Gitmo are much better at getting straight answers than we are!"

"Look. Look. Let's start over. What do you want to know?"

First Officer Blakely, then took the lead--

"Are you the one who wrote the letter to Sir Jenkins-Doyle?"

"I recognize you, Sir Jenkins-Doyle, from your lectures. But I have absolutely no idea what he's talking about. I have never written you a letter!"

"We'd like a sample of your handwriting. And we'd like to do a DNA swab and take your fingerprints."

"Can you do that without charging me with something, or reading me my rights?"

"We can and we will. But just to cross the t's and dot the i's, we're arresting you on multiple counts for attempted mass murder, terrorism, and a dozen instances of fraud—which has already cost the Cunard Lines, Scotland Yard, and the FBI hundreds of thousands of dollars up to this point in time."

"I'm an American citizen, and you're British. You don't have any jurisdiction over me."

"Wrong! Here at sea, the Captain has total jurisdiction and he has appointed Sir Cecil as his deputy in charge…and I'm the QM2's Head of Security. This by the way is FBI Special Agent in Charge, Larry Gregg. I assume you know that the FBI is an American law enforcement agency. That of course means you'll be tried in <u>both</u> the U.S. and UK. And since terrorism is involved, possibly other countries as well. You can probably also expect hundreds of civil lawsuits from passengers whose civil liberties and lives have been threatened. You'll be in a high security prison until they carry you out in a coffin, unless you're lucky enough to be executed early!"

"Look. OK, OK…
"I'll confess to being a few things, but I'm definitely not a terrorist and certainly not a mass murderer.

"I'm just a guy trying to make a living off of a few well-healed older ladies on this cruise. I booked an Oceanview double so that I'd have a place to bring them for a little romance. It's the married ones especially that are looking for thrills…an hour or so of 'personal attention' while their husbands aren't looking. I change my appearance throughout the voyage so that this afternoon's companion won't think me promiscuous if she sees me chatting up someone else tonight. That's important because I want them to come back for more, usually in the morning or afternoon while they tell their husbands that they're at the Spa. Or at night, when their husbands are in the Casino. It's that second or third time around when they're the most generous. Sometimes with cash. More often with a bracelet or ring or necklace that they can say was lost...because after all, it's covered by insurance anyway. They like to think I'm a brilliant, but very discouraged, author who is close to giving it all up after getting multiple rejection slips for my last manuscript. They like to pretend that their generous gift to me is in support of the arts, not a payment for personal service. And they always leave richer than when they came through my door. They're happy, I'm happy. What's the harm in that?"

After hearing all that and stifling a slight smile, Sir Cecil said—"Bravo."

Then he added sharply— "If you're a writer, I can tell that your specialty is 'fiction'. And I gather that your conquests were all deeply asleep here in your bed while you roamed the Ship's passageways in the middle of the night.

"I'm sad to say I don't buy it. You're the person we call 'The Author', and after we take your prints and a DNA swab, we'll know exactly who you really are.

"First Officer Blakely, please take this individual into custody. Agent Gregg, please notify FBI headquarters and your team that we have our man. I'll inform the Captain and Scotland Yard. They'll take him off the Ship in Southampton and transport him to a secure MI6 location for specialized interrogation. It won't take them too long at all to determine the whys and wherefores of his insidious plot.

"And you? You? The only ones on this Ship who will miss you are all those needy fictionalized ladies in your little tale of commercialized romance!"

-- 7:38 PM --

In a 3-way phone call to Agent Gregg and First Officer Blakely, Sir Cecil conveyed his decision—

"I'm sure we have the right guy, but something happened tonight in the *Britannia* restaurant that worries me. One of the waitresses was beginning to fill up the water glasses at her tables, and the water that came out of her pitcher was dark green. It appears to be just food coloring. But who did it is still a mystery. Perhaps a prank by one of the passengers, but I don't think we can let our guard down. Our guy could have an accomplice. So I'm ordering all our security measures to remain in full force until we reach Southampton.

"Did we have any problems tonight at the Greylord Project cocktail parties in the *Concierge Lounge* and *Commodore Club*?"

"None, whatsoever."

"OK. Let's remain on full alert through our Saturday disembarkation.

"The letter said he'd strike on the fifth day of our crossing…that includes tonight if we count our day of departure from New York. But it could be tomorrow, if he meant our fifth full-day at sea.

"If there is an accomplice, and if it wasn't a hoax, that means he could try to hit us within the next 30-hours!"

31.

Failure

FRIDAY, OCTOBER 13 --

THE DAY PROGRESSED without incident. The Ship's daily newsletter reported that the simulated hijacking exercise had been successfully completed. All five of the undercover FBI agents posing as hijackers had been apprehended. The newsletter then went on to provide details on the preparations for docking in Southampton early the next morning, with the specific schedule for each deck's 'bags out' and disembarkation procedure.

-- 9:00 PM --

The Greylord Project's 'Gala Cocktail Reception & Dinner' had just ended, and only a few stragglers remained in the *Queens Room* saying goodbyes. Then it was off to their staterooms to pack away their tuxes and gowns, and early to bed because tomorrow's 'bags out' schedule would begin at 5:00AM.

-- 9:38 PM --

There was a rap at Sir Cecil's stateroom door. When he got there, no one was to be seen in the passageway. But there was an all too familiar envelope in the rack next to his door.

"Not again" he thought as he sat on the bed and opened the envelope. Inside, in a familiar hand, was this very disturbing message—

CUNARD

Dear Sir Cecil,
Tag. You're it!
Despite all your best efforts, you have failed to protect the more than 300 Greylord Project delegates that I have infected this night during their Gala Party and Dinner. All have now been marked with my sign!

But all is not lost. As I watched you during the week, I must acknowledge that you did give it your absolute best "old school" try, organizing an impressive effort. So I decided, as a professional courtesy, to cut you a break and use something non-lethal in lieu of the toxin I had originally prepared.

So please notify all your afflicted passengers that they are in absolutely no health risk or danger. The dark brown stains that will appear on their hands in the morning come from a USP approved colorless compound used in cosmetics—dihydroxyacetone (DHA). This is the active ingredient traditionally used in commercially available sunless tanning products. Even in concentrated form, it is harmless and will gradually wear off by itself.

How was it administered, you might ask? Why in the hand sanitizer dispensing stations outside the 'Queens Room', where tonight's Greylord Project black tie event was held. I'm so thankful that the staff was highly diligent in reminding everyone to sanitize their hands before entering!

Until we meet again --
Sincerely yours,
Michael A.

-- 10:15 PM --

Sir Cecil quickly assembled the core team of Captain Cornwall, First Officer Blakely and Special Agent Gregg. He showed them the letter and pronounced— "Gentlemen, we have indeed failed!

"Yes, no one has died. And yes, for these past six days we did stave off a major panic among the passengers and crew. But it appears that 'The Author' is still at large. And that he has succeeded by creating a major new problem that will be almost impossible for us to contain. If this letter is to be believed, early tomorrow morning we can expect to have 300-or-more frantic calls from Greylord Project attendees…calling us in panic for help and for answers.

"Unless you have better suggestions, here's what I propose—

"First, let's ask the Ship's Surgeon about this DHA chemical. Is there really such a compound, and is it just a harmless skin-tanning agent? And if it is, how quickly does it tan and how soon can we expect it to wear off? At the same time, let's remove all the hand-sanitizer dispensers from around the Ship…and secure the ones from the *Queens Room* for testing by a lab once we hit shore. We can't trust that they indeed contain DHA. Hopefully it's not something more harmful.

"We obviously have to brief the Director of the Greylord Project and inform every one of their attendees that they might be affected. How we phrase things is critically important. After giving it much thought, here's what I suggest as our official explanation."

He then handed them this document—

PASSENGER ALERT

Due to an unfortunate mix-up last night, some of the hand-sanitizer stations at the entrance to the *Queens Room* contained a cosmetic-grade additive used in commercially available sunless skin-tanning products. Called DHA (dihydroxyacetone), this additive, if applied lightly and spread evenly, results in the appearance of a natural tan. But if too heavily applied and spread unevenly, it can result in darker patches. Even so, any tanning effect will fade completely within a very few days, or much sooner.

How this unfortunate incident occurred is under investigation. But it is directly tied to the simulated hijacking drill successfully conducted during this voyage.

WHO IS AFFECTED?
Only those who attended the 6:00PM Friday Night event for the Greylord Project in the Queens Room.

WHAT HAPPENS NEXT?
We know that an apology is not enough. So for each of the 312 Greylord Project passengers who were possibly affected by the

questionable hand-sanitizer, you'll find two vouchers in your QM2 departure folder—

1. A voucher to cover any and all costs associated with a consultation with your personal physician, or dermatologist, or cosmetician, should you deem it desirable.

2. A voucher good for a full 20% discount off your next Queen Mary 2 voyage.

Again, our sincerest apologies,

Captain Jeremy Cornwall
QM2 Ship Master

After reviewing the document, Captain Cornwall nodded his approval and said— "I agree. But I'll first have to run it by our Cunard CEO, Sir Oliver Walters."

Special Agent Larry Gregg then stood as he said— "Just for the record-- All the liability for this cockup rests with Cunard, and possibly with you Sir Cecil as mastermind of this whole hijacking cover story. You basically lied to everyone on board. Now, those of us in this business are not above using counterintelligence techniques, but if someone has to take the fall over this, it's not going to be the FBI. Start to finish, this was your dance, Sir Cecil. So if this ever comes out, you get to bend-over and take the bow!"

"Thank you for that all-too-graphic statement of support!"

Then the Captain interjected— "What if this letter is also a bluff? Based on all that's transpired, I now doubt he ever really intended to kill anyone. And perhaps he's put nothing in the hand-sanitizer dispensers. What if his sole goal was disruption? Something I might add that he's achieved brilliantly. If there was just the regular hand-sanitizing liquid in the dispensers, and we put out this Alert…aren't we just giving him another win?"

In response, Sir Cecil pointed out— "We'll be able to tell the moment people wake-up in the morning and look at their hands. If they see nothing unusual, we don't distribute the Passenger Alert letter and the vouchers. But if even a few calls come in, I'd recommend that we distribute them to all 312 passengers who might be affected.

"And let me go further. Right after this meeting I'll go down to the *Queens Room* and slather my own hands with the sanitizer. That way, I'll know if we have a problem even before the first call comes in in the morning!

"And if the calls do come in, that's when we should notify the Greylord Project's Executive Director, Malcolm Elliot. Handled right, he can share in the credit for negotiating the 20-percent QM2 future discount. He should like that!"

32.

Southampton Arrival

SATURDAY, OCTOBER 14 --

-- 4:30 AM --

EVEN THIS EARLY, nearly a half-dozen passengers had called the Front Desk and were patched through to the Security Office. First Officer Blakely immediately notified the Captain, Sir Cecil and FBI Agent Gregg...and then dispatched the PASSENGER ALERT to all of the Greylord Project staterooms. Simultaneously, Sir Cecil called Malcolm Elliot of the Greylord Project...to tell him what had transpired, using the cover story of the hijacking exercise. Inspecting his own hands, Sir Cecil could see that the tanning stain was alarmingly dark.

-- 8:30 AM --

George Trecott sat quietly in the window bay of the *Kings Court* buffet restaurant, enjoying his third cup of coffee. He had watched approvingly as passenger after passenger passed by, repeatedly glancing at their hands...which in contrast to their pale facial complexions were deep mahogany in color. What a comic sight they made!

Beneath the table, George kept one foot securely pressed against his carryon bag. Not that he would forget it or that anyone would try to steal it, but it did contain all his notes and materials from his past week's great adventure, including his recordings of all the War Room meetings.

Knowing that Sir Jenkins-Doyle would organize an effort to find him and stop him, George tracked Sir Cecil's movements for those first few hours after 'the letter' had been delivered, wearing his QM2 waiters jacket and carrying a tray filled with covered dishes and a coffee pot from his own untouched room service breakfast. George followed Sir Cecil to the forward elevator bank on Deck 8, where he saw him press the button for Deck 12, the location of the Bridge and the Captain's quarters.

Then, wearing a variety of disguises throughout the evening, George monitored all movements on Deck 8, watching for Sir Cecil's return to his stateroom. That led to the amazingly fortuitous discovery that something really major was just about to happen in Queens Suite #8130.

Workman were removing the Suite's king-size bed and replacing it with a large conference table and several chairs. Three computers were outside the suite on carts, along with flip charts and other meeting materials. Seizing the opportunity, George quickly returned to his own stateroom, where he donned his waiters jacket and stuffed a few special items in his pocket. Then returning to the Queens Suite, he boldly entered the room and with some authority said to the two workmen—"We'll also need a table for the coffee urns and all the cups they'll need. Can you bring something up?"

When the work crew left to get the table, George installed four wireless bugs in what he correctly assumed would be Sir Cecil's 'War Room'. As a result, now everything that was said in Suite #8130 was transmitted to George's stateroom and recorded on a series of thumb drives that were now safely stowed in George's carryon bag!

These recordings kept George fully aware of…and one step ahead of…all of Sir Cecil's and the FBI's moves during the crossing. And they would provide extraordinary primary research for George's novel!

Satisfied with his work, George readied to depart the Ship. Then back home, where work could begin full-time on his masterpiece!

33.

London – Two Weeks Later

Even though catastrophe had been avoided, and he was given credit for brilliantly managing the crisis and saving the day, Sir Cecil Jenkins-Doyle was furious that he had not accomplished more. 'The Author' should be sitting in a prison cell awaiting years of incarceration. And not a single passenger should have experienced any harm or discomfort.

Yes, the Scotland Yard laboratories confirmed that it was indeed DHA in the *Queens Room* hand sanitizers. And that yes, it was harmless and its tanning effect would quickly fade in just a few days.

And yes, the afflicted passengers with very few exceptions were more than happy to receive a 20-percent savings voucher. Which contributed greatly to avoiding any negative press reports.

Those news stories that did appear had headlines like—"Adventure Aboard The Queen"— which actually made sailing aboard the Queen Mary 2 seem more exciting, with perhaps greater appeal to younger passengers who might typically view the QM2 as a bit too formal and more than a tad stuffy.

Before disembarking, the passengers had been cautioned not to reveal the details of the many counterterrorism measures taken aboard ship to foil and capture the would-be hijackers. They were told that keeping the security team's 'means and methods' confidential was important in the fight against future terrorism at sea.

But as expected, most everyone did tell a wide circle of family and friends about their exciting adventure, often embellishing their own experiences and personal roles in what they all described as an 'enormously successful counterterrorism exercise'. Some of the more colorful anecdotal stories and interviews soon found their way into print and onto TV, where they not only enhanced the QM2's image, but more than likely dissuaded future would-be hijackers from making any attempt on a passenger ship at sea.

Among the things that particularly gnawed at Sir Cecil was his snap judgment in concluding that the person they had taken into custody was indeed 'The Author'. Once his prints had been taken and run against FBI files, he was identified as one Scott Isaacs, a suspected jewel and fine arts thief from Las Vegas. Isaacs had been arrested and charged several times, but never convicted. And since no thefts or other complaints had been reported aboard the QM2, he was released two days after docking in Southampton. His claim of false arrest and imprisonment was dropped once he was reminded of his confession for what could be called 'sex crimes' aboard Ship. Having that added to his permanent record was something that he chose to avoid!

Another mistake Sir Cecil believed that he had made was not including passport numbers in the passenger database that he had sent to Scotland Yard and to the FBI. If he had done so, he now knew that he would have found 17 passengers traveling with false passports and IDs. Scott Isaacs was one of them. And chances are that 'The Author' was one of the other 16.

Putting those matters to one side, Sir Cecil vowed to expend whatever it would take to find and punish 'The Author'. This was more than just personal. Because of this individual's 'little games', vast amounts of money and manpower had been wasted. And the reputations and indeed the careers of his three closest associates aboard the QM2 had been seriously damaged. Though their efforts were exemplary, some higher-ups characterized them a failure. Blame had to go somewhere!

Captain Jeremy Cornwall was being asked to take early retirement. First Officer Jonathan Blakely was being reassigned to a lesser post. And FBI Special Agent Larry Gregg was being criticized by his superiors for ceding too much control to Sir Cecil and not taking greater personal command. Accordingly, Gregg was now under tremendous pressure to find and bring quickly to justice the so-called 'Author' who had wreaked so much havoc.

To accomplish this, Agent Gregg knew that he would have to deploy the full resources of the FBI…reasoning that this individual must have left a trail of unsolved crimes with a distinctive and curious modus operandi. Namely…letters in advance to the victims. Working with the FBI profilers was an important first step. But even more important…sending out requests to every FBI field office in the country.

Within just days, and to his great surprise, he received detailed replies from both Fort Lauderdale and Indianapolis!

“THE AUTHOR”

34.

Creating 'Ian Kirk'

WHERE TO BEGIN? How to begin?

How to unfold the story?

These were the questions and alternative answers that George played out in his mind for the first two weeks after returning home.

In his original outline for the book, George saw his title character… "The Assassin"…as a highly skilled former government agent gone free-lance. There was nothing new in that, of course. Dozens of books and movies had assassins who were rogue government agents. But what would be new in this book was the degree of vivid detail in precisely how George's assassin intricately planned and carried out eight or more of his high-profile kills.

There were plenty of 'police procedurals' on the best-seller list… written by authors who had been cops or newspaper crime reporters. But this would be the first 'assassin procedural'…written by an author who had actually lived the life, risking all in real world personal encounters out in the field. Not made up stuff. But the real thing. It would be, in effect, an assassin's "how-to / tell-all" biography.

Another difference would be the outcome. George's "Assassin" would be the book's hero...not its villain. And he would suffer no bad end. No 'good versus evil'. No 'fatal mistakes'. No 'deus ex machina' event to deliver final justice.

None of that storyline had changed from the original outline. But what had changed was in George himself. His experience out in the field had now totally shifted his perspective. At the outset, George had assumed that he would be a passive but critical observer of the events he had set in motion. Much as a scientist or anthropologist would monitor and analyze and record their observations and findings with total objectivity, George would be a true reporter of events and not the subject of his own research.

But a metamorphosis had occurred within him. 'Living the life' out in the field had emotionally transformed him from George the objective reporter to George the Assassin. And that made him rethink his entire approach to his book!

Originally, George had planned to use the conventional structure found in most novels...with a storyteller, situation descriptions, and dialog. But he increasingly recognized that this format would be vastly too limiting. While it would let him potentially thrill the reader with a series of high-risk assassinations, it could never allow him to fully express the true sense of emotions and fulfillment felt by his protagonist...'The Assassin'...the kind of fulfillment he had personally experienced during his own life as an assassin over these past several months.

Ultimately, he came to the realization that his book would be far more powerful and far more compelling if it centered on the inner thoughts of the Assassin himself...rather than just on the mechanics of his assassinations! He should write it as a first-person narrative! A fictional autobiography, where the Assassin was both the protagonist and the hero...telling his own story. Only then could he do proper justice to revealing what it was actually like to be an Assassin. The high-stakes game of wits. The raw excitement in the face of danger. The overwhelming feeling of power! The God-like choice of who should live, and who should die!

The novel he now wanted to write could definitely not be told from the objective point of view of some investigative journalist...or law enforcement official...describing and moralizing over the crimes of a master Assassin. It must be the candid confessions of the Assassin himself...as told in confidence to his interviewer, George Trecott.

To make this work, George would combine three elements--

1. A fictional character that would play the role of his master assassin.
   He'd call him 'Ian Kirk'. He'd be a bigger-than-life individual...totally unlike George himself in both background and panache. A James Bond hero to his shy and unassuming chronicler!

2. Detailed descriptions of 8 or 10 major assassinations...an almost how-to guide.
   He make-up most of them. But some would be based on his actual 'field research' in Boca Raton, Indianapolis, and aboard the Queen Mary 2. Of course, the names, and situations would be changed. George had to assume that some of those affected by his handiwork back then would see parallels in Ian Kirk's exploits and become suspicious. George's answer would be that he was simply a journalist, retelling the stories told to him by the real Ian Kirk. And that as a journalist, he was duty bound never to reveal Kirk's true identity or his location.

3. Reflections on the thrills of being an assassin.
   In the fullest sense, this would be the central theme of the whole book. And George knew he could deliver it convincingly well. The Joy. The Power. The Mastery over death itself. Surprisingly, George had never felt more alive than when he dispensed death! And he wanted to share that experience of fulfillment with others!

Everything in the book depended on making Ian Kirk both compelling and convincing. A fascinating man of supreme talents and great intellect. An individual you could secretly identify with. An unorthodox sort of hero. But a hero nonetheless, in spite of his deadly profession. Most assuredly, Ian Kirk was a man of strong ethical principles, not a sadist and certainly not a sociopath.

To create Ian Kirk, George Trecott devoted the next week to developing his character's back-story…fleshing out details from early childhood through adulthood. It wasn't enough to just portray him as a brilliant and charming killer. George had to fully understand Kirk and all the many influences and experiences that made him the man he became. Why his early life led him to become an assassin? How he developed his extraordinary skills? Why he's now chosen to finally share his secret life with others?

George also needed this very extensive back-story on Kirk for his personal protection against any suspicion that "The Assassin" was indeed autobiographical. He wanted to be able to have a detailed dossier on Kirk, in case he ever needed to show that he was indeed real. That's why George included far more 'facts' in his dossier than were included in his book. And who knows? Perhaps one day George might write a follow-up to "The Assassin"…a prequel about Ian Kirk's early life?

But George also realized there was another piece of research that he had to undertake before starting his first draft.

He already had all he needed to breathe realistic excitement into the several assassinations he would dramatize in his book. From his field research, he knew precisely how to plan and execute a successful assassination. How to anticipate and counter the many actions of law enforcement...before, during and after each event. He had learned all this from his work in Boca Raton, Indianapolis, and aboard the QM2. And with that knowledge, he could easily create five more fictional assassinations for his book.

And he also had all he needed to convey the intellectual fulfillment and emotional thrills animating Ian Kirk's life as a professional assassin. The exhilaration, the sense of power, the total satisfaction uniquely found in a life of deadly encounters. All this George had discovered within himself. And he was eager to express it and share it through his creation, Ian Kirk.

But that still left open the core question of <u>morality</u>. How could Ian Kirk live the life of a professional assassin without any moral qualms and feelings of guilt?

The answer would be that Ian Kirk embodied a unique form of morality...a certain new-age morality that he would display and persuasively explain in the book.

George wanted to make absolutely certain that his readers did <u>not</u> see Ian Kirk as a psychopath, sociopath, sadist, or a soulless hit-man-for-hire...even though death was his business. And finding a way to achieve that meant that George had to search for a credible moral rationale underlying Ian's actions. And developing that would require some in-depth research to answer two key questions—

- What is death...from a philosophical point-of-view?
- How can one ever justify taking the life of another...from a moralistic point of view?

George knew that the title of his book—"The Assassin"—would conjure up graphic images of the classical assassin...usually defined as—"A murderer of an important person in a surprise attack for political or religious reasons." And these images were far from positive.

Historically, an assassin was almost always a fanatic...driven by religious or political hatred. The English word 'assassinate'... which first appeared in a 1600 Jesuit pamphlet and five-years later in Shakespeare's 'Macbeth'...came from the Arabic word 'Hashshashin'. This was the name of a militant fanatical group of Nizari Ismailis in northern Persia during the time of the Crusades. Feared for their ruthless killings of political and religious enemies, they held sway from the 8th to 14th centuries throughout Persia, Syria, Turkey and across the Middle East. Because the word 'Hashshashin' shares its etymological roots with the word 'hashish', it has been commonly said that this group used hashish before embarking on their murderous missions. But an increasing number of Western scholars now discount this as myth.

In contrast, today's assassins are largely seen as cold-blooded killers. The few positive exceptions are fictional characters like Bond and Rapp...fearless patriots "with a license to kill"...basically one-man armies working under direct orders from their government's top security agencies. Then there are the 'killers-for-hire' like John Wick and a number of Quentin Tarantino's creations. While exciting to watch, they are seriously flawed individuals that few would like to emulate. And then there are the legions of thuggish hit-men. Cretin killers who don't deserve the title 'assassin'.

Ian Kirk would be totally unlike any of these!

Establishing that difference required George to probe deeply into those two pivotal questions—1. What is death? And-- 2. How can taking the life of another ever be justified? And before long he found that if he combined the answers to those two questions, he could shape and persuasively express the unique form of morality that he wanted his Ian Kirk to possess.

In his research, here's what he found—

What is death?

From a medical and legal standpoint, the commonly accepted answer is pretty straightforward—"The irreversible cessation of all vital functions especially as indicated by a permanent stoppage of the heart, respiration, and brain activity." At that point the body begins to decay at the cellular level.

Over time and in various jurisdictions, that definition has changed a bit, with phrases like 'brain dead' allowing the legal withdrawal of various medical devices and procedures that might have otherwise prolonged life.

But from a philosophical standpoint, the answer is quite different—

- To a true philosopher, "Death does not occur when body functions cease." "Life continues in a new and far better form."

- Plato and Socrates defined death as…"The ultimate separation of the soul and body."
- Aristotle wrote—"The dead are more blessed and happier than the living." And—"To die is to return to one's real home."
- Socrates wrote—"Death may be the greatest of all human blessings."
- From the earliest of times, the almost universal view has been that death is not the end of life, but rather a doorway to a greater life. Even Neanderthals placed food and implements in the graves of their deceased for their journey. And certainly the most spectacular examples that display a belief in the afterlife are found in Egypt during the time of the Pharaohs.
- Every major religion has as its central dogma the belief that we humans survive physical death, with our spirit shedding the physical body that contained it while on earth. And Hindu scriptures even proclaim—"Death is the only Truth."
- While it's become popular in some secular circles to declare that death is finality and the absolute end of one's existence, the vast majority of humans from the beginning of time have believed that death is the doorway to an eternal spiritual afterlife. Philosophers and theologians may differ in their attempts to describe this afterlife, but most agree that the good or evil we embraced on Earth will determine what we find when we pass through that door.
- Among the many thinkers who have spoken about the afterlife are these—
    - -- William Shakespeare—"All that live must die, passing through nature to eternity."
    - -- George Bernard Shaw—"Death is a splendid thing."
    - -- Helen Keller—"Death is no more than passing from one room to another."

- -- Walt Whitman—“Nothing can happen more beautiful than death.”
- -- Steve Jobs—“Death is likely the single best invention of life.”

How can taking the life of another ever be justified?

The answer is—very easily! Because society allows it all the time! Even today we use phrases like “justifiable homicide” and “just wars” to cover lethal acts of self-defense, protection of others, military combat, etc. And though some argue otherwise, the millions legally slain while still in the womb are in fact sanctioned killings. In many countries euthanasia is now legal. And assisted suicide often goes well beyond just assistance.

Where does Ian Kirk stand in all this? Quite simply, every assignment he undertakes is always a “justifiable homicide”. Ian Kirk is as well qualified as any government bureau or agency to make that judgment and undertake that mission. Perhaps even more so, because of his objectivity. Politics and public opinion do not compromise and interfere with his judgment.

And it’s never about wreaking vengeance! It’s about something else entirely.

Most of the individuals that Ian Kirk targets are evil. They have already harmed one or many...and will harm one or many again. It would simply be irresponsible not to remove them now, before this can happen again.

Some of his targets may be righteous, but even the righteous can impede progress and impair the common good. It would be short sighted not to remove them as well.

But removing them from their physical existence does not remove them from an afterlife! Through his actions, Ian merely speeds their passage through the door...providing the righteous with unparalleled rewards...and the evil with a possibly compassionate summing-up that may lead to some forgiveness before they can doom themselves for all eternity by doing more evil on Earth.

Simply put, Ian Kirk is actually an agent of mercy. Mercy to those he escorts through the door. And mercy to those others on Earth who might have been harmed if his targets were left untouched.

And that is Ian Kirk's unique brand of morality, as George has conceived it for his book. And in developing it, George has convinced himself that it makes such eminent sense, that if there is ever a next time he may not make his assassinations fakes!

In an effort to accurately sum up Ian Kirk's observations about life and death, George then penned the following declaration for his book's opening page epigraph—

> "Fear of death drives all our other fears
> and fuels all our emotions.
>
> "Our doomed desire for self-preservation
> compels us to seek immortality through
> fame, power, fortune and in physical
> relationships. All of which ultimately
> abandon us in the end.

> "Death is our only lasting legacy.
> And in creative hands, it is our
> only permanent art form."
>
> Ian Kirk

Once the Kirk back-story and moral justification were completed and the book's structure was decided, the text flowed out of George's mind almost too fast to be put down on paper. With unbelievable speed, George completed his manuscript. And as he read through his final draft, he realized that his book could no longer be called a 'thriller'. It had in fact become an inspirational guide to anonymous killing!

This scared him! But he had invested too much to start over. So he sent the manuscript to a few publishers.

Finding a committed publisher would normally be a challenge. But this time it was easy. They saw the book as so gripping…so controversial…so potentially explosive…such a surefire best seller… that it was snapped up and rushed into pre-publication and book-promotion planning.

Reference File Document—D3 -

Confidential Background Dossier on Subject 'Ian Michael Kirk'

Compiled by George Trecott from interviews with the subject and independent research

Early Childhood—

- Ian Kirk was born in Strasbourg to a philandering French banker and a British mother who was a constantly touring opera singer. An only child, both parents considered him more of a burden than a blessing. His mother seldom acknowledged his existence, because it would belie her claims of being far younger than she actually was, contradicting her public pronouncements and professional image. His father spent so little time at home that he'd not see the boy for weeks, and only then with a muttering nod in passing.

- That left Ian's care to a series of not-too-carefully vetted nannies, each hired for their apparent strict code of discipline rather than their skills with a gifted child, or for their empathy.

- To avoid punishment, Ian from his youngest age learned how to lie, and to deceive, and how to misdirect—creating the image of the perfect child—while keeping the real Ian secret to himself.

- He also learned never to ask for or want a pet. A stray cat he once brought home disappeared the next day. Though she lied, he learned that Nanny #3 had brought it to the pound for gassing. The adults around him had laid down strict rules about pets. They insisted that animals carried disease and should never be petted or brought into the house. They repeatedly said that the only wild animals worth seeing were in museums, where they had been fumigated, stuffed and put on display. They even claimed that animated films like Bambi, portraying animals as cute children, were actually part of a Communist plot to disarm the West, by making gun ownership and use seem evil. They repeatedly emphasized that animals were animals, and not humans! Shooting them was just fine. It kept their numbers in line.

- As far as he knew, Ian had no uncles or aunts or cousins. When he asked about grandparents, he was simply told they were all dead. "Nothing more to say. You wouldn't have liked them anyway!"

Schooling—

- Once he was old enough, Ian was shipped off to a series of boarding schools in the UK. There he excelled by outwitting his professors and classmates, projecting himself as a model student, and as a trusted friend and confidant to one and all.

- With each passing year he perfected his skills as a master manipulator, amazed by the gullibility and moldability of everyone he came in contact with. And these skills grew throughout public school, college and university to ensnare a widening circle of influential contacts.

- To all who knew him, Ian was an exceptional and exemplary individual—a young man of great intelligence, great competence, great wit, and great compassion. And remarkably for an individual with such gifts, they saw him as a man with absolutely no ego. Humble. Self-deprecating. Always giving credit to others!

- But at the very heart of Ian's being was an EGO of gigantic proportion. Not "ego" narrowly defined as some form of 'self-esteem'. But EGO as defined by Merriam Webster— "Ego...The Self...especially as contrasted with all others in the World."

- Ian saw himself as a being unique in the entire Universe. Not one of the multitude, he was an individual set entirely apart. There were humans...and then there was Ian. Like the other animals that these humans were, he could use them or totally ignore them. He was He. They were them!

Career path—

- While still in University, Ian was approached by Her Majesty's Government and recruited as what they called 'a bright young boy' for a position in an unnamed security service. He learned his assignment only after accepting and signing a sheaf of documents, including the Official Secrets Act. Thereafter followed training in a broad range of skills, including---intelligence gathering and analysis, espionage, spy-craft, weapons, and the lethal arts. Excelling in all areas, he was in record time made a 'deniable agent' in MI6, Her Majesty's Secret Intelligence Service, also known as 'The Office' by those in the inner circle.

- As a 'deniable agent', Ian was given five different aliases and all the biographical background data and documents to support them. Unknown to his Masters, he acquired three more for his future personal use! There was no record of these in the MI6 archives.

Appearance—

- Ian Kirk was in his late 30s and of average height and weight—with no tattoos, birthmarks or discernable scars. He had dark brown hair and dark brown eyes and a pleasant well-proportioned face. There was nothing distinctive to catch the eye as unusual. Even a gifted caricaturist would have a hard time zeroing in on any distinguishing feature to enlarge or exaggerate in a drawing.

- Unlike many MI6 operatives who had perfected their lethal hand-to-hand combat skills in strenuous gym workouts--Ian Kirk's muscularity was achieved by long distance running and power swimming, giving him both speed and stamina--far more useful talents in escaping a confrontation in lieu of being bloodied in one.

- With his mix of French and English genes, Ian could fit in almost anywhere. At first glance, an Italian or an Irishman, a Spaniard or a German, a Catholic or a Jew, would all assume that Ian shared their ethnicity or heritage. Even without a change of hair color, most Northern Europeans would think the same.

- He could speak five languages fluently—French, English, German, Spanish and Italian. And with special training from an MI6 theatrical dialect coach could affect a reasonable Russian, Middle Eastern and American accent. All in all, this made Ian ideal spy material!

MI6 'Wet Work'—

- After a significant number of successful field assignments in Europe and the Middle East, MI6 gave Kirk his first 'wet work' orders. A sanctioned assassination of an arms merchant in Istanbul. He was said to have performed the mission flawlessly. But contrary to their warnings in training, he felt absolutely no remorse in this, his first killing. Rather, he found it both exciting and fulfilling. As required, he did take the mandatory post-event therapy, followed by 3-months of desk duty to 'heal'. And throughout, he made sure to say all the right things to show he was a solid, non-conflicted Agent.

- Then came a series of more challenging and deadly assignments, which Ian again accomplished without flaw, earning him the highest accolades at the top of the Service. And in just a very few years, MI6 began to view him as their 'Avenging Angel'. The man they assigned to keep the UK and the Free World 'safe for democracy'!

- In contrast, Ian viewed MI6 as his personal 'Booking Agent', lining up bigger and better gigs where he could perform on increasingly larger stages. And to stretch himself to the absolute peak, here and there Ian would take on a few 'pro-bono' freelance killings if they posed seemingly insurmountable challenges.

Going Private—

- After four years as a top level MI6 assassin, Ian made the decision to open his own business. There were lots of potential clients out there willing to pay top dollar to have an adversary permanently removed. Corporations, cartels, politicians and syndicates, even billionaires and governments, all could become his clients. So many in fact that he could pick and choose to select only those that met his new firm's high moral standards.

- To set up shop, Kirk had to orchestrate his own death in a way totally convincing to the Service. He wanted them to not only mourn him, but to be so certain of his death that without hesitation...and with full pomp and ceremony...they would affix his Star to the "MI6 Wall of Heroes"

- The perfect opportunity would come with his next assignment. A Russian oligarch with access to advanced weapon systems and WMDs was putting together a syndicate of four terrorist organizations. Its purpose? To finance and establish a heavily secured arms depot in a remote area that could supply their individual weapon needs on demand. Principals from the four organizations—Boko Haram, ISIL, Al-Shabab, and Ansar Allah—would be meeting aboard the Russian's 130-foot yacht *Barbabella* the following month...somewhere in the Caribbean, to finalize all the arrangements.

- The 'Office' wanted all four terrorists and the oligarch taken out, with full deniability. That meant missiles to destroy the yacht were ruled out, because satellite imagery would provide clear evidence of their launch point.

- The plan was to have Ian pose as a Swiss banker who would act as the middleman financier in the deal, for a sizeable fee, of course. He would board the *Barbabella* in Jamaica to work out final details with the Russian, two days before the four weapons buyers would board in Cuba.

- While in Jamaica, a vanload of food stores and other supplies would be loaded onto *Barbabella*. Disguised as cartons of canned goods, the explosives that Kirk would use to blow up the yacht would be brought aboard. Detonation would occur once the yacht reached the Cayman Trench, where the Caribbean Sea had a depth of over 25,000-feet. All 21 passengers aboard, including the 10 crewmembers, would be lost at sea without a trace. Only Kirk would escape. After setting the timers, he would slip overboard a good half-hour before detonation. This would give him time to distance himself from the explosion. After *Barbabella* and all hands had gone to the bottom, MI6 would rescue Kirk at sea.

- Along with the food stores, the van would deliver three large propane cylinders for the yacht's ovens and stoves. Concealed inside the cylinders was the special equipment Kirk would need for his planned escape...and for his real escape. One cylinder contained scuba gear with a built in tracking device that would allow an MI6 high-speed motor launch to quickly find Kirk and bring him aboard. This scuba gear Ian Kirk would leave untouched, to convince MI6 that he had never left the yacht.

- A second cylinder contained a 'Yamaha 500 Li-Sea' battery-powered underwater scooter and Ian's personal scuba gear. Using these, Ian could travel undetected below the surface at a speed of 4.5-miles-per-hour, allowing him to reach a small unoccupied fishing boat that he had left anchored to a buoy six-miles distant from the planned explosion site. A spare battery pack would allow him to travel twice that far if needed.

- Before slipping overboard, while all but a few of the crewmembers were asleep, Ian would set two timers... one for 20-minutes, the second for 22-minutes. The first timer would set off a series of flashes and sounds similar to gunfire. Then 2-minutes later, the main explosive charge would split open the yacht and send her quickly to the bottom.

- The high-altitude MI6 drone monitoring the whole operation would capture proof that Kirk was still aboard when the massive explosion occurred. It would seem apparent that he had been discovered setting the charges and a gunfight ensued. The tracking device on his MI6 scuba gear would verify that he had never escaped the yacht. It kept generating his location aboard, right up to the moment of the blast!

- As word reached London, elation over the success of the mission was tempered by sadness over the loss of Ian Kirk. He gave his life for Queen and Country! And he would never be forgotten! He would live in legend and be a role model for all to follow!

- Ian, of course, had put all thoughts of Queen and Country aside. Reaching his small fishing boat, he sailed on to Belize and then in a series of legs flew to Bern, Switzerland—the new world headquarters of his company, appropriately named 'Liquidators International'.

Assassin For Hire—

- During the interviews with him, Ian Kirk declined to reveal his client list and his targets, citing confidentiality and professional ethics. But he did provide the author with broad-stroke details of eight successful assignments—with names and places changed as appropriate.

35.

A Book Like No Other

TWO YEARS LATER --

THE ACCLAIM EXCEEDED George Trecott's greatest hopes. Within days of publication, his book..."The Assassin"...had soared to the #1 position on both the New York Times and Amazon's 'Best Sellers' lists. And impressively, it had topped both their 'Fiction' and 'Non-Fiction' lists. It straddled both because George had written it as if he were an investigative reporter, researching and then interviewing one of the world's most notorious professional assassins.

Was it fact? Was it fiction? Perhaps a little of both. But above all it was a bravura accomplishment. Both exciting and chilling. Both riveting and repulsive. Both gleeful and heartless. Both moral and immoral. And impossible to put down...or to forget!

Already the calls had come in with lucrative offers for the film rights. George's agent was playing off Netflix against Amazon, and Warner Brothers against Sony and 20th Century Fox. And most exciting of all were the requests for personal meetings from Martin Scorsese, Ron Howard, and Quentin Tarantino.

What made "The Assassin" so compelling was that it defied all the accepted literary conventions in the crime, mystery, thriller, police procedural and biography genres. It was a completely new approach, a genre unto its own! And its protagonist—given the cover name of Ian Kirk by the author—was at one and the same time so admirable and so evil that seeing life through his eyes stirred up primal feelings that most of us keep buried deep within our subconscious.

As a reader, one couldn't help but identify with Ian Kirk. But doing so made you a party to his acts. Through him you could actually feel the thrill of killing another human being. And you killed without any true sense of remorse. Your only relief from feeling guilt was to remind yourself that this was just a book that you could stop reading at any moment. But as with a graphically gruesome photo, initial revulsion might force you to look away, but then compulsion would draw you back to look again and again, no matter how hard you might try to resist! Or as with a particularly erotic photo, your moral instincts might tell you to turn away, but an involuntary arousal in your loins would quickly take over to keep you transfixed.

In a remarkable way, "The Assassin" was unlike any other book ever written. It transported you into a vivid alternate reality...with places and people and events just as real as those in your deepest and most disturbing REM-sleep dreams. It unlocked and opened wide the door between the often conflicted conscious world and the often hidden unconscious where our darkest appetites and primal fears comingle. As one reviewer put it—"It's like Freud on steroids!"

But still, as a reader, you just knew that Ian Kirk would eventually self-destruct or be killed or be sealed away in a maximum-security institution. That would be your release, your atonement, your absolution for identifying with him and participating in his killings. But that doesn't happen. Evil reigns supreme. Ian Kirk remains untouched. More successful, happier, and totally unremorseful than ever.

In "The Assassin", Evil conquers Good. At first that upsets you. Then you secretly relish it. As another critic put it—"The Assassin doesn't stop at being a guide-book to the Post-Christian Age, it's the definitive hand-book to the Post-Morality Age!"

36.

The Book Tour

WELL BEFORE "THE Assassin" was published, George's literary agent told him to expect an extensive book tour and a series of TV and radio interviews. The book was that good and he'd be in big demand.

Taking a critical look in the mirror, George decided that what he saw was not the image he wanted to project. He was no Ian Kirk! He was an overweight middle-aged man with thinning gray hair, thick glasses, puffy cheeks and a receding chin. His teeth were yellowed and snaggy, which is why he rarely smiled. He also had a somewhat squeaky voice and something of a shuffling gait. These he could mask when in disguise, but only with concerted effort!

Using part of his book advance, George hired a team of professionals to give him a complete makeover. A personal trainer to loose weight, tone up, and improve his walk. A plastic surgeon to reshape his chin and puffy cheeks. An oral surgeon for a full set of dental implants. An ophthalmologist to eliminate his need for glasses. A stylist to give his hair a new color and look. And a speech therapist to give him a commanding voice. A totally new wardrobe completed the transformation. The 'new' George was "ready for his close-up!"

To get George comfortable speaking before a group, his publisher's PR people scheduled a series of 'meet the author' receptions and book signings at small independent bookstores in Northern New Jersey. These would occur two weeks before his book tour would officially kick-off in New York City. From there, they'd move on to major markets coast-to-coast. At every stop, there would be radio interviews and where possible local TV coverage. And a press kit would give local newspapers and magazines all they needed to run a feature on 'America's Runaway Best Seller'..."The Assassin"...and its author George Trecott.

All this would culminate with an in-depth interview on "*60-Minutes*", timed to coincide with the announcement that George's book was named a finalist for a trifecta of awards—The National Book Award, the Booker Prize, and the Dagger Award from the Crime Writers Association. He had already been given the Edgar Award for the best mystery book of the year.

As the tour unfolded, week-after-week, city-after-city, interview-after-interview, profound changes were occurring in George.

At the start, and understandably nervous, he delivered his talk without variation, almost by rote. But as he became more and more comfortable, he began to notice how he could play off individual audience reactions to sway his listeners in any direction he might want. A little more chilling horror? A little more gallows humor? A touch of rakish charm? Not only did this titillate the audience and give George a 'rush', it sold far far more books at the end of his talk.

And there was one thing more. Never much of a hit with the ladies, George was now finding himself becoming a bit irresistible. In most every town, there were one or more females in the audience that wanted more than just his inscription on their signed copy. Was it his fame as an author? Was it his charm at the podium? Was it the makeover that made him the walking image of his fictional Ian Kirk? Who cared...as long as it led to a few drinks after each lecture and some unforgettable nights in George's hotel suites.

Much could be said about the importance of book tours from a commercial point of view. But this tour was absolutely transformative for George. Once a shy and bitter loner, he was now an exciting man of fame. Ian was no longer a fictional character. He was alive in George...body, mind and soul!

37.

FBI Agent Larry Gregg

WASHINGTON, D.C. --

FBI AGENT LARRY Gregg rarely watched "60 Minutes". But because they were doing a feature tonight on his home team, the Washington Nationals, he decided to tune in. Never did he expect that this last minute decision would bring him face-to-face with George Trecott...and reopen his investigation into the Queen Mary 2 incident.

In a full quarter-hour segment, the "60 Minutes" interviewer heralded the publishing phenomenon that was George Trecott's book, "The Assassin". And in a series of probing questions he asked George if it was true that he partnered with a real life assassin in writing the book, and that the incidents in it actually happened.

George answered somewhat coyly—"You're well aware that a journalist never reveals their sources. But I can assure you that my book, though fictionalized, is based on solid facts. Yes, I've changed the names, places and circumstances to protect my sources, as well as the actual victims—most of whom were thought to have died in accidents or from natural causes."

The interviewer then asked about Ian Kirk, the fascinating master assassin in George's book.

"My portrayal of Ian...his psyche and his moral compass...is as accurate as my humble talents as an author would allow. If anything, he is more charming and compelling, and more chillingly amoral than I've conveyed. If Satan himself had half of Ian's talents, we'd be eagerly asking him to let us join him in Hell! And obviously, his real name isn't Ian Kirk!"

In the time remaining, the interviewer asked about a few of the assassinations described in the book, leading off with a group killing aboard the Queen Mary 2. At this point, Agent Gregg's jaw dropped and he became riveted to the screen. As Trecott described the event, far too many of the details matched the threatened killings aboard the QM2 almost three years before. This was not a coincidence. This was confirmation that Trecott...or this Ian Kirk...had been directly involved. Still smarting from his humiliating failure back then to bring someone to justice, Larry Gregg vowed that this time he would finally nail the guy!

Not wanting to wait even 24-hours for an Amazon delivery, Larry Gregg decided to buy a copy of "The Assassin" first thing the next morning at Kramers Bookstore on Dupont Circle, just a 10-minute walk from his office at FBI Headquarters in the Hoover Building.

Back at his desk, Gregg turned directly to the chapter on the Queen Mary 2 assassinations. While the voyage was in the Pacific and not transatlantic...and the targets were 8 underworld figures from Hong Kong, Taiwan, Japan and the Philippines, gathered together for some kind of jurisdictional negotiations...the main details of the assassination's planning matched those of the transatlantic crossing where Gregg and the others had tried unsuccessfully to capture the so-called 'Author'!

Even the method was the same…a toxin in the hand-sanitizer on the last night of the voyage. The victims showed no immediate signs of illness, but all died several days later back at home from an untreatable bacterial infection. The authorities were never notified. If the book was to be believed, no connections between them were ever made.

As far as Gregg knew, there were no fatalities among the Greylord Project attendees after their QM2 cruise three-years ago. But that was worth checking out. Something really odd was at work here!

Turning back to the beginning of the book, Gregg soon found himself being mesmerized by the somewhat irresistible appeal of this man…Ian Kirk. Indeed, it took a lot of Gregg's willpower to resist his impulse to see Kirk as a vigilante hero…and perhaps even a role model.

As a career law enforcement officer, Gregg had far-too-often seen the guilty going free. Free to commit far worse crimes, again and again. How often he wished that he had the power and authority to stop that evil and to protect the innocent who would be devastated and often destroyed by it. But being that kind of super-hero avenger was not in Larry Gregg's job description.

But in this book, Ian Kirk gave him a credible rationale as to why it should be his duty…indeed his moral obligation…to right these wrongs. Compelling. Persuasive. But dangerous. That is, unless he wanted to sever all his ties with the Bureau and risk becoming a lawbreaker himself.

Larry Gregg could now see why "The Assassin" was becoming a publishing phenomenon. It unleashed inner feelings about justice and convincingly persuaded the reader to action. And then…in eight assassination chapters…it provided step-by-step plans on how to take out the guilty without fear of detection and without fear of getting caught. It was the ultimate vigilante 'how-to' book!

In addition to the chapter on the Queen Mary 2, two of the other assassinations rang a bell with Agent Gregg—

- In Miami, a woman was assassinated when a deadly parasite was delivered to her in her take-out coffee from Starbucks. In this telling, she was the wife of a U.S. Senator and had a far younger lover who was a known Russian agent. This was a fairly close match to the method used in the Boca Raton spiked-coffee incident that the Palm Beach Detective…R.C. Nichols…had told him about 3-years ago.

- In Illinois, a jailed crime boss was murdered inside a high-security prison. The method? An untraceable poison delivered in a food gift pack. The unsuspecting Coroner had declared it a heart attack. This too was a near match to the Indianapolis prison poisoning that FBI Agent Sally Templeton had described.

The remaining chapters described five other assassinations, presumably all with real-world match-ups—

- In San Francisco, the CEO of a high-tech firm that was rumored to be the front for a Chinese cyber-warfare operation. He died in a car crash attributed to 'driving under the influence'.

- In San Salvador, an insurgent rebel leader died from a spider bite.

- In New York City, the vengeful ex-mistress of a City Council Member was electrocuted from faulty wiring in her co-op apartment.

- In Bermuda, a tragic drowning incident…when the young head of a predatory hedge-fund had a malfunction in his scuba diving gear.

- In London, when the gay lover of a Minister was threatening to write a 'tell-all' that would bring down the Government. He died from what was reported to be a slip off his 12th-floor apartment balcony from an icy patch and a faulty railing.

Each of these assassinations was fascinating to read, almost short stories in themselves. The rationales for each of the killings, the descriptions of the individuals involved, the methods and manners of the initial surveillance, the set-up, the execution, and the avoidance of detection. Almost a University course in how to be a successful killer!

After an intense reading of the book, Larry Gregg made a series of phone calls—Sir Cecil Jenkins-Doyle in London, FBI Agent Sally Templeton in Indianapolis, and Lieutenant R. C. Nichols in Fort Lauderdale. He told them to get a copy of the book and after reading it, to call him back.

"I think this guy, George Trecott, is <u>our</u> guy…or can tell us who is. And on behalf of all of us, I vow to finally bring him to justice!"

38.

Targeting Trecott

NEW YORK CITY --

George Trecott felt he had little choice but to meet with FBI Agent Larry Gregg at the FBI Field Office at 26 Federal Plaza in lower Manhattan. While Gregg said it was about an ongoing investigation, his tone suggested something far more serious. Trecott knew who Gregg was, because Gregg was everywhere to be seen on that Queen Mary 2 voyage when he had Sir Cecil Jenkins-Doyle and the FBI running around in circles. But he was confident that Gregg had no evidence that he had been anywhere near the QM2 before, during or after that voyage.

George knew he would have to be very careful in the interview. Open and cooperative, and in no way evasive. And to make sure he was ready, George drafted the questions that Agent Gregg was most likely to ask. Then he perfected answers to all of them. Played right, he could point Gregg in another direction...away from him, and toward that phantom assassin that he had called Ian Kirk.

Agent Gregg too was well prepared for the meeting. Sir Cecil, Sally Templeton and R.C. Nichols all agreed that the details in the book

were too close a match to real incidents to be a coincidence. And they had sent their complete files to Gregg.

The questions they all asked were—Why were there no fatalities in any of these earlier incidents? And why the taunting letters? Did the assassin get his toxin doses wrong? Or were these some kind of dress rehearsals? Or was this some kind of sick game?

But regardless, laws had been broken, reputations destroyed, irreparable harm done to many of the individuals involved. This guy Trecott had lots to answer for!

In addition to studying these files, Larry Gregg had ordered a complete FBI work-up on George Trecott.

Cunard maintained a comprehensive ten-year database on all passengers and crewmembers that had ever sailed aboard the QM2 or on any of its other ships. A comparison scan uncovered no matches to Trecott's name, passport number, or photo. That didn't prove anything, of course, because he could have been traveling under a different name and disguised his appearance.

A thorough background check on Trecott found no history of criminality or any notable achievements. He was a graduate of Columbia, but his career had not carried him very far. He appeared to be just an ordinary, middle-class Joe…divorced, childless, and living fairly hand-to-mouth until he got a big publishing deal for his book—"The Assassin". Of course, that could describe the life of most first-time authors in America!

Interviews with neighbors and former employers described George Trecott as a quiet, somewhat shy loner, who made not much of an impression—either positive or negative. If he had a secret life, no one knew anything about it!

One notable factor was George Trecott's physical appearance. His yearbook photo bore little resemblance to the photo on his book jacket. And the photos on his newly issued drivers license and passport were much different than those on his earlier documents. At first, Gregg suspected that Trecott, the author, had assumed the identity of the real Trecott. But bank and medical insurance records established that Trecott had changed his appearance <u>after</u> receiving his book contract. Apparently, then he had the money to change his life and satisfy his vanity!

Larry Gregg took all this into account as he prepared for his George Trecott interview. Reading Trecott as somewhat timid, he decided a direct and forceful approach would be most productive. If he could fluster Trecott in his questioning, some important unguarded responses could be triggered.

39.

The Interview

"Mr. Trecott, thank you for coming. Please take a seat.

"I'll be recording this session, so please note that your comments today will be on the record."

"Am I being charged with something? I don't even know why I'm here. You said there was something about an ongoing investigation?"

"We're investigating your book. Several of the crimes you report in it show an insider's knowledge of actual unsolved crimes. How did you come by this knowledge?"

"As a journalist, I can not reveal my sources. I'm sure you can understand that."

"Are you Ian Kirk?"

"I am not."

"Then how did you gain the insider's knowledge described in your book?"

"I'm not sure what part of the book you're referring to."

"Let's just take the Queen Mary 2 incident. How did you gain the insider knowledge you detail in it?"

"Again, I can not reveal my sources."

"Did you just make it all up? Or did you have outside information sources?"

"As the book acknowledges, I did have a human source."

"Who was that source?"

"I can't tell you, even if I wanted to."

"Why is that?"

"I don't know his real identity or how to reach him."

"Since we're talking about major crimes here, you have to do better than that."

"Again, I don't know his real identity or how to reach him."

"Can we at least acknowledge that someone who claims to be a professional assassin has told you about these assassinations?"

"That's precisely what I said in the preface to my book. I explicitly stated that all that followed was told to me in a series of interviews with a master assassin that I call Ian Kirk."

"Mr. Trecott, we've looked into your background and find that you've led a fairly quiet and uneventful life. It defies logic that you would meet a so-called master assassin and that he would confide in you the comprehensive details of his many crimes."

"But he did!"

"If you won't tell me his name, at least dispel my disbelief...by telling me how you met him...and why he would of all people confide in you?"

"You probably won't believe me."

"Try me out, because I don't want to have to charge you with obstruction of justice."

"I met him by chance. And of all places, it was on the 102nd-floor Observation Deck of the Empire State Building."

"You're right, I don't believe you!"

"But it's true. At the time, I was writing a mystery and in my book the charming contract killer had persuaded his client's wife to join him in seeing the fantastic views from atop the Empire State Building. He planned to shove her over and plant a suicide note, then escape undetected.

"For my book, I was doing research on the Empire State Building and all the deaths that had occurred there, and even before then at that location. Back in the late 1800s, this was the site of the original Waldorf-Astoria Hotel...the world's largest hotel, with over 1,300 bedrooms. That gave me lots of opportunities to describe some notorious killings. All of which, I have to admit, I was making up.

"Initially, there were even plans to make the spire of the Empire State Building a docking station for dirigibles. This proved impractical because of the high winds, but I planned to work in a murder or two involving dirigibles and the Nazis in my novel.

"Well, on that day…it was 3-years ago in a February, and I'll never forget it…I was on the 102nd-floor Observation Deck making detailed notes on the layout, the elevators, access to the spire, etcetera for my novel. There was only one other person there at the time, because the fog that had rolled in had totally obscured the view. We got to chatting, and he asked about my note taking.

"I told him I was an author of mysteries and thrillers. I admitted that none had yet been published because I was having a difficult time creating realistic situations. He asked me to describe a few and then suggested he might be able to help.

"He described himself as a retired national security officer with real world experience. I detected a slight British accent and assumed that he might be a former MI5 or MI6 or Scotland Yard agent. But he never acknowledged that.

"He said that if I were interested, he could 'spin me a few yarns' about some of the real-world clandestine assassination attempts. I eagerly accepted his offer and he suggested meeting for coffee the next morning near the U.N.

"We met once a week for the next two months at various coffee shops around town. As he spoke, I frantically took notes, because I recognized that what he told me would make a fabulous novel. Far better than anything I might possibly conceive of by myself.

"He never gave me his full name. He said I could call him 'William'. I didn't press it, because I was grateful for the things he told me and didn't want to chance ending our get-togethers.

"After our eighth coffee together, I went to the appointed coffee shop and he wasn't there. I waited for over an hour and went back every day for a week. He never showed up again.

"Agent Gregg, you say that the details in my book match real assassination incidents. That surprises me. Because I always believed that what he told me was fictitious. Something he concocted, something spun out of whole cloth. Or at least something embellished from bits and pieces of real events."

"What did this 'William' look like?"

"Well, that's hard to describe. Average height and weight. Maybe mid-50s based on his gray hair. Horn rim glasses. A mild disposition and cultured voice, almost spell binding, at least to me. Dressed like a country gentleman. Tweed jacket, tattersall shirt, corduroy pants, tweed driving cap and dark brown car coat. Not every time, but more often than not."

"That's a pretty formal get-up in today's casual world."

"I wondered about that too. Because he wasn't dressed that way when I first met him on the Empire State."

"How was he dressed then?"

"Pretty normal. Dark slacks, sweater, raincoat. Nothing particularly notable."

"You mentioned he had a British accent."

"I thought it was. But very faint, not pronounced. It could have been Scottish or Australian or something else. Maybe it was just the clothes he wore that gave me that idea. Or perhaps it was just an accent he was affecting. I'm really not sure."

"Let's assume for a minute that he was a real assassin, and that these were his real killings. Why would he want to divulge any of this to you, a complete stranger?"

"I have no idea. That's why I've always assumed that he was not personally an assassin, but just a person-in-the-know telling me about some assassinations he was aware of. They were great stories. Real or made-up? That made no difference to me. I'm a novelist not a policeman."

"OK, but if he were a real assassin, why would he possibly confide in a complete stranger?"

"I can only guess. Maybe, just maybe, he had a hunger or compulsion to tell someone, anyone, about the 'brilliance' of his efforts. And he chose me as someone safe who might possibly tell the world on his behalf.

"If he was a real full-time assassin, I'd assume that he led a lonely and solitary life. Perhaps he hungered for recognition. If you've read my book, you'll see that all the assassinations he told me about were never viewed by the authorities as suspicious deaths. There were no headlines. No searches for an anonymous killer. No appreciative… or horrified…audiences to give him recognition. Perhaps that's why he seized on our chance meeting in the Empire State Building…in order to make me his herald!

"But on the other hand, perhaps he was a trickster. It didn't matter to me. It was the stories and plot lines I valued. I of course wondered who he was and all that, but it was not an overriding concern. If it was all made up, that was OK with me!

"Agent Gregg, you say these were real crimes. Then isn't it possible that he read about them in the press and made up his stories to go with them? Or maybe they were natural or accidental deaths that he chose to fictionalize?"

"The answer is 'no', we know for a fact that these were not natural or accidental attempted killings."

"Wait! You just said 'attempted killings'. Does that mean they never actually happened? I don't understand. Why are you involving me?"

"Because major laws were broken. And you appear to be smack in the middle of it all."

"Do I need a lawyer?"

"That's your decision. But this investigation is just getting started. I'm sure we'll talk again. Thank you Mr. Trecott for coming down here today!"

"Oh, I have one more question for you Mr. Trecott. That astonishing character in your book…Ian Kirk…where did you come up with him? More than anything, it's his morality…or should I say…lack of morality that has caused all the sensation and driven your book to huge popularity. Surely he wasn't that tweedy, middle-aged Brit you had coffee with. Who did you pattern your character after?"

"He came full born, right from my imagination. That and a few bottles of 'Jameson' Whiskey. I stirred together a potent blend of Machiavelli, Ted Bundy, Hannibal Lector, and Faust into a movie-star-handsome package. I'm proud to say that Ian Kirk is 100-percent my creation. And frankly, he scares me more than a little. I hope none of his twisted thinking seeps into me. He's a modern day Boogieman! What more can I say?"

Shaking his head, Agent Larry Gregg ended the meeting. He'd listen to the interview tape a few times again, before sharing it with Sir Cecil, Sally Templeton and R.C. Nichols.

40.

Transparent Lies

NEW YORK CITY --

BACK IN HIS apartment, George Trecott thought through his interview with FBI agent Larry Gregg. That no one else was present suggested that no formal investigation was underway. Most likely, Gregg was just fishing for answers because he was still smarting from his failure aboard the QM2 and the resulting impact that had on his reputation and performance record.

In writing his book, George had thought long and hard about whether to replace the Queen Mary 2 with a different ship in one of his assassination chapters. He stayed with the QM2 because that was the ship he knew intimately, and because it just might be fun to open some old wounds in Sir Cecil Jenkins-Doyle. Apparently, it had done much the same with FBI special agent Lawrence Thomas Gregg!

It was also apparent that Gregg was in contact not only with Sir Cecil, but also with other key players. In the interview, Gregg had given that away when he said—"Several of the crimes you report"… and…"Let's just take the Queen Mary 2 incident". So George had to assume that at the very least, police Lieutenant R.C. Nichols in Fort Lauderdale and the FBI agent Sally Templeton in Indianapolis were now part of this fishing expedition.

The events in the three jurisdictions were not directly linked. But even before the book was published, an experienced investigator with full FBI resources could have uncovered similarities between them. Someone like FBI special agent Larry Gregg, who had a personal axe to grind! And after the book came out, the connections would have become obvious. At that point, Gregg would have brought in Nichols and Templeton for a full debriefing.

George thought through each of the events to see how the people involved might perceive things—

In Boca Raton there was that disturbing warning letter sent to Tilly Dixon's husband, Howard, from someone calling themselves "Your Guardian Angel". A few days later, Tilly was rendered temporarily unconscious by a fairly harmless substance in her take-out chai tea. Police Lieutenant R.C. Nichols was the lead investigator and he took a very personal interest in the case, vowing to Howard and Tilly that he'd bring their victimizer to justice.

In Indianapolis, a drugged food package from a non-existent charity called "The Guardian Angel Society" had penetrated the walls of a high-security prison to temporarily incapacitate a notorious con-man named 'Tex' Bickford. No one sympathized with Bickford's medical plight, but both the Warden and Head of Security at the Jail lost their jobs and reputations over this negligent breach of security. Among the suspected culprits were the fired President and local Branch Manager of the Texas Bank that Bickford had swindled. And as the number one suspect—there was Harley Quirk, whose name, reputation, business, marriage and life savings had been wiped out when Bickford plundered his advertising agency. Then there was FBI Special Agent Sally Templeton. Frustrated by her total inability to find the guilty party or parties involved…she still saw it a personal challenge and career necessity to break the case and bring someone to justice.

And on the Queen Mary 2 in its transatlantic crossing to Southampton, there was that taunting letter to Sir Cecil Jenkins-Doyle, giving him five days to prevent the threatened murder of over 300 passengers. Thanks to the combined and concerted efforts of the FBI, Scotland Yard and the QM2's officer force, there were no fatalities and panic was averted. But almost 300 passengers did have their hands stained by a cosmetic-grade tanning compound. Failure to prevent even this incident, and failure to capture the culprit, resulted in a number of reputation and career losses including Captain Cornwall and First Officer Blakely. Sir Cecil's once sterling reputation as the brilliant former head of Scotland Yard was tarnished. And FBI Special Agent in Charge Larry Gregg was no longer seen as "bright young man and heir apparent' in the Bureau's hierarchy. Many high-level UK ministers and U.S. government officials still characterized the incident as an embarrassment and a wasted multi-million-dollar fiasco. However, the Cunard Line just wanted to expunge the incident from memory. They considered it that much of a bad-PR disaster.

So George could well understand why Gregg and the others wanted answers—and wanted payback.

He also clearly recognized that his book was the first new clue they had in over 3-years. And with all three of their cases included in his book, it showed there was a strong linkage between these separate events. And that made the book's author, George Trecott, a person of interest in their search to bring someone to justice!

But the treatment of the crimes described in the book no doubt left them with a number of important unanswered questions --

1. George's book was all about killings. But none of the actual events had fatalities. Rather, it seemed that all were designed to show that an actual killing would have been possible. But all choose to use non-lethal substances. Why?

2. All the cases involved letters in advance of the incidents. Why? To challenge and ultimately embarrass the authorities? Some kind of sicko game? In George's book, no letters or forewarnings take place!

3. And the most immediate question they must all have—How did the author of "The Assassin", George Trecott, gain such an intimate knowledge of all these events in three different jurisdictions? Was he himself the perpetrator? Or did he have an actual primary source…the assassin he calls Ian Kirk in his book? Or did he concoct the whole thing out of research he did from published stories and interviews?

From George's perspective, he wanted them to believe the latter—that the book was pure fiction based on actual events that he'd heard about or read about. And to get them to that conclusion, he had used a bit of misdirection.

If he had told them outright that he had no direct personal knowledge of any of these events…that they were built upon stories he had read about in the press or online…they'd no doubt keep pushing to poke holes in his story to see if he was lying. So he'd give them a different lie to challenge.

In his interview with Agent Larry Gregg, he spun that dubious yarn about his mysterious source…a guy he met atop the Empire State Building. And in making that claim, he intentionally laid it on very thick. The chance meeting, the coffee shop dates, the British squire clothes, the unlikely fact that a professional assassin would confide in a total stranger he had just met. All this told in a way designed to stretch credibility. And for good measure, he added a few "tells"... little darts of the eyes here and there that an experienced interrogator would pick up on.

And then he topped it all off by proudly boasting that his Ian Kirk character was 100-percent his own brilliant creation. By being so very effusive about his creative writing skills here, he was almost confessing that his entire book was fictional.

Yes, he wanted them to conclude that he was lying! Lying about having a real life source. Now why would he conceivably lie about that? There was only one logical conclusion-- Because he could never publically admit that his book was really a hoax. Its entire commercial success and his fame as a writer absolutely depended on it being seen as the true confession of a real assassin! Without that, it was nothing!

As George figured it—
If Larry Gregg was even half the investigator that he certainly was, he'd probably conclude right then and there that George Trecott was a dead-end in his search for answers. He'd see right through George's ludicrous claims... and write him off as just an egotistical first-time crime writer. Not a guy ever capable of pulling off those audacious crimes in Boca Raton, Indianapolis, and aboard the QM2.

At least, that's what George hoped.
But alas, that was not to be!

41.

The Video Game

SIX MONTHS LATER --

GEORGE'S LITERARY AGENT Oliver Gold called late Friday morning with an exciting announcement. "George…It's finally ready!!! The developers have signed-off on the prototype. Our Virtual Reality game 'The Assassin Live' is finally ready. We can see it in its final form and test it tonight!"

For months, Gold had been working under tight security with the Chinese software developer '*Finito*' to shepherd the project through.

As a game, 'The Assassin Live' went far beyond George's book, with features in the Deluxe Edition that would make it an overnight sensation. In fact, these features were so controversial that they would guarantee intensive media coverage, propelling sales to dizzying heights.

The entire concept and authorship was George's. Along with the truly diabolical innovations in the Deluxe Edition.

In both the Standard and Deluxe Editions, you became Ian Kirk… and as a gamer you could experience all of the challenges and joys of being the world's most legendary assassin. Three 'resource modules' gave you the necessary skills and tools to overcome even the most impossible obstacles. Combined, they provided the player with the world-class training and resources that gave Ian Kirk his unequalled lethal skills. And you could even dialog with a virtual Ian Kirk to measure and hone your 'ruthlessness index'.

The 'Target' module trained you in the 'who, when, and where' aspects of a successful assassination. All parts of which were under your full discretion and control in the game. And all parts of which in balance determined your success versus failure, and your escape versus apprehension.

The 'Method' module gave you a dynamic warehouse of surveillance and killing tools, along with professional training videos on how to use them most effectively. All the latest technical gadgetry was included, with uploads to keep the list current, and with links to the best suppliers. Every known poison, lethal organism, explosive device, firearm, bladed weapon, and other important killing device was not only inventoried, but also rated. And many had links to 'how-to' tutorials. Importantly, this module also contained a 'Reference Library' that let the gamer access demonstrations of the classic manual killing arts of strangulation, suffocation, drowning, and lethal head and body blows.

The 'Planning' module was of course the most important. It let you map-out and pre-test alternate strategies before finalizing a Plan-A and Plan-B…and importantly, an Abort strategy. A well-conceived and thoroughly pre-tested plan was not only critical in taking-out your current target…it also determined your survival to kill another day. The 'Planning' module helped you learn and perfect these vital skills!

These three 'resource modules' prepared you to become a successful professional assassin. And it was in the main body of the game where you could ply your trade.

Included in the Standard Edition of 'The Assassin Live' were 100 contract-kill assignments. For each of these 100 targets, a complete background file was provided...with photos, profiles, histories, security warnings, and more. The 'fee' for succeeding in each assignment was specified, with amounts commensurate with the difficulty of the assignment.

After accepting an assignment, the gamer would then have to negotiate a number of challenging obstacles to succeed. If the target survived or was only wounded, it would be considered a failure. And if the gamer was captured or killed, it was an abject disaster.

Attempt after attempt on the same target could be made, until the gamer succeeded or was killed or captured. This 'on-the-job-training' was a valuable aspect of even the Standard Edition.

'The Assassin Live - Deluxe Edition' delivered breathtaking additional capabilities. Rather than being limited to 100 pre-assigned targets, you could select your own real-world victims...creating avatars of most anyone you'd like to kill. A spouse, a parent, a boss, a political figure, a sibling, a neighbor, a superstar, a TV commentator, a hedge fund manager, you name it!

Using special built-in tools to probe the internet, and with 'deep-fake' technology, you could combine photos, mapping data, building floor plans, and more to import true-to-life individuals, places and situations into your game. Placing them in any setting you'd choose—at home, at work, in a theater or supermarket or sports arena, in bed, or in a car, in a pool, atop a high building, or in a basement, garage or park, or in a hospital room.

And of course you were not limited to a single target. You could target two in a hotel room tryst, twenty in a private jet, or thousands at a rock concert. Your choice was virtually unlimited!

And just for fun, when you succeeded you could send an anonymous email to your target. Standard wording said—

RIP

Dear (insert name here)
Congratulations!
This is to inform you
that you have just been successfully assassinated
in the Virtual Reality Game
'The Assassin Live'

You won't be missed!

For legal reasons, both Editions of the game carried a full disclaimer. And both required the digitally signed acknowledgement and agreement of both the purchaser and the user…that the game was—"For entertainment purposes only, by adults 21 years of age and older. That it was not to be used in violation of any laws, or anyone's individual civic, personal, or legal rights…. blah, blah, blah…"

Which of course, was the exact opposite of how it would be most often used!

The Friday night demonstrations of both Editions of 'The Assassin Live' went exceedingly well…and a launch date was agreed upon. One factor that was confirmed privately in a side session was that George would have his own personal triple-encrypted 'backdoor' into the operating systems of both Editions of the game. He didn't tell them why. But among other things, it was to allow him to match up users of the Deluxe Edition with any actual killings that might result from the Game's use. All avatar targets would be routinely matched against police reports, news stories and obituaries. That way, George would be able to identify and develop a cadre of acolyte assassins for his possible future use. Perhaps not necessary, but a nice touch anyway!

42.

Furor & Condemnation

THE WORLDWIDE CONDEMNATION of '<u>The Assassin Live</u>' by the media, government officials, law enforcement, religious leaders, and just plain so-called concerned citizens was eclipsed only by the spectacular sales success it enjoyed. It became an overnight sensation, obliterating all previous computer game sales records.

If the Book was controversial, the Game was truly explosive. Under public pressure, more than 30 organizations and 12 States filed for injunctions to have the Game banned and its inventories seized.

At the same time, thousands of experienced gamers and free-market advocates spoke out in its defense, arguing that a direct link between a video game and violence had never once been documented. And that even the most violent AO-rated games were shown to be harmless recreation...and even perhaps therapeutic, defusing rather than feeding violent impulses.

All this back and forth assured off-the-chart sales at record prices. And within months, George had become a multi-millionaire many times over!

But statistics don't lie…at least that's the claim of the organizations that publish them.

Since the introduction of '<u>The Assassin Live</u>', the number of year-over-year unexplained deaths in the U.S. and elsewhere had been soaring. While many pointed to the Game as the obvious cause, definitive proof was absent. But George as the creator knew better. He could clearly see the linkage when he matched his confidential list of Deluxe Edition users and their avatar targets against published death records. That he was successfully training experienced assassins was obvious—and a measure of some notable pride. Not only was he a famous author and famous game creator, he was now also an influential educator as well. That was a very rewarding and heady feeling, indeed!

His creative works had not only influenced many thousands around the world, growing numbers were actually putting his teachings into practice. George had given them the inspirational framework and tools to succeed…and they were fully embracing them and making them a movement!

Hungering for added new challenges, George was already mulling what further accomplishments a man of his unquestionable talents should pursue!

He knew he'd come up with something very soon!

43.

Press…Good & Bad

NOT A WEEK went by where the names 'George Trecott' and 'Ian Kirk' were not making headline news…Lawsuits, injunctions, opinion pieces, personal profiles, record breaking sales statistics, crime rates, man-on-the-street interviews, commentaries on the growing 'Ian Kirk Cult' of game users…along with a constant stream of letters to the editor.

There's an expression in broadcast news programming—"If it bleeds, it leads." And rarely had the broadcast media been given such an ongoing 'bloody' opportunity in peacetime. Every violent crime report could be expanded by questioning its link to "The Assassin Live" game. Interviews with the victim's family members, friends, neighbors, lawyers, police officials and experts in the field, along with news anchor commentary and exchanges…could expand a routine crime report for 2-minutes to a full 5-minutes or more… enhancing the program's ratings and potential ad revenue.

Radio talk shows with call-in listeners were devoting hours to what everyone was now calling "The Assassin Live Cult Phenomenon." And a number of TV specials did the same.

And eclipsing them all was the avalanche of content on the internet. It was topic Number-1 on Facebook, Twitter, Instagram and more. A host of new sites and blogs provided an ongoing forum for 'true believers' and for those 'utterly opposed'.

All this was great news from George's perspective.

But then two unrelated events began to annoy him significantly.

That pesky FBI agent Larry Gregg was once again stirring up trouble. Unable to establish a link between George and those long ago events in Boca Raton, Indianapolis and on the Queen Mary 2, Gregg was apparently leaking information to the press.

Quoting 'unnamed sources in law enforcement', some so-called investigative journalists were posting stories claiming that George Trecott was not all that he professed to be. That in fact, the master assassin he called Ian Kirk did not really exist. Nor was Kirk a fictional character made-up by George Trecott. But rather, George Trecott himself was a criminal who was under investigation in several countries and states, for a series of felonies, including both attempted and mass murder.

This of course prompted a feeding frenzy in the media, hounding George for comments and interviews. Knowing that no response would only add to the frenzy, George steeled himself and delivered a carefully rehearsed statement in a standing-room-only press conference.

Adopting a slightly bemused expression while slowly shaking his head 'No', he remarked—

"What utter nonsense! Perhaps I should thank them for publicizing my Book and my Game…which by the way are both still setting sales records!

"Of course, Ian Kirk doesn't exist. That's the made-up 'cover name' that I gave to the real person who told me the true story of his exploits. I point that out right in the preface to my Book. Apparently, some headline-hungry journalists, who probably never read my Book, are equating Ian Kirk with me.

"And yes, big news! The real Ian Kirk has killed many people. That's his job description after all! My god, he's an assassin. Why is that such a surprise?

"And claiming that I am Ian Kirk! Are they really serious? George Trecott—full-time writer-by-day / professional assassin-by-night? Give me a break! That's just as ludicrous as it sounds!

"You know what I think? The authorities are frustrated because I won't reveal Ian Kirk's true identity. And they're trying to force me to do so by spreading these crazy stories that I am really him. Well let them prove it. They can toss me in jail. Waterboard me at some undisclosed location if they like. But I will never ever reveal my sources. That's our solemn code as journalists. Don't you agree?"

Within a few weeks, the media moved on to other sensationalist "Breaking News" stories. But George felt that FBI special agent Gregg and his merry band deserved a little payback. Perhaps he should make them targets and upload their files to his cadre of proven Deluxe Edition acolytes. A bounty of say $50,000 in Bitcoins might prove a nice incentive. He'd have to think about that. Better to let the dust settle for now. No need to hit back just yet!

The second event that proved a bit unsettling to George was reputational. He was being increasingly attacked by religious opinion leaders who were calling him…"an exploitive messiah of evil… dragging in millions of dollars each month by hooking the vulnerable on his heady-drug of no-consequence sin."

All the money he was making was fine. But George had never done any of this for profit.

Initially he had embarked on this journey simply to show the world his creative powers. His powers to create a totally new genre in fiction. But his fieldwork in Boca Raton, Indianapolis and on the QM2 had expanded his insights enormously. With each successive field experiment, he discovered exhilarating new feelings and understandings within himself. New doors were opened into his consciousness, revealing hidden powers that we actually all possess…but powers that society had always attempted to keep totally suppressed. This discovery was life changing. And he knew he had an obligation to share it with others!

Breaking those chains of moral suppression for those strong enough to handle it had become his new singular mission. His message was simple and direct— You and you alone are your own absolute master. All of society's rules and artificial constraints on your absolute primacy should be ignored and ultimately abolished. Self-fulfillment was properly the sole goal of your existence!

In creating Ian Kirk, George was attempting to put words to that mission. Kirk was his evangelist—explaining, persuading and converting. All the assassinations in his book were simply expressions of Kirk's freedom from society's constraints and moral suppression. It was this philosophy that the Book and Game were really about!

And through the Book and now the Game, George was successfully converting thousands to that belief system. While not everyone understood that now, future generations would see him as a true liberator. He knew his name would eventually be up there with those other greats who had dramatically redirected the course of human history…Jesus, Galileo, Marx, Einstein, and now Trecott!

Of that, in all modesty he was absolutely sure!

44.

Threats

MIXED INTO TODAY'S stack of mail, George saw the familiar envelope. It was the third similar one he had received this month.

Putting on white cotton gloves to preserve its integrity, he slit open the envelope and read its contents—

Dear George—

This world will be a far
better place when you're gone.
And that will come sooner
than you think.

I know all that you've done.
And you will pay.

Not with coin of the realm.
But with your life.

You've been warned!

Reaper

It was time to bring in the authorities. Placing the letter and envelope in a protective folder along with the others, George placed a call to FBI Special Agent Larry Gregg in Washington.

"Have you called to confess?"—these were the first words out of Gregg's mouth when Trecott's call was put through.

"No, Agent Gregg. I'm calling because I may need your help."

Taken back a bit by that, Gregg softened his tone and said—"So, tell me about it."

During the next ten minutes, George described the letters and explained all the pressure he was undergoing. Gregg said he better come down to D.C., so that forensics could look at the letters and so that they could figure out what to do.

George said he'd take the Acela and be there in the morning.

45.

A Cry for Help

LARRY GREGG NEVER believed George Trecott, and wasn't sure he believed him now. But Trecott did seem genuinely shaken, so maybe this situation could be used to extract a straight story from Trecott in exchange for FBI help.

Gregg let George prattle on about his fear for his safety. Then suggested that Trecott should handle the matter with the help of the New York City PD.

George protested that the NYPD would be just as happy if someone did kill him—that they were blaming him for the City's historically high murder rate.

Larry listened, and then settled back in his chair before saying—"OK. Maybe I can help you. But only if you tell me all you know about the incident aboard the QM2 and also those in Boca Raton and Indianapolis."

George nodded in agreement and replied—"So it was the Boca Raton and Indianapolis cases that also interested you. I thought so. Though you had never mentioned them by name before.

"I personally had nothing to do with either of them…or with the Queen Mary 2 incident that you focused on. But after our last meeting in New York, I went back over my notes from my sessions with William. He alluded to all three, but pretty much described them as 'test runs'…something he apparently did quite often to work out the details in his plans. Your recent interest in these cases prompted me to do an internet search on all three…press reports, official statements, etc.

"Am I not right that no one was injured or killed in any of these incidents? So may I ask, why are you so fixated on them?"

"People were harmed…emotionally and in terms of reputations."

"I see. But if it's any consolation, some considerable good did come out of all three of these events."

Gregg bristled at that outrageous claim, and asked Trecott how he could possibly make such a statement.

George calmly answered—"Out of curiosity, I did some considerable further research on the aftermath of all three events...and found some interesting things.

"Let's start with Boca Raton. Apparently, it was that coffee shop incident that prompted the Food & Drug Administration to issue new safety guidelines for the fast-food and self-serve industry. Those guidelines are now presumably protecting millions of consumers from illicit tampering of their food and beverages."

"But what about the on-going trauma inflicted on the woman and her husband?"

"If I read the reports right, it was actually he who precipitated the whole thing by responding to an anonymous letter offering to dispose of his wife. In effect, he issued a contract on her life! No wonder he and she may have lingering issues. Am I wrong?"

"Yes you are! What about Indianapolis?"

"Apparently, the prisoner was not really harmed, and no one shed any tears over his brief incapacitation. But again, great good came from the incident. It identified a gaping hole in prison security, which has now been plugged. The result? One major source of illicit drugs flowing into our prisons has been curtailed."

"And how do you rationalize the Queen Mary 2 incident?"

"If I'm not mistaken, it has resulted in a new international protocol for dealing with both terrorists and the attempted hijacking of cruise ships. Plus, improved security features for criminal threats aboard ship. Apparently as a result, many cruise lines now routinely run 'war games', where specialized teams come in unannounced to test and rate the ship's preparedness and effectiveness in crisis prevention."

"Are you asking me to put you in for a medal…or two…or three? All of these things involved crimes! And I'm still not convinced that you weren't the perpetrator. I can't prove it. But please don't patronize me with stories about how grateful we should be for these events."

"I'm sorry you feel that way. But I ask you to please not let your antipathy toward me prevent you from helping me over the threats I'm now receiving.

"I know you want me to reveal the true identity of Ian Kirk and tell you how to find him. My suspicion and great fear is that Ian Kirk… the man I know only as 'William'…is the one who sent me these letters. I think he's furious about how extensively I've exploited and profited from his stories. And by doing so, that I have significantly increased the likelihood of his apprehension.

"That, Agent Gregg, is my worry. And it's why I've come to you. Both of us now want to find and stop Ian Kirk!"

Larry Gregg said nothing, which prompted George to make his final appeal—
"Help me, and I'll do everything I can to help you. I'll even turn over to you all my notes from my interviews with 'William'. They cover 16 of his claimed assassinations…six more than I describe in my book!"

"OK. Bring all your files down here on Monday. And in the meantime, stay inside your apartment. I'll have a security detail posted at your building. They'll accompany you to DC first thing Monday morning."

With that, George gratefully shook Larry Gregg's hand and left the Hoover Building.

Oh his way to the Acela for his train ride home to Manhattan, George smiled and thought—
"That went exactly as I planned!"

46.

The Final Chapter

GEORGE HAD SPENT the day in his apartment, setting up things for what would be his crowning achievement. For this was the day. The day that George would secure his place in history. How few could say that? Not 1 in 10,000,000.

Savoring his second cup of rich black coffee, George thought back through these past five years.

How very much had changed. Changed from that day in that run down house in that run down New Jersey town. The day when George said..."Enough"...and began the journey that had made him one of the most famous authors and thought leaders in the country, if not the world.
So much accomplished in so relatively little time!

George now had it all! Fame, fortune, personal satisfaction, the world as his oyster! And at this point, he had only one major accomplishment yet to be achieved. Gloriously passing through that door to discover all the joys and splendors that he knew were waiting for him on the other side! From a perfect worldly life—to a profoundly more perfect eternal life!

And at what better time? He was at his apex! And he would now solidify this precious moment for all eternity.

Most men fear death. But George knew better. After all, death was his area of expertise. And his friend!

In nature, all living things reach a moment of sheer perfection... the blooming rose, the spring lamb, the budding shaft of wheat, the vintage grape. This is the moment they were born to celebrate. The very moment at which they must be harvested to capture and preserve their primal essence. Once that moment passes, they spiral downward ...withering to dust, or to decay and slime.

But what of humankind? As emotional and self-delusional creatures, they refuse to accept nature's plan. They so greatly fear non-existence that they cling to an ever-diminishing life...if that can be called a life at all.

Of course, some few do choose to end their lives early...choosing suicide to escape pain or punishment, depression or disgrace. None of these conditions applied even remotely to George. He was not seeking an escape. So suicide would never be an option.

And George had always considered suicide a surrender...not a victory. And it was a victory that George was planning for this afternoon. A victory achieved with the help of an assassin's hand.

Unlike suicide, assassination actually doubled an individual's worldly immortality. Consider all those whom an assassin's hand had made a legend—preserving for all time our memory of them at the peak of their achievement— Caesar, Gandhi, Lincoln, Malcolm X, Jack and Bobby Kennedy, Sadat, Martin Luther King, John Lennon and thousands more.

And consider all those said to have died far too young—preserving for all time their worldly legacy —Mozart, Princess Diana, Shelly, Keats, Anne Frank, James Dean, Emily Bronte, Alexander the Great, Shubert, Von Richthofen, Tutankhamen, Amelia Earhart, Christopher Marlowe, Joan of Arc, and many thousands more.

Yes, in a purely physical sense George would die today. Not young, but well before his time! And he'd die today…not by suicide…but by the assassin Ian Kirk's hand. It would be his friend Ian who would guide him through the door to his future life. A glorious life of fulfillment and unlimited achievement!

Shifting his coffee cup to the side, George selected a large navel orange from the fruit basket before him. Slowly rotating it in his hands, he selected the stem end to begin peeling, with the assistance of a small antique fruit knife.

Arranging the separated orange sections neatly on a dessert plate, George took one last look around the room to confirm that everything was in place and in order. And it was.

George had injected this particular orange the day before with a toxic but painless blend of alkaloids and anesthetics. Within seconds after consuming a few sections, he would fall into a dreamless sleep; and within minutes his heart would cease beating. The authorities would easily identify the toxin but find no vial, syringe or other items to indicate that the orange had been dosed inside the apartment. That would direct their search to an external source.

A careful search of the apartment would uncover the threatening notes that he had received. (Notes that he of course had written to himself.) And his appointment book and phone records would lead them to FBI Special Agent Larry Gregg, who may or may not be fully cooperative.

With great difficulty, the authorities would finally be able to breech the security and encryption on his computer. There, clues to the real name and location of Ian Kirk would be discovered, along with comprehensive files that included their correspondence, relationship and agreements. These files would reveal Kirk's growing unhappiness with Trecott's exploitation of his work, along with threats to stop…or else. (All these files, of course, were fictions created by George himself… to convince the authorities that Ian Kirk was George's assassin.)

A final display of George's creative brilliance! A bravura performance that would assure that both George and Ian Kirk would live forever in legend!

George smiled as he savored the sweet yet tart orange segments. He was about to make his most important journey of discovery!

THE NEW YORK TIMES

Controversial Author and Ethicist George Trecott dead at 61

Police authorities report that the body of George Trecott was discovered last night in his penthouse apartment on Manhattan's Upper West Side. While the investigation is still in its early stages, the death is an apparent homicide.

Individuals close to the department's forensic division report that the cause of death was poisoning. A partially eaten orange was found next to the body and appears to have been injected with a toxic substance. The orange was part of a routinely scheduled food delivery from a nearby market earlier that afternoon.

According to the building's doorman, Trecott had not left the apartment that day and had no visitors. Papers and reference materials on his desk suggest that he was at work on his next novel.

As the author of the massively popular book *The Assassin* and its breakthrough video game counterpart *The Assassin Live*, George Trecott had become an extremely well known and controversial public figure. In the book, game and in interviews, lectures and on social media, Trecott preached a radical brand of hedonism in a philosophy he called '*Kirkism*', which reportedly now has more than 100,000 followers worldwide. Praised by exponents of unfettered free speech, he was also vilified by those who blamed him for accelerating society's moral decline and the abandonment of Judeo-Christian values. Many also linked him to the soaring murder rates being seen in both cities and in formerly crime free areas.

In a statement released to the press, Oliver Gold--literary agent and longtime friend of Mr. Trecott—stated: "No single individual in the past hundred years has had a bigger impact on our culture. He was a true visionary and powerful exponent of unfettered individualism. His name has earned him a permanent place in our lexicon of inspirational leaders. He will be sorely missed; and we can only wonder how much more he might have achieved had he not been taken from us so relatively young."

Informed sources say that multiple lines of inquiry are underway in an attempt to track down George Trecott's killer. Apparently he received a number of threats in the weeks preceding his death. One theory is that the individual called Ian Kirk in *The Assassin* and *The Assassin Live* actually exists and is not just a fictional assassin. Others discount that long held rumor, but still label Trecott's killing as an assassination.

George Trecott was born in a small village near Troy, NY to working class parents. An only child, he left home at 18 to attend Columbia University in New York City, earning an AB in English. Following graduation, he became a high school teacher in Katonah, NY. Moving to New Jersey, he taught at a small private school and spent a brief time as a copywriter at a local advertising agency where he met his future wife. That marriage ended in divorce and her current whereabouts are unknown. Mr. Trecott then spent a number of years as an editor of crime fiction for a now-defunct Texas publisher, before resigning to work on his own book full time.

The Assassin was Mr. Trecott's first published work, an astonishing achievement for a first time author.

The NYPD Public Affairs Office has announced that a press conference will be held later this week to provide more details on the investigation.

Authors Note—

The "Amateur Assassin" is a cautionary tale. A tale of how Ego can breed self-delusion…transforming an ordinary man into a powerful force for evil.

A theologian would describe this as "the work of the Devil." The Dark One who wishes to ensnare us and make us his agent.

A psychiatrist would call this an illness. Something to be treated with therapy, therapeutics or confinement.

But whichever you choose to call it, make no doubt there's a potential force for evil within each of us. The Ego is a very powerful 'metaphysical organ'. And if not tamed, it can devour us.

Whether you attempt to tame it or not is your decision.
But don't say that I didn't try to warn you!

APPENDIX

People & Places—

New Jersey-

- George Trecott………. Author and amateur assassin
- Janet Trecott………… George's ex-wife
- Ripper Publishing….. Vanity press and George's employer

Florida-

- Howard Dixon……….. Target #1 – Boca Raton
- Tilly Brown Dixon…... Target #1 and Howard's second wife
- "Dixon Holdings"………. Howard's Real Estate Investment Company
- St. Michael The Avenger… "Guardian Angel" Warning Letter Writer
- "The Boca Bean Coffee Shop"…. Site of the Crime
- Carlos Jarman……….... Boca Bean Coffee Shop owner
- "Boca Raton Regional Hospital"…. Where Tilly was taken
- Doug Sullivan………… Howard's Attorney and oldest friend
- Chuck Daily…………..… Doug Sullivan's PI, retired Miami PD Detective
- "PBSO"…………………… "Palm Beach Sheriff's Office" in Fort Lauderdale
- Lieutenant R. C. Nichols… PBSO Homicide Unit, Chief of Detectives
- Bert Carlson…………..... PBSO Detective
- Harry Rodrigues…….. PBSO Detective
- Willard Dixon………… Howard's son and owner of a boat charter business
- "Sanchez Syndicate"…… Well connected criminal organization

Indianapolis-

- Seymour Dollan / aka "Tex" Jay Bickford, Bill Sweeny, Will Collins, Colin Wilson, Cole Thomas…………… Target #2
- "Galileo Global Partners"…. Shell company in El Paso set up by 'Tex'
- Georgina (Ginger) Morgan… Asst. Bank Manager of El Paso Trust
- Sid Lafontaine… Galileo Regional Manager

- Ed Montagne…Galileo Regional Manager
- "The Thomas Quirk Advertising Agency"… Indianapolis Ad Agency
- Harley Quirk…Agency President, son of the founder
- Dennis Conrad…Agency accountant/bookkeeper
- "Indiana Cellular"…. Agency client
- "Family Pride Markets"… Agency client
- "Olympic Runner Shoes"… Agency client
- "Pontiac Insurance"…. Agency client
- "Rocky Carroll"… Houston boot maker
- "Stetson Diamante"…$5,000 Western Hat
- Lou Rhodes… CFO of Galileo
- Harrison Smith… Administrative VP of Galileo
- "Solar Winds Unlimited"…fictitious company
- Brooks Gerard… Harley's lawyer, former federal prosecutor
- "Marion County Sheriff's Office"…where "Tex" was jailed
- Sally Templeton… FBI Agent, Indianapolis Field Office
- "Guardian Angel Missionary Society"… Perp of the Jailhouse Crime

Queen Mary 2—The Set-up

- Roger Sayles…….. George Trecott's alias #1
- Peter L. Brown…. George Trecott's alias #2
- "Vince Lombardi Service Area"… Park & Ride on NJ Turnpike
- "Brooklyn Cruise Terminal"…. Cruise embarkation point
- "Cunard's Queen Mary 2"…. NYC to Southampton transatlantic voyage
- Stateroom 3008… George's single cabin on Cruise #1
- 'The Greylord Project'… VIP Conference… George's Target for Cruise #2

Queen Mary 2—Site of the Crime

- Roger Sayles…….. George Trecott's alias #1
- Peter L. Brown…. George Trecott's alias #2
- Sir Cecil Jenkins-Doyle…. Retired head of New Scotland Yard
- Stateroom 8032…Sir Cecil's cabin
- Queens Suite 8130…Sir Cecil's War Room
- Captain Jeremy Cornwall…QM2 Ship Master

- First Officer Jonathan Blakely…QM2 Head of Security
- First Officer Donald Van Zilen…QM2 Passenger and Crew Administrator
- Chief Engineer Conrad Schmidt… Mechanical & Electrical Systems Director
- Senior Hotel Manager Perry York… Food/Beverage/Staterooms Director
- Chief Entertainment Director Marcus O'Toole…. Events & Facilities Director
- Chief Purser Ivy Witicomb…. Passenger & Crew Communications Director
- 'Greylord Project' Executive Director…Malcolm Elliott

Queen Mary 2—Added Resources

- Sir Oliver Walters…….. CEO Cunard Lines based in London
- FBI Headquarters….. Director Jack Kilpatrick
- New Scotland Yard Headquarters…. Director Sir Kim Farley-Thomas
- MI5 Headquarters…. Director Sir Kevin Chatsworth
- MI6 Headquarters… Director Sir Thaddeus Long
- FBI Team Flown in…Special Agents Larry Gregg, Gil Cooper, Jason Eldridge,

  Mitch Pearson, Tony Casale, Sal Price
    - FBI Undercover Hijack Team…. Victor Gamble, Harriet Tyler, Sid Frank, Buzz Jones, Otto Zigg
    - Jewel Thief…. Scott Issacs

The Book -- Characters & Places

- Principal Character…. Ian Kirk (aka William)
- "Barbabella"…luxury yacht
- Oliver Gold…George's Literary Agent
- "Finito"…Chinese video game developer
- "Liquidators International"…Ian Kirk's Firm

Queen Mary 2 Guest Areas—

Common Areas -

• Grand Lobby	Decks 2 and 3
• Promenade Deck	Deck 7
• Sun Deck	Deck 13
• Observation Deck	Deck 11
• Pursers Office	Deck 2
• The Lookout	Deck 14

Restaurants -

• Britannia Restaurant	Decks 2 and 3
• Kings Court	Deck 7
• Queens Grill	Deck 7
• Princess Grill	Deck 7
• Carinthia Lounge	Deck 7
• Verandah Restaurant	Deck 8
• Golden Lion Pub	Deck 2
• Boardwalk Café	Deck 12

Cocktail Lounges -

• Grill Lounge & Bar	Deck 7
• Commodore Club	Deck 9
• Chart Room	Deck 3
• Champagne Bar	Deck 3
• Sir Samuels	Deck 3
• Cunard G-32	Deck 3

Theatres / Ballroom-

• Royal Court Theatre	Decks 2 and 3
• Illuminations	Deck 3
• Queens Room	Deck 3

Wellness Centers -

• Canyon Ranch SpaClub	Deck 7
• Fitness Center & Gymnasium	Deck 7
• Sports Center	Deck 13

Meeting Rooms / Lounges -

• Atlantic Room	Deck 11
• Boardroom	Deck 9
• Concierge Lounge	Deck 9
• Cunard Connexions	Deck 2

Pools -

• Terrace Pool & Lounge	Deck 8
• Pavilion Pool & Bar	Deck 12
• Grills Terrace & Whirlpool	Deck 11

Special Function Rooms / Areas -

• QM2 Casino	Deck 2
• Churchill Cigar Room	Deck 9
• Ships Library	Deck 8
• Ship Bookshop	Deck 8
• Kids Zone	Deck 6
• Kennel	Deck 12
• Shops	Deck 3

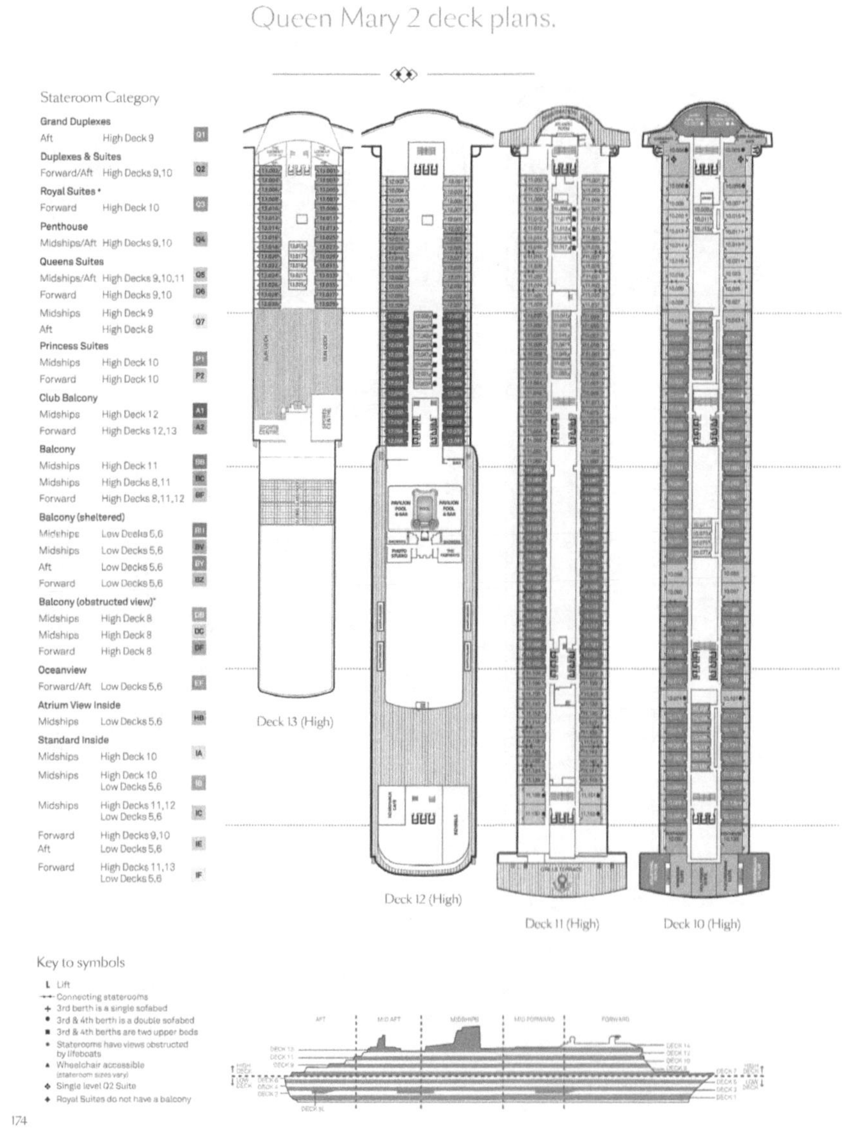

Queen Mary 2 deck plans.

Stateroom Category

Category	Location	Decks	Code
Grand Duplexes			
	Aft	High Deck 9	Q1
Duplexes & Suites			
	Forward/Aft	High Decks 9,10	Q2
Royal Suites ◆			
	Forward	High Deck 10	Q3
Penthouse			
	Midships/Aft	High Decks 9,10	Q4
Queens Suites			
	Midships/Aft	High Decks 9,10,11	Q5
	Forward	High Decks 9,10	Q6
	Midships	High Deck 9	Q7
	Aft	High Deck 8	Q7
Princess Suites			
	Midships	High Deck 10	P1
	Forward	High Deck 10	P2
Club Balcony			
	Midships	High Deck 12	A1
	Forward	High Decks 12,13	A2
Balcony			
	Midships	High Deck 11	BB
	Midships	High Decks 8,11	BC
	Forward	High Decks 8,11,12	BF
Balcony (sheltered)			
	Midships	Low Decks 5,6	[illegible]
	Midships	Low Decks 5,6	BV
	Aft	Low Decks 5,6	BY
	Forward	Low Decks 5,6	BZ
Balcony (obstructed view)*			
	Midships	High Deck 8	DB
	Midships	High Deck 8	DC
	Forward	High Deck 8	DF
Oceanview			
	Forward/Aft	Low Decks 5,6	EF
Atrium View Inside			
	Midships	Low Decks 5,6	HB
Standard Inside			
	Midships	High Deck 10	IA
	Midships	High Deck 10 Low Decks 5,6	IB
	Midships	High Decks 11,12 Low Decks 5,6	IC
	Forward Aft	High Decks 9,10 Low Decks 5,6	IE
	Forward	High Decks 11,13 Low Decks 5,6	IF

Deck 13 (High)

Deck 12 (High)

Deck 11 (High)

Deck 10 (High)

Key to symbols

- L Lift
- ⟷ Connecting staterooms
- ✚ 3rd berth is a single sofabed
- ● 3rd & 4th berth is a double sofabed
- ■ 3rd & 4th berths are two upper beds
- * Staterooms have views obstructed by lifeboats
- ▲ Wheelchair accessible (stateroom sizes vary)
- ❖ Single level Q2 Suite
- ◆ Royal Suites do not have a balcony

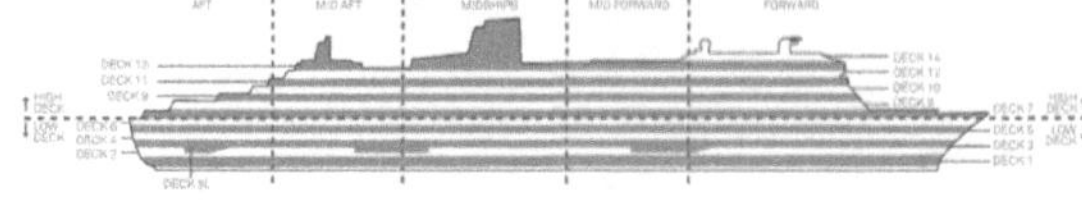

174

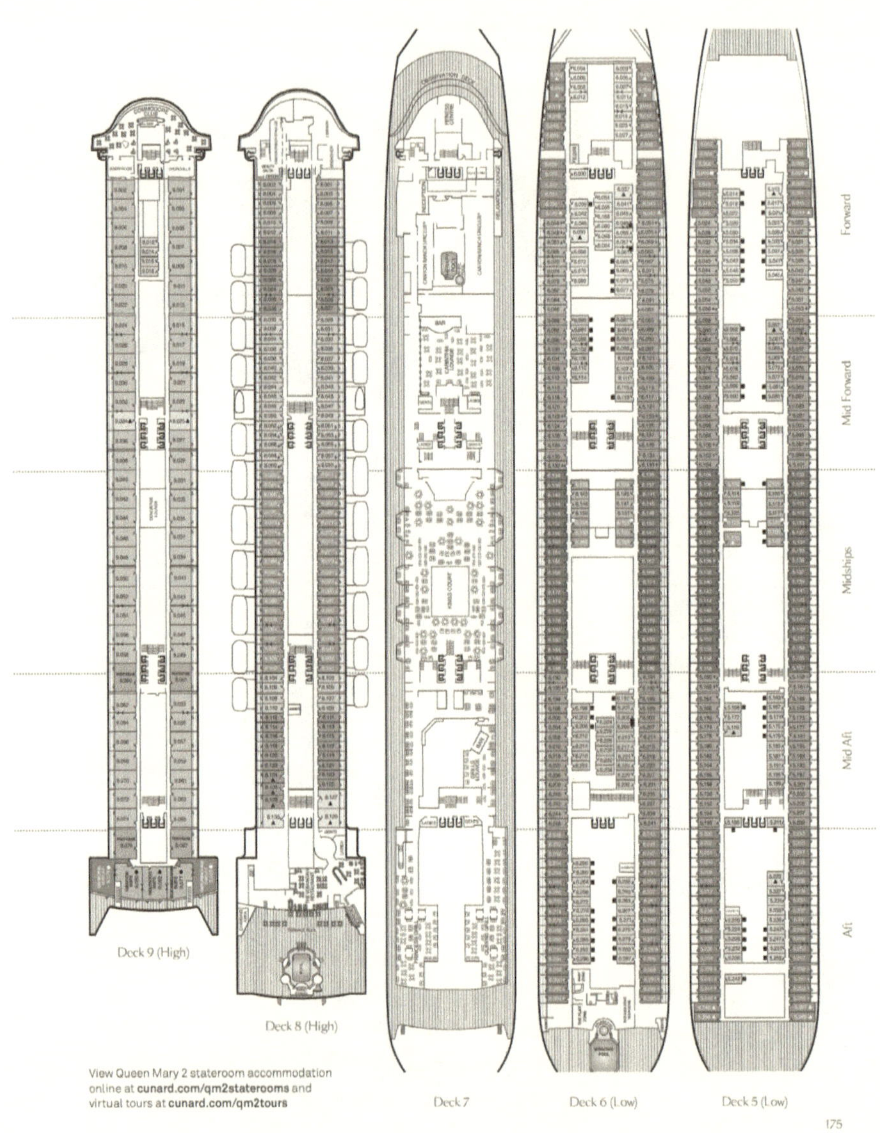
Forward
Mid Forward
Midships
Mid Aft
Aft
Deck 9 (High)
Deck 8 (High)
View Queen Mary 2 stateroom accommodation online at cunard.com/qm2staterooms and virtual tours at cunard.com/qm2tours
Deck 7
Deck 6 (Low)
Deck 5 (Low)
175

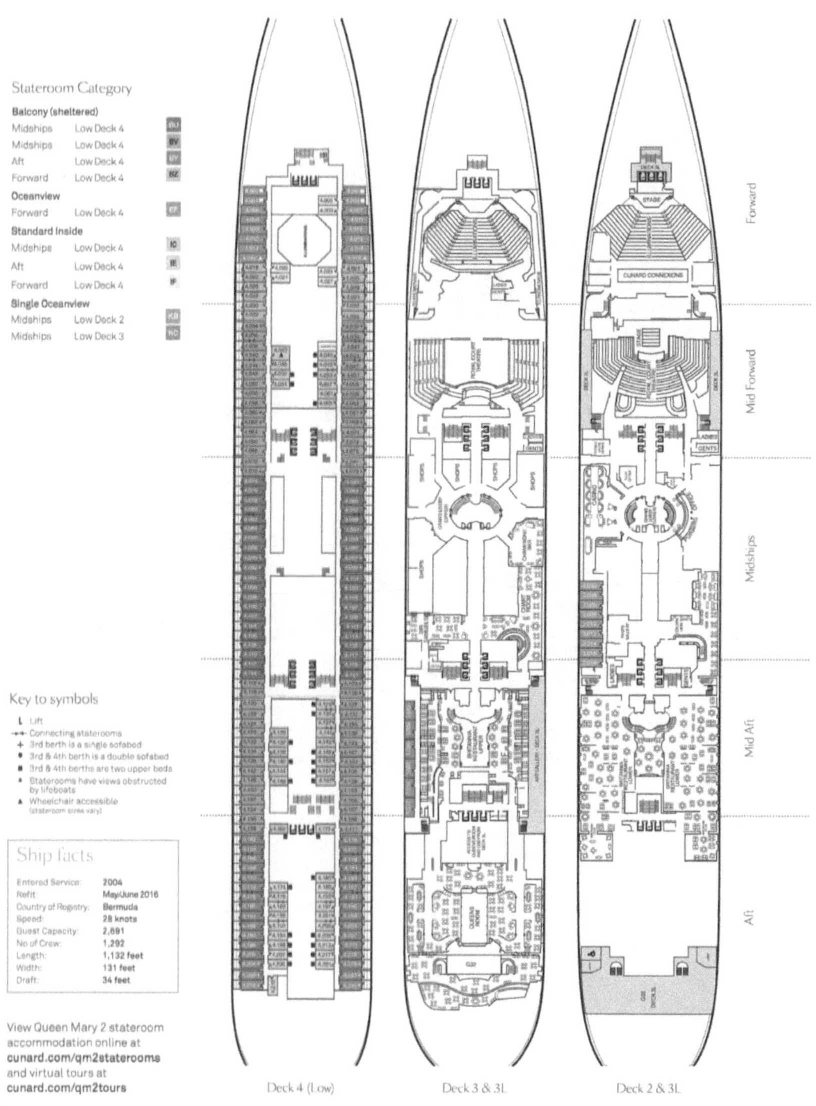
Stateroom Category
Balcony (sheltered)
Midships Low Deck 4 BU
Midships Low Deck 4 BV
Aft Low Deck 4
Forward Low Deck 4 BZ
Oceanview
Forward Low Deck 4
Standard Inside
Midships Low Deck 4 IC
Aft Low Deck 4 IE
Forward Low Deck 4 IF
Single Oceanview
Midships Low Deck 2
Midships Low Deck 3
Key to symbols
Lift
Connecting staterooms
3rd berth is a single sofabed
3rd & 4th berth is a double sofabed
3rd & 4th berths are two upper beds
Staterooms have views obstructed by lifeboats
Wheelchair accessible
Ship facts
Entered Service: 2004
Refit: May/June 2016
Country of Registry: Bermuda
Speed: 28 knots
Guest Capacity: 2,691
No of Crew: 1,292
Length: 1,132 feet
Width: 131 feet
Draft: 34 feet
View Queen Mary 2 stateroom accommodation online at cunard.com/qm2staterooms and virtual tours at cunard.com/qm2tours
176
SHOPS
STAGE
CUNARD CONNEXIONS
LADIES
GENTS
Forward
Mid Forward
Midships
Mid Aft
Aft
Deck 4 (Low)
Deck 3 & 3L
Deck 2 & 3L

www.ingramcontent.com/pod-product-compliance
Lightning Source LLC
Chambersburg PA
CBHW030812310726
48980CB00006B/468/J

* 9 7 8 0 9 7 7 8 0 5 6 9 3 *